SHARP SHOOTIN' COWBOY

VICTORIA VANE

sourcebooks
casablanca

Published by Sourcebooks Casablanca, an imprint of Sourcebooks, Inc.
P.O. Box 4410, Naperville, Illinois 60567-4410
(630) 961-3900
Fax: (630) 961-2168
www.sourcebooks.com

Printed and bound in Canada.

MBP 10 9 8 7 6 5 4 3 2 1

Praise for *Slow Hand*

For John, my true-life romance hero

Chapter 1

Mojave Desert, Southern California

LYING ON HIS BELLY BEHIND AN OUTCROPPING OF rocks, Reid squinted into the scope of his rifle. He was sweating like a pig in his dirt-encrusted ghillie suit and didn't even want to *think* about how he smelled after three days in hundred-plus temps. He shifted his body. His legs were numb from hours of observation, but he still felt the gravel chewing through the suit and into his skin.

"You got plans after this, *hermano*?" asked his spotter, Rafael Garcia. They'd met during basic eighteen months ago and had done two tours together. Six months after returning, they'd both earned the coveted Scout Sniper hog's tooth they proudly wore around their necks.

"Nothing special," Reid answered. "You?"

"Oh yeah. Big plans, considering this is our final weekend of freedom and the last chance to score some ass. You need to come along this time."

Reid squinted through his riflescope at the village below where the USMC had re-created a near-perfect model of their mission theater, complete with hundreds of Arabic speakers who wandered the streets and haggled in the staged marketplace. It was quiet below; maybe too quiet.

"No can do, Raf. I've got phone calls to make and a ton of shit to take care of before we deploy." In truth, he was still licking his wounds.

What pissed him off most wasn't so much getting dumped, as he'd half-expected that, but her chosen method. That's what really sucked. Rather than a letter or even a phone call, she'd sent a Dear John text on New Year's Eve: Can't wait for u anymore. :(So sorry Reid. Take care. Tonya.

After two years together, she hadn't even allowed him the satisfaction of tearing up a letter. Five months later, he still wasn't over it. After seeing so many guys dumped during deployments—and now having experienced it himself—he'd banished any thought of women from his mind.

"C'mon, *hermano*," Garcia cajoled. "You've still got all next week to take care of that shit. You gotta get some while the getting is still good. We're looking at eight straight months of *chaqueta*."

"*Chaqueta?* Jacket?" Reid translated with a frown.

"No, man." Garcia grinned, fisting his hand and mimicking jacking off.

"You speak English as well as I do. Why can't you just use it?" Reid asked.

"You're not in Wyoming anymore. You need to learn some Spanish. Hispanics are the fastest growing minority. Especially here in SoCal. Who knows? We may even outnumber you *gringos* before the end of the century. Just think of it as broadening your cultural horizons."

"Yeah? Well, I think my cultural horizons are gonna expand real soon, considering where we're headed."

"And the *hijos de puta madres* over there will kill

you for touching their women. Shit, they don't even let you look at them. For the next eight months, we'll all be doing *punetas*."

Garcia was right. The coming months would be almost monastic. No sex. No booze. A supreme test of both celibacy and abstinence. Most of the grunts would spend the next week drinking 'til they puked and fucking anything that moved. He didn't judge, but that didn't mean he wanted to be part of it.

"Tell you what, *esé*," Garcia continued, as he raised his binoculars, "if you go this weekend, I'll even take you someplace where your cowboy ass will feel right at home."

"In Southern California?"

"Yeah. We have rednecks in *tejanos* out here too. *Mierda*," Garcia swore softly. "Insurgent sighted at two o'clock. He's got an RPG shouldered."

"Fuck. Can't see him."

This was the final test of a grueling, sleep-deprived seventy-two hours, and he was about to fail. Reid pulled back from his scope to blink the dust out of his eyes, then scanned for his target again. "Sighted," Reid confirmed with relief. "Got the son of a bitch in the crosshairs."

"Too slow, *hombre*. He's already taking cover. Looks like he's going to launch from behind that concrete wall."

"The hell he is." At twelve hundred yards, it was the longest shot Reid had ever attempted, but his bipod supported the deadliest weapon he'd ever fired. The M82A3 with fifty-caliber rounds could certainly handle the distance and even a concrete wall. Hell, it could probably take out a fucking tank from a mile away.

"Wind call?" he asked.

"Steady at seven miles per hour. No cross breeze," Garcia replied.

Reid doped his scope.

"Push it left point two," Garcia instructed.

"You sure about that?" Reid had estimated point three. He was rarely off, but Garcia knew his shit. He'd proven to be the best spotter in their class.

"Yeah, I'm sure. You gotta trust me." Garcia echoed his own thoughts, but Reid was accustomed to relying on his instincts. It was hard to turn that over to someone else. "Tell you what," Garcia continued, "if you miss the mark, you're off the hook. If you hit, you're the designated driver."

To any other guy that kind of bet might provide incentive to miss, but Garcia knew him too well. Reid took pride on *never* missing a shot and had an entire trophy room of big game back in Wyoming to prove it.

"All right by me." Reid made the necessary adjustment and honed in once more on his target, a silhouette behind a concrete wall that stood over half a mile away.

One shot. One kill. The scout sniper mantra. It was time to take it.

Reid inhaled slow and deep. Exhaling, his finger tightened on the trigger. He held the next breath for a three count and then slowly and deliberately squeezed. The recoil rammed his right shoulder. The discharge blasted his ears. Three seconds later, half the concrete wall disintegrated before their eyes.

"*Mierda!*" Garcia lowered his spotting scope with a grin. "That thing's a fucking cannon. So, are we gonna take a taxi or do you wanna drive?"

Chapter 2

"I DON'T KNOW WHY I LET YOU DRAG ME HERE. YOU know as well as I do that I'm gonna hate this place."

Yolanda pouted. "C'mon, *chica*. When was the last time you had any fun? You've had your nose buried in your books for months, and now you're gonna be working all summer in the middle of nowhere. Just give it a chance, OK?"

"There's plenty of other places we could have gone besides a redneck club," Haley groused.

"But this place has the biggest dance floor in California. Four thousand square feet to shake your booty."

"You're the dancer, not me." The club scene wasn't Haley's thing. At all.

"Don't be such a wet blanket. It'll be fun."

Haley cast a disparaging eye over the line of girls in their cowboy boots and ass-squeezing Daisy Dukes. "The place is a bit testosterone-challenged, don't you think?"

Yolanda laughed. "Don't worry about that. In a couple of hours, it's gonna be swarming with horny marines."

"Great. Do you ever think of anything else besides partying and guys?" Haley rolled her eyes.

"You're the one who mentioned testosterone," Yolanda said, grinning.

Although they'd been best friends since junior high

school, she and Yolanda had vastly different priorities. Haley didn't even try to keep up with Yolanda's
revolving-door love life.

"Rarely." Yolanda winked at her. "There's a lot more
to life than books, Haley, but don't take my word for it.
It's time you discover for yourself."

"What's the point?" Haley argued. "I don't have time
to date."

"Who says anything about dating?" Yolanda replied.
"We're just here to have a good time, right? It doesn't
have to lead to anything. Look," Yolanda continued, "if
you don't want to be accosted by horny marines, just
stay out on the floor. You don't even need a partner.
They play mainly line dances here, and most of those
guys are too macho to line dance."

"I'm just going to make an ass of myself."

"It's why we came early," Yolanda countered. "So you
can take advantage of the lessons. If you don't catch on,
no problema. They'll mix it up later with some freestyle
hip-hop. C'mon. At least give it a chance. It'll be fun."

"Yeah, barrels of fun," Haley mumbled.

They moved slowly up the line.

The big, bald, unsmiling bouncer held out his hand.
"ID."

"You'd think they'd be a bit friendlier," Haley muttered as both girls fished out their wallets.

Yolanda presented her license and promptly received
an over-twenty-one bracelet.

"Pay to the right," he said. "Next."

Haley received a scowl when she presented her ID.
"Put out both hands."

She complied and got a big black "X" on the back

of each with a Sharpie. Great. If she wanted ink on her body, she'd have gotten a tat.

"We enforce the law," he warned. "Try to drink, and we'll boot your ass. Pay to the right."

She stepped to the counter already feeling like a felon.

"Twenty bucks," the cashier announced without even looking up.

Haley presented her debit card.

The woman shook her head. "Cash only."

"Cash? Who carries cash anymore?"

"No cash. No entry."

"Just a minute. Let me find my friend." Haley searched the crowd for Yolanda, but she'd already gone inside.

"You're holding up the line."

"But I don't have any—"

"I got it." A soft, whisky-smooth baritone sounded from behind her.

Haley spun around to meet a solid wall of chest. Her gaze tracked north of the button-down western shirt to meet a pair of sky-blue eyes shadowed by a well-worn Stetson. Built like a rock, with dimples to boot, this tall cowboy stirred interest in places she'd ignored for a very long time.

He stepped up to the cashier, flipped his wallet open, and handed the woman two twenties.

"I'll pay you back as soon as we get inside," Haley blurted. "I have a friend—"

Blue Eyes shook his head. "It's no big deal. I got it. If it bothers you that much, you can pay me back later on with a dance."

"Thanks for the easy terms, but I'm not much of a dancer." Haley's mouth stretched into an involuntary smile. He really was hot, and a charmer too.

His answering smile morphed into a crooked grin revealing even, white teeth. The night was starting to look up. Her gaze tracked to his blue eyes again. Way up. She'd never gone for that type before, but when he gazed down at her with a heart-skipping grin stretching his mouth… *Holy cow…boy*.

"That's a bit of a relief actually," he said. "I manage a passable two-step, but that's about the limit of my repertoire." He nodded to the gap that had broadened between them and the door. "Wanna go inside now?"

Haley tensed under the sudden contact of his big, warm palm on her lower back. It was a light touch that still set every nerve ending on alert. Discomposed by her own response, she fought the instinct to pull away. Forcing a breath, she willed herself to relax, and let him guide her toward the door.

Once inside, he offered his hand. "I'm Reid."

She eyeballed him anew. A handshake? Was he for real? "You're not from around here are you?"

"No, ma'am." His annoyingly disarming grin lingered. She didn't trust how easily she responded to it, to him. "Born and raised in Wyoming."

"Wyoming? So you're the genuine article and not one of those jokers?" She inclined her head to the throng gathered around the mechanical bull.

He shook his head with a scoffing sound. "I earned my spurs on the real thing."

She glanced down at his boots, expecting to see them. He chuckled. "I don't wear 'em unless I'm ridin'."

"So are you going to show them how it's done?"

"I got nothing to prove. Besides, there's no comparison. A mechanical bull can't stomp you into the dirt or plant a horn in your ass."

"Are you working on one of the ranches out here?"

"Nope. I've hung it all up for the U.S. Marine Corps."

"You're a *marine*?" she repeated in dismay.

"Yup. Corporal Reid Everett of the Third Battalion First Marines."

Damn. Damn. Damn. Why did the only guy she'd taken any interest in since God knows when have to be a marine? The revelation instantly snuffed out any flicker of interest. A potential fling with a hot cowboy was one thing, but a jarhead was completely out of consideration.

"Nice meeting you, Reid." She turned away.

He laid a hand on her arm, his brows meeting in a subtle frown. "Not quite the reaction I'd expected..."

"My father was a marine," she explained.

"*Was?*"

"So I'm told," she responded, tight-lipped. "I never knew him. I'm going to find my friend now."

"Wait a minute. Wha'd I say?" He looked confused and maybe even a bit hurt, like she'd locked his wheels up and sent him skidding.

"It's not what you said. It's what you *are*."

Just another whore-mongering marine. They were all just a bunch of horny dogs. Her own father had been one of them—impregnating her mother, never to be heard from again.

The grunts from Camp Pendleton had an especially long and well-earned history. She'd even done a research study on it for one of her college classes. Since the USMC established their base in 1942, the number of illegitimate births within a one-hundred-mile radius of the base had skyrocketed nine months after every major troop deployment. The data was undeniable. *Semper fidelis* certainly didn't apply to the women they left behind.

"I'm not into marines, Reid. But don't worry, there are plenty of women here who would be more than eager to give you a memorable pre-deployment send-off."

Not daring to look back, Haley made a brisk retreat.

Reid stared after the petite blonde in consternation. Although he'd arrived without the slightest interest in getting laid, that was before he'd eyed her. She seemed so different from all the rest. Reserved. Almost aloof. Dressed in a pale yellow sundress with a long, loose braid down her back, she'd stuck out like a sore thumb compared to the others in their belly shirts, miniskirts, and booty shorts.

He'd wondered what all that gold silk would look like loose and kissing the dimples of her ass. He shook his head in mild disappointment. Guess he'd never find out.

"*Ay! Cabrón!*" Garcia appeared at Reid's side with two bottles of Dos Equis and a shit-eating grin. He offered one of the long necks. "Who was that hot little *rubia*?"

"Dunno." Reid accepted the beer with a grimace. "Never got her name." He still couldn't figure her abrupt about-face. She'd begun to soften toward him, only to turn frigid as ice in the blink of an eye. "I gathered she's not partial to jarheads."

"Then best cut your losses, cause you sure as shit aren't going to score there. Maybe you should try a

Chicana? Just pick one and ask her to slow dance. There're plenty of hot little *mamacitas* on that floor who'd go for that six-three frame and pretty-boy face."

Reid took a swig of beer. The dance lessons had finished with a manic performance of "Cotton-Eye Joe." The lines broke up with dancers dispersing toward the various bars.

"Here's your chance, bro. All you gotta do is offer her a drink. I'll even teach you to say it in Spanish: *Quiero comer tu coño*."

Reid eyed Garcia with suspicion. "I thought *comer* was 'to eat.'"

"Eat, drink." Garcia shrugged. "It's all the same in Spanish."

"I'm not falling for it, Garcia. I've been around you long enough to have a pretty good notion of what *coño* means."

"Hey man." Garcia raised his hands. "Just doing you a favor. That phrase is sure to come in handy for you one day."

"I appreciate your concern for my dick, *amigo*, but I'm really not interested in chasing tail. Blonde or Chicana. I'm perfectly happy to leave the field open, chill with a couple of beers, and shoot some pool."

"Suit yourself, *cabrón*. But the only balls I'm interested in are right here." He cupped his crotch with a smirk.

The blare of hip-hop music drew their attention back to the floor. Couples were already pairing for some up-close freak and grind, while a few girls were twerking in groups.

"*Mira ese culo!* Look at that ass, man." Garcia

gestured to a curvy brunette. He upended his bottle, emptied it in one long swallow, and then handed it to Reid. "Target sighted, *hermano*. Time to engage."

—~~~—

Haley didn't know why she'd let Yolanda drag her to the club. She didn't have time for guys. She was far too busy with work and school to even think about them. Or had been. Until the cowboy. He'd definitely made her *think*, but her budding infatuation died a premature death the moment he'd declared himself a leatherneck. Maybe she wasn't being fair, but the deck was firmly stacked against him.

She already wanted to leave, but Yolanda had driven. Unless her friend chose someone else to take her home tonight, she'd be stuck here until closing. Haley looked around the club with increasing dismay. She hated dancing and was surrounded by marines.

She scouted the dance floor and spotted Yolanda holding up her hair and doing a body roll, sandwiched between two guys. Maybe she'd be driving herself after all. By the look of things, Yo was gonna get a ride of *some* kind.

Yolanda spotted her and waved frantically, beckoning Haley to join her and the two guys. Haley answered with a sharp headshake. If she was going to be stuck here all night, she really needed a drink. She formed a fist with her thumb raised to her lips, the universal drink sign. Yolanda nodded acknowledgment and then ground her booty into her new partner.

Haley considered the acetone wipes Yolanda had shoved into her purse. A few minutes of scrubbing in the bathroom would erase the black marks on her hands. She weighed the consequences. If she got caught, she'd get tossed out on her ass. It was definitely worth the risk.

Moments later, Haley exited the restroom, hands thoroughly cleansed of black marker. She then discovered an ATM at the back of the club and whipped out her debit card. After collecting her cash, she headed for the nearest bar, only to be intercepted by four different guys sporting buzz cuts. She rolled her eyes. More marines. It wasn't too hard to brush them off *yet*, but the night was early and they weren't fully tanked.

She could really use that drink, but the bartenders would ask to see her bracelet before taking an order. With her friend on the floor, her only option was to ask one of the grunts to buy the drink for her. Opting for the devil she knew, the cowboy, Haley scouted the bar. At least she had the excuse of paying him back. She had enough cash to cover her debt and still buy a couple of cocktails. She found him a few minutes later shooting pool with a cadre of his leatherneck buddies.

"Hey, cowboy. I have something for you." She slapped the twenty on the table where he was setting up his first shot.

Her unintended innuendo was met with silence as his baby blues darted up from the table to meet her gaze. The rest of the group eyeballed her up and down with open interest, making her feel like she'd entered a wolf's den.

She bit her lip, wishing she'd said something else. "I-I mean I found an ATM. I can pay you back now."

His tawny brows met. "Said I didn't care about that."

He pushed the twenty across the table and turned his attention back to the cue.

That was it? A brush-off? Haley's hackles rose. Was this his idea of payback for her earlier snub? *I don't think so, cowboy*.

"All right then." She parked her hip on the edge of the table, blocking his view of the balls. "If you won't take it from me, play me for it."

He stepped back from the table, his gaze sweeping over her with open cynicism. "You want me to play you?"

His partner at the table sniggered. "If the cowboy won't take you up on it, I will. I'll play you like a sonata, baby."

Straightening to his full height, the cowboy shot his buddy a dangerous look. She guessed he was a few inches over six feet and wondered how much of that was the boots. Probably only an inch or so. Without them, he'd still tower at least a foot above her five-foot-two inches.

She dropped another twenty. "Double or nothing? Eight ball, nine ball, nine ball kiss, Chicago, Chinese, Rotation 61," she rattled off the game variations.

A buff marine in a muscle shirt flashed a lecherous grin. "I'll rotate you sixty-nine, sweetheart." No doubt about it, they were already halfway to shit-faced.

Haley ignored him. "Slop shot, call shot. Your choice, cowboy. Loser buys the drinks."

Reid considered the blonde who'd brushed him off like a fly from shit less than an hour ago. When he'd paid her cover he hadn't expected anything in return except maybe a dance, but now she'd positioned herself squarely in his crosshairs.

"So you think you're a player, eh?" Reid eyed her with renewed speculation, wondering what game she was really playing.

"Only pool," she answered as if reading his mind. "A better question would be what kind of *player* are you?" She slid off the table, letting the double entendre hang.

"Guess you'll just have to find out for yourself. Mind if the lady steps in?" he asked the cluster of marines. The request was purely rhetorical. They all knew he was staking his claim, but he'd still sweeten the deal. "Tell you what, give us some space, and I'll buy you all a round."

"Go on," she urged the grunts as if shooing chickens, adding with a grin, "I'm sure Corporal Everett doesn't want any witnesses when he gets his ass handed to him."

The marines dispersed toward the bar with muffled guffaws.

His interest ramped another notch, Reid propped his cue against the table and cocked his head to study all five-foot-nothin' of her. She was probably no more than a buck ten soaking wet, yet had the balls to go toe-to-toe with him. "You sure talk big for such a puny little thing."

"I laid my money down, didn't I? What are we playing?" she asked.

"Let's just keep it a simple game of eight ball." He offered her a cue. "Ladies first?"

"No. Lag for break. I play by the rules." She set up two balls for the shot.

He came up beside her and leaned over the table, his

cue poised. "Always?" He was close enough to smell her, fresh and sweet like ripe strawberries. "Sometimes it's more fun to break 'em."

She snorted and chalked her cue. "Says the guy whose entire life is dictated by the USMC for what, the next four years?"

"Six more. I signed on for eight."

"*Eight?*" she pulled back with a surprised look. "What kind of idiocy is that?"

He stiffened. She had no qualms about speaking her mind, for damn sure. Lucky she was an attractive female. Good-looking women could just about get away with murder. Hell, many had. It was an injustice, or maybe God's idea of a joke, but facts were facts. Men had a long history of making life and death decisions guided by their dicks. His was already exerting a great deal of influence.

"Back home we have another word for it. It's called *patriotism*."

"Don't get your feathers all ruffled," she came back. "I just don't understand anyone's desire for that kind of life."

"The military creates order out of chaos. That often applies as much to the individual as to the mission."

"That may be, but there are plenty of other ways than the military to 'find yourself.'"

"I s'pose so," he replied. "But look how many people waste years of their lives in college only to end up flipping burgers."

She tossed her head. "And killing skills are so much more practical in life?" Her voice and eyes challenged. Taunted. But he wasn't about to take her bait.

"The Marines teach more than killing. Look...er... Hell, I still don't even know your name."

"Haley," she answered softly. "Haley Cooper."

"Look, Miz Cooper, we obviously don't see eye to eye on this issue, so let's just drop it and play."

They completed the lag shot, both balls bouncing off the table to return to the head rail. Reid's ball was closest, a millimeter from touching the rail. He considered the table. "Looks like it's gonna be ladies first after all."

"You sure you want me to break?" She flashed him a smug smile. "You might live to regret that decision, cowboy."

Reid stood a couple of steps behind and slightly to the right, perfectly positioned to scope her out as she set up her shot. Every movement was too damned distracting. Her dress clung to her ass, riding up as she bent over the table, but not as far as he'd like. He guessed she was a distance runner by the look of her lean and shapely legs. He found his gaze caught in a loop, tracking up and down between her legs and ass.

She broke, and then straightened, tugging her skirt back down over her legs. "You haven't said what your job is, Corporal Everett."

"Scout sniper." He flushed, knowing what was coming next. She'd try to put him on the defensive.

"You're a *sniper*?" Her eyes widened. "Isn't that the same as an *assassin*?"

He felt his color deepen another shade, but was careful to keep his expression and voice neutral. "A scout sniper's primary function is to conduct close reconnaissance and surveillance in order to gain intelligence on the enemy and terrain. By necessity, he must be skilled in long-range marksmanship from concealed locations in order to support combat operations."

"Wow. That was a mouthful. Did you quote all that from some soldier manual?"

"A U.S. Marine isn't a *soldier*."

"What's the difference? You both make war, don't you?" She studied him as if she knew she'd ventured onto treacherous ground but was still determined to see how far he'd let her tread.

"The Marine Corps' primary mission isn't to *make* war but to *protect* this country and those who can't protect themselves, Miz Cooper." He continued unapologetically. "Unfortunately, sometimes that does mean war and killing." She was intentionally pushing his hot buttons, but he was accustomed to maintaining rigid self-control.

"So you actually think some people *deserve* to die?" Her face was flushed, and her green eyes blazed.

"Some do," he answered levelly. There was no way to win once an argument got emotional. "I'm a peaceful man who believes in minding my own pastures, but I also believe in good and evil. There are a lot of very bad people in this world. Certainly the ones who fly airplanes through skyscrapers. When that kind of thing happens, I believe in doing whatever it takes to protect our own."

He could see her getting more worked up by the minute, and damned if he wasn't also—just not in the same way. She'd been baiting him from the start, spewing arguments that usually just pissed him off, but in this case, it was turning him on.

His gaze locked on her mouth. Her tongue darted out as if she read his thoughts. She drew a breath as if to formulate another rebuttal, but he'd had enough. Before her lips could spout off any more of the Pacifist Tree Hugger's Manifesto, he pulled her into his arms and silenced her with his.

———

The kiss came without warning, and Haley was too stunned at first to react. He began gently enough, his lips sliding over hers, hands cupping her face, thumbs stroking her jaw, and then he grew more insistent, his tongue probing the seal of her lips. His callused hands were simultaneously firm and gentle, and his lips paradoxically soft and commanding.

Mere seconds had her head spinning and stomach fluttering. She was slipping fast and not about to let him pull her in any deeper. Part of her wanted to give into it, to see where it might lead, but the other half resented his audacity. Her pride won out. She resisted the urge to soften, to open to him, then stiffened, pressing her hands against his chest.

He released her instantly.

She stepped back, knees weak and pulse racing. "I didn't come here looking to hook up."

"Neither did I. But sometimes unexpected things happen." His gaze locked with hers, a look of speculation gleaming in his eyes. "When they do, it's best to just go with your gut instinct."

"That so? Well all my instincts scream 'no marines,' so don't let it *happen* again."

Suddenly remembering the cue in her hand, Haley turned back to the table. It took all of her will to focus back on the game. She could hardly believe how he'd nearly unraveled her with a single kiss. Then again, no one had *ever* kissed her like that. She made her break, pocketing the one, and then moved methodically around the table, calling each shot as she sank every solid. Only the eight ball remained, but it was trapped behind two stripes.

Reid's lips curved with smug certainty. "Looks like I'll get my turn after all."

"Don't count your chickens, cowboy." She laid down her cue and searched the wall behind her for a shorter one. "Jump cue," she said in answer to his silent question.

"You're kidding right?"

"Nope." Approaching the table, she angled for her shot. She could almost feel his eyes on her ass. She glanced over her shoulder. Sure enough. He was leaning against the wall with both arms crossed over his broad chest, his gaze zeroed in on her behind.

"Enjoying the view?"

"Sure am," he confessed, unabashed.

He was sadly mistaken if he thought he'd unnerve her. Keeping him in her peripheral vision, she widened her stance and stretched out over the table. All signs of smugness evaporated from his face. He tugged on his jeans.

Haley grinned, reveling in her small victory, and then prepared for a bigger one. "Eight ball, side pocket," she declared with confidence. On a three count she took the shot, jumping the stripes to pocket the eight. "Yeah baby!" She threw down the cue and fisted the air, gloating in her triumph.

Reid gaped at the table. "I'll be goddamned. How did you learn to do that?"

"My grandpa was a regional pool champion."

"That bit of information was mighty sneaky to withhold."

She shrugged. "You didn't ask. Loser buys. I'll take a mojito."

His gaze darted to her hands. "No bracelet? Thought you never broke the rules."

"I said I *play* by them. That's not quite the same. Are you gonna buy me that drink or not?"

Reid signaled a waitress, ordering a beer and a Coke. "Sorry, sweetheart," he answered her scowl. "I might bend a few rules, but I do abide by the *law*. And you aren't legal yet...not for drinking anyway." His gaze swept slowly over her, inciting ripples of heat in its wake.

"You're wasting your breath," she insisted, but her gaze wavered from his.

Reid Everett oozed the kind of quiet, sexy confidence that inspired both trust and stupidity. He was self-assured without arrogance, supremely comfortable in his own skin, the kind of man who made smart girls do dumb things. Her will was growing weaker the longer she stayed with him. Her brain told her it was time to go, but she couldn't quite bring her feet to comply.

Yolanda's appearance was her saving grace. "Thought you might be getting thirsty, *chica*." She had two drinks in hand and a marine in dress blues hot on her tail. She handed Haley a cosmo, not her drink of choice, but it would have to do.

"Haley, this is Corporal Rafael Garcia. *Rafi, esta es mi major amiga,* Haley." She eyed Reid with interest. "Who's your friend?"

"Garcia's better half," Reid answered with a smirk.

"Oh yeah?"

"Corporal Reid Everett, also with the Thundering Third. Raf's my spotter."

"I'm Yolanda Rojas." She raked Reid from Stetson to boots. "You look more like a cowboy than a marine."

"Most of us don't wear dress blues on liberty, but I s'pose Garcia here needs all the help he can get."

"Ay, Rafi!" Yolanda tugged his sleeve. "Are you going to let him get away with that?"

"He's one to talk, sporting the *tejana*," Garcia shot back. "Most of the guys in this place only wear it for one reason."

"That's them. This is me." Reid shrugged. "This is my uniform of choice in Wyoming."

Suppressing a smile, Haley watched the exchange over her drink. Reid leaned down to murmur a warning. "Get caught with that and they'll toss us all."

"Then let's find a table, *hombre*." Garcia steered them to a newly vacated spot in the corner.

A short while later, Haley's mood had lightened. Maybe it was the alcohol, but she was actually enjoying herself. Reid and Garcia continually razzed each other while Yolanda flirted outrageously with both of them. It didn't bother Haley. Yolanda was fun, flighty, and notoriously fickle, but tonight she'd obviously set her sights on Rafael.

Garcia bought another round of drinks, then he and Yolanda headed once more to the dance floor where he pulled her into an indecently close two-step.

"Yolanda and Rafael seem to have hit it off," she remarked, eager to keep the conversation on neutral ground.

Reid was slouched back in his chair watching the room. "Garcia's a good man and a helluva marine, but he likes to play fast and loose."

"Then they're well matched. Yolanda's a party girl."

"What about you?" he asked. "You don't seem the party-girl type."

"Me? No." She laughed. "I'm a bookworm and a certified monogamist."

He took a sip of his beer. "So am I. The monogamy part, not the bookworm. Hated school. It's why I joined the military instead of college."

She snorted. "You really think I'm gonna buy that monogamy line?"

"Not trying to sell it. Just stating a fact. I've been with two women in my life."

"Two?"

"Yeah. The first was my best friend's older sister, and the second was my younger sister's best friend. We dated for a coupla years after high school."

She still didn't believe him, but curiosity got the better of her. "Best friend's older sister? So you were seduced by an older woman? This I gotta hear."

"I don't kiss and tell."

"Really? But isn't that all you guys talk about in your down time? Getting laid?"

"I don't deny there's a lot of that kinda talk, but you gotta understand how it is. We're deployed for months at a time. We're physically and mentally pushed to the brink. A man's got to have something to look forward to. Under those conditions, it's usually the thought of a woman."

"So you're trying to justify filthy talk as a morale booster?"

"I s'pose so." His gaze met hers and then dropped back to the table. "You'd best push that drink over here now."

"Why? You want some?"

"No, they're checking IDs. Don't—"

His warning was too late. Haley had already turned around. The glare of a flashlight blinded her. "Crap," she muttered.

"Hands on the table please."

She set her teeth with a sense of impending disaster. The bouncer directed the beam of light to her hands. "No bracelet?"

"It must have fallen off." Her lie wasn't remotely convincing.

The bouncer shone the light in Reid's face. He tipped his hat back. "There a problem?"

"Yeah. We enforce the drinking laws here."

The flashlight darted over the beer bottle and half-full martini glass that sat in front of him, then back to Reid's face. Sometime during the confrontation, Reid had managed to slide her cosmo to his side of the table. Maybe she was off the hook after all.

"You a two-fisted drinker?" the bouncer asked.

"Yeah," Reid offered, wooden-faced. "Those are both mine."

The bouncer picked up the glass and sniffed. "What kinda pussy drinks a cosmo?"

Reid's jaw twitched, but his voice remained level. "I guess that would be me."

"Yeah? What about the lipstick on the rim? You wear that too? I wanna see some ID. Now. Asshole." His hand came down on Reid's shoulder.

Reid's gaze tracked to the hand and then returned to the bouncer's face. His expression grew deadly. "I advise you to remove your fucking hand from my shoulder before I remove it permanently from your wrist." His threat was slow, soft, and crystal clear.

Haley felt an unexpected thrill. She blamed the alcohol.

The bouncer beckoned to the cop making rounds at other tables.

"Shit," Haley murmured under her breath. Now her recklessness was going to get them arrested. She felt a sudden surge of guilt. Other than kissing her, Reid had behaved impeccably all night. The guy certainly didn't deserve a black mark on his record.

"The drink is really mine," Haley blurted to the cop.

"She with you?" he asked Reid.

"Yeah. She's with me." He volunteered his military ID card.

The cop's expression softened infinitesimally. "What company you with?"

"The one-three, officer. Just finished scout sniper training and getting ready to redeploy."

"Oh yeah? You've already done a tour?

"Two. The last was in Anbar province, Iraq. Looks like we're going back for another round of that shit."

"Yeah? I was a gunnery sergeant with the one-one in Desert Storm." He shone the light on Haley again. "Your boyfriend here just saved your ass, girlie, but you'll both be leaving now. See them out," he instructed the bouncer and then moved on to another table.

Chapter 3

"BUT—BUT I STILL HAVE A FRIEND INSIDE. WE CAME together," Haley protested.

"C'mon." The asshole bouncer took her by the arm.

"Big mistake." Reid stepped in. He had little tolerance for bullies, let alone one who'd lay hands on a woman. "Hands off her. Now. I already told you what I'd do, and I'm about itchin' to make good on my promise."

Chest puffed, the bouncer moved into Reid's space. "All you marines think you're such badasses, don't you? The minute you put on the uniform, you're fucking Superman."

Reid shrugged. "The Corps' reputation speaks for itself. A marine is your best friend or your worst enemy…and I ain't exactly feeling the love right now." He wasn't the brawling type, but Reid never backed down when pushed to the wall. "This is your last warning," Reid threatened.

The bouncer met him stare for stare. "You're gonna have to knock me down."

Reid tensed. He knew the musclehead had a good forty pounds on him, which might give him the advantage of brute strength, but he'd be slow and clumsy. He'd have to strike first and fast. The dumbass would never know what hit him.

He was about to do just that when Haley interposed herself between them, hands anchored on her hips. "This is ridiculous. Do heightened testosterone levels kill brain cells or something?"

Both men stared down at her dumbfounded, their mutual antagonism temporarily forgotten.

"Let's just go, Reid." She grabbed his arm, dragging him in the direction of the door. Reid hesitated, his eyes never leaving the bouncer. For a moment the asshole looked like he'd follow them out, but then turned away with a shrug.

Once outside, Reid shook his head with a chuckle.

"What's so funny?" she demanded.

"Just taking a mental inventory," he replied. "First, I get my ass kicked at pool. Then, I barely escape arrest for contributing to the delinquency of a minor. After that, I'm harassed by an overzealous, steroid-enhanced gorilla looking for a brawl, which by the way, would have landed me in the brig. All this within two hours of meeting you. You are a whole lot of trouble in a tiny little package, Haley Cooper."

"I never should have involved you," she replied, looking contrite.

"It's all right," he said. "To be honest, I can't even remember the last time I got thrown out of a bar."

"It wasn't my intention to cause you any trouble. I'm really sorry."

"I'm not," he countered. "Just wish I'd gotten at least one punch in. That bouncer deserves to get his ass kicked."

"Let it go. It's bad enough as it is. They're not going to let either of us back in that place for at least six months."

"Does that bother you?"

"Well, no," she confessed. "I hate clubs. I'm just glad Yolanda wasn't there. She would have throttled me if she got banned from her favorite trolling spot."

"Then it is all for the best," Reid said.

"Why's that?"

"Now she can't drag you back here again. Problem solved."

His answer elicited a laugh. He liked the sound.

"But what about you?" she asked. "You can't come back either."

"Doesn't matter to me. I don't dance, and there're plenty of better drinking holes a lot closer to base. Besides, I'm gonna be gone for the next eight months anyway."

"Iraq?" she asked. "I heard what you told the cop. You've already been there?"

"Yeah. I've been to that hellhole."

"And now you're going back again?"

"Yup. Jarheads are all stupid as shit like that. We believe in completing the mission. Can I drive you somewhere?"

She considered the offer. "Yolanda brought me, but I'd hate to ruin her night by asking her to take me home so early. On the other hand, I live forty-five minutes in the opposite direction from you."

"I don't mind."

"What about Garcia? Didn't you ride together?"

"He's smart enough to dial a taxi. Where do you live?"

"San Jacinto."

"My truck's over there." He pointed and then settled his hand on her lower back for the second time that night. Her skin was warm through the cotton dress, yet she shivered.

"Cold?" he asked.

"It's a bit chilly, but nights are always cold at this elevation. I should have brought a jacket."

"I keep one in the backseat of my truck. You can borrow it."

They walked across the parking lot in silence broken only by the crunch of gravel underfoot and the music blaring from inside the club. He clicked his key fob to unlock the truck.

"This is your ride?" she asked.

"Yeah, it's mine." He was glad he'd had his F-350 washed and detailed. Although he didn't own a lot, he tried to take good care of the few possessions he had.

She eyeballed his pride and joy with disapproval. "Do you have any idea how wasteful this vehicle is?"

He shrugged. "S'pose I know better than you do, since I tank it up every week."

"Don't you care anything about the environment?"

"Look, Haley, before you get back on that high and holy horse of yours, remember where I come from. A Prius ain't exactly equipped for farm and ranch work."

She closed her mouth.

He opened her door.

She hesitated again, a wall of wariness once more surrounding her. "You are just offering a ride, right? You aren't expecting anything else, are you?"

"Like what?" he prompted.

"A lot of guys would think—"

He shook his head. "You've got to stop painting all men with the same brush. No strings, Haley. I'm not that kinda guy. I just want to be sure you get home safe. That's all. Besides, it's only nine o'clock on a Saturday night, and I don't have any plans other than packing my stuff."

"When do you leave?"

"Next week. You wanna send Yolanda a text to let her know you're leaving with me?"

"Do you mind?"

"Course not."

She pulled out her phone while he retrieved his Carhartt jacket from the back. He suppressed a chuckle as he dropped it over her shoulders. The coat nearly swallowed her up. He handed her into the cab, circled around to the driver's side, and climbed in.

"Damn it," she cursed. "My phone's dead!"

"Here." He fished his iPhone from his shirt pocket. "Use mine."

He waited while she typed out her text.

A moment later, the phone chirped. "Is that her answer?"

"Yes. She says go on ahead and not to worry about Garcia. She'll drive him back to base." She added dryly, "You might have figured out she has a thing for guys in uniform."

"A perfect match." He grinned. "Garcia has a thing for girls with a thing."

She laughed again. He could get used to that.

They headed toward I-215 north. In silence. She shifted frequently in her seat as if restless. The cab seemed smaller, the air heavier. He glanced frequently in her direction. He was feeling pretty edgy himself, but knew how to hide it.

"I make you nervous?"

"No! Of course not." Her denial sounded too forced.

"Hungry?" he ventured at length. "It's still early. Want to go get a burger or something?"

"No thanks. I don't eat meat. People can survive perfectly well without killing animals for food."

"Why doesn't that surprise me," he mumbled.

"Mind if I turn on some music?" she asked.

"Go ahead. Anything but that hip-hop crap is fine with me."

She looked up from the tuner. "You don't like it?"

"Nope. And I hate that kind of dancing too. Guess I'm kinda old-fashioned that way."

"I don't like rap or hip-hop either."

She scanned several stations. The breezy lyrics of "Breakfast at Tiffany's" by Deep Blue Something filled the air. *You say that we've got nothing in common, no common ground to start from...* She grinned. "Apropos, don't you think? I agree with you on the dancing, by the way. If I'm going to copulate with someone, I'd rather do it in private than in the middle of a dance floor."

"Copulate? Strange word choice. Sounds a bit... clinical."

"Yeah, well, I guess my brain is trained to think in scientific terms."

"Why's that?"

"I'm a biology major. Pre-vet actually. I've taken almost everything I can at Mt. San Jacinto Community College. I'll be transferring soon to UC Davis."

"Oh yeah?"

"I *hope* to get into the veterinary college, but it's

pretty competitive. I'm doing a summer internship at a wolf sanctuary to improve my chances."

"A wolf sanctuary? In Southern California?"

"Yes. It's run by a group that wants to reintroduce wolves to California."

"Yeah," he scoffed. "Because that program's been such a raving success in the Rockies."

"What do you mean? Conservationists have saved them from the brink of extinction."

"Wolves have been saved all right. And if they keep multiplying at the current rate, it's our livestock that'll be on the endangered list."

She crossed her arms. "People should eat less meat anyway. It's unhealthy."

Reid cursed under his breath. "Ever been around a wolf, Haley?"

"No, but I've worked at dog kennels for years."

"Wolves are *not* dogs," he argued. "You need to get that straight from the start. Don't think that a wolf can be tamed or trained. Or even a wolf cross. They might be cute and furry, but they're damned dangerous animals."

"They still deserve our respect and our protection. All animals do."

"I don't argue that. I like and respect animals too, but predators like wolves and grizzlies need to be kept in check."

"What do you mean by that?"

"I mean their numbers need to be managed."

"You mean by *killing* them?"

"When necessary," he said.

"So you're one of *them*?" She shook her head. "Why should that surprise me? I can partly understand people who hunt game for subsistence, but the ones who consider hunting and killing pure sport are another matter."

"There's something you need to understand before you pass judgment. I was born hunting, tracking, and shooting. I held my first rifle at about six years old. Killed my first elk at twelve. My family runs a hunting outfit just outside Yellowstone. It's been our livelihood for three generations. "

"And I suppose you have all those animal heads mounted on your wall as trophies?"

"I do. A whole roomful. And I'm not going to apologize for it. I like hunting and shooting, but I've never killed anything just for the hell of it. We eat all the game animals. And every predator I've ever taken has been at the behest of the Fish and Wildlife Managers. Trophy hunting helps maintain the ecological balance."

"Nature did fine on its own until people like *you* almost wiped out the predators."

"People like *me*?" He mumbled another epithet.

"Yes," she declared. "And someone has to make it right."

"And you think that's *you*?"

"Not me alone, of course, but there are a lot of people who care about wildlife and the environment."

"So you're one of those green-living crusaders."

His mockery put her further on the defensive. "Maybe I am, but certainly no more zealous than *you* are."

He grinned. "So you're actually saying we're *alike*."

She exhaled an exasperated huff. "Don't twist my words. There's a huge gulf of difference between you and me. I like animals *alive*, and you like their heads on a wall."

"That's not fair and you know it. I've always been surrounded by animals. I was raised with dozens of dogs, cats, and horses. They've been a huge part of my life."

"Then how can you hunt? I just don't understand it. Why kill wild animals when we raise millions of domestic ones for consumption?" She opened her mouth to sound off again and then closed it with a sigh. "I'm not going to convince you anyway, am I?"

"Nope. And there's no sense wasting any more breath on it. Let's just agree to disagree."

"If we avoid all the things we disagree on, what's left to talk about?"

"We've hardly exhausted all the possibilities."

"Next exit. Turn right," she instructed. "Then left at the second light."

They drove another mile in protracted silence.

"Turn here," she said. "It's the first house on the left."

He pulled into the drive, put the truck in park, and cut the ignition.

"Thanks for the ride, Reid. It was kind of you." She reached for the door.

"Wait a minute," he stalled. He didn't want her to go. Not yet. Although her opinions annoyed the hell out of him, her big green eyes drew him in. He'd never felt this kind of contradictory attraction before. Politics be damned; in this moment nothing mattered but his desire to taste her again. "Don't go yet. I want to try an experiment."

Her gaze narrowed. "What kind of experiment?"

"A simple one. I bet if we tried real hard we could find a number of things we can agree on."

She snorted. "I doubt it. We stand on opposite sides of

every issue as far as I can tell. Besides, what's the point if we have to *try*? Most people connect over common interests and shared views. We have none of those."

"Being on different sides doesn't necessarily make us enemies. Good people are allowed to disagree. Some of the best solutions to the hardest problems result from differing minds coming together, meeting in the middle. Humor me, Haley. How about we just start with one thing and see if we can't build on that?"

His gaze honed in on her mouth. He moved closer, close enough to feel her soft, sweet breath caressing his face. He waited. He'd made his intent clear. The next move was hers.

"Like what?" she whispered, licking her lips.

There it was again, that subtle invitation.

"This," he answered.

～⁂～

His lips met hers in a soft exploration that asked, rather than demanded. She didn't stiffen or retreat this time, but leaned into him by fractions. His mouth was gentle, tender, and teasing, as if savoring the kiss. She couldn't help responding to the warm, wet slide of his lips. Despite their differences, her body had been thrumming with anticipation the entire drive, even secretly craving this.

He slid to the center of the bench seat, cupping her nape, and angling his head, but still made no effort to exert total control. Instead, he coaxed with small flicks and darts of his tongue. It seemed he was right after all. It *was* possible to meet in the middle. She opened to him with a sigh. He drew her sideways onto his lap, deeper into the kiss. Their breath mixed and moans mingled as his questing tongue met hers in long, lush strokes that sent warm ripples to the place between her thighs.

She pushed his hat off.

He cupped her breasts with both hands, gently squeezing.

She whimpered with the growing need to feel his hands on her bare skin, his mouth on her breasts. His callused fingers answered one of those wishes, gliding down her body and under her skirt. Slow and deliberate, he inched upward toward the apex of her thighs. She answered with a moan as his warm fingers explored beneath her panties, delving into her wetness. She clenched her thighs together, trapping his hand. His mouth never left hers as he circled and stroked her, continuing to ramp her need until she shuddered with the first spasms of pleasure.

"Good God." She broke breathlessly from the kiss. "You sure know how to get a girl all hot and bothered."

She drew her skirt higher to straddle his thighs, squirming against his erection but rather than moving to penetrate her, Reid withdrew his fingers and slowly eased her back with a deep, regret-laced sigh.

Her gaze darted to his face. "What's wrong?"

"This is about to get way out of hand, sweetheart. I didn't mean for it to go so far. I'm not about to do this parked in your front yard."

"You wanna go somewhere else?" she asked. "I can't take you inside. I live with my grandparents, and they're kind of old-fashioned about these things."

"Then we have something in common," Reid said. "So am I."

"But I don't understand. I thought you…we—"

He shushed her, pressing a finger to her lips. Another shudder of desire rippled through her at the smell of her own essence. "It's not a good idea to start something up when I'm leaving in a few days."

"Who says this has to lead to anything?" Haley quoted Yolanda. She throbbed with the need he'd incited but now refused to relieve.

His blue gaze met hers. "I do. As much as this pains me, *and believe me it does*, this ain't gonna happen tonight."

"Tonight is *all* there is, Reid. I thought this is what all you marines wanted. I don't understand you at all." She wanted to grind her teeth in frustration.

"I'm not so hard to figure out. I said I don't do hook-ups. Neither do you, by the way. When I get you in my bed, I want to take my time and do it right."

"In your bed?" She laughed. "Who says you'll ever get another chance after this?"

"*I do*. Now give me your number."

"Not likely. As you just said, there's no point in getting further involved. You're leaving."

"But I'll be back," he countered.

"And I'll be gone. UC Davis is over five hours away. Besides, I have a strict no-marine policy."

"Then what was this?" he asked softly.

"A momentary lapse of reason, but I'm quite recovered from it." Not exactly the truth, but she was burning with resentment. She'd offered to do something she *never* did, and he'd rejected her.

There would be no second chances.

"Give me your number, Haley."

He tried to kiss her again, but she pulled away and reached for the door. "Good-bye, Reid. Thanks again for the ride."

This time he didn't stop her. She listened for his engine as she walked to the front door, but he didn't burn rubber like she'd expected. The porch light flickered. Her grandpa opened the door with a look of surprise.

"You're home early." He gazed past her shoulder to Reid's big, black truck in the drive. His brows met in a scowl. "Who's that? And where's Yolanda?"

"Just a friend, Gramps. I had a headache and Yolanda wasn't ready to go, so he offered me a ride."

"You aren't asking him in?"

"No. I told you I have a headache. I'm going straight to bed."

He touched her sleeve. "Is that his jacket?"

"Oh shoot! I forgot I was wearing it."

Reid had started the truck and was backing out. She tore off the jacket and waved it madly overhead. He paused, nodded acknowledgment, but then pulled out without it, leaving her looking after him.

"Guess he doesn't want it back."

"Or more likely"—her grandpa winked—"he needed a good excuse to return."

Chapter 4

REID'S BALLS ACHED ALL THE WAY BACK TO BASE. HE'D wanted her something fierce. He wanted more than anything to feel himself moving deep inside of her and knew she'd been as caught up in the moment as he'd been, but tomorrow, she would have relegated him to the lowest depths of hell. Maybe later he'd kick himself for passing up the opportunity, but the last thing he wanted was to reinforce all her prejudices about marines.

Besides that, he'd been raised to believe that anything worth doing deserved to be done right. A girl like Haley Cooper wasn't a fast fuck on the seat of his parked truck. He had a strong hunch she'd be worth his time and effort.

The following morning, he was still thinking about her. Maybe it was just the challenge that appealed to him, but he couldn't get her out of his head. He was damned if he could figure it out. They had nothing in common, but their attraction was as real as any he'd ever felt.

He'd intentionally left his favorite jacket behind. The prospect of going back for it, for her, would give him something to look forward to over the next eight months of purgatory.

She'd refused to give him her number, but he still had the text she'd sent Yolanda from his phone. Worst-case scenario, he'd call her friend and ask for it, but it would probably be easier to get it through Garcia. In this situation, his spotter was definitely his best in.

Reid was sprawled on his rack restlessly flipping through TV channels when Garcia dragged into the barracks looking haggard as shit. "Rough night?" Reid asked.

"She fucking wore me out."

"Is that a complaint?"

"Hell no," Garcia replied. "I think she might be *the one*."

"Oh yeah? Think you could get Haley's number from her?"

"What? She wouldn't give it to you herself? Even after a lift home? Guess she was the only one who got a ride, *eh hombre*?" Garcia laughed. "If scoring is that hard for you, maybe you'd better give up on women and just stick to the rifle range."

"Fuck you, Garcia," Reid grumbled. "Just get it for me, okay?"

Later that day, Garcia handed him a slip of paper with a smirk Reid was tempted to smack off his face. He snatched it from his buddy's hand without comment and punched it into his phone contacts. He then pocketed his phone only to whip it back out. He wanted to call but resisted the urge. Instead, he quickly typed a text. Thinking about u Haley Cooper…Reid.

Moments later his phone vibrated. U forgot ur jacket.

He texted his response. I'll get it from u when I come back.

No marines… she replied.

Give me a chance & I'll change your mind.

Four days later, the Third Battalion First Marines boarded three commercial jets bound for Kuwait City. For twenty-two hours, they paced the aisles and watched movies — *Ocean's Eleven*, *Men in Black*, and *Die Another Day*. *Black Hawk Down* played twice by request. The incident in Mogadishu was a brutal reminder of the similar Blackwater incident, and why they were returning to Iraq. The arrival of the Thundering Third meant there would be a reckoning for the spilled American blood.

Reid didn't fear death. He'd already had enough close calls to know it was out of his control anyway. Death in a hot zone was random and unpredictable. It was never safe. He'd learned that on his first deployment two years ago.

They'd spent weeks on Failaka Island in Kuwait training for an invasion when America's finest were literally caught with their pants down. Two squads from Bravo were stripped down to their skivvies and kicking back on the beach when an old white truck came barreling out of nowhere, spraying fire. Having used blanks for the training exercises, the marines had no ammo. No armor. No cover on an open beach.

Growing up in Wyoming, with the constant presence of grizzlies, wolves, and mountain lions, Reid was in the habit of carrying — even if taking a shit. Out of two dozen marines, he was the only one with his sidearm and live ammo. While the others dove into the surf, he'd returned fire.

The incident earned him a commendation and a spot in scout sniper school, but the damage was done. Two green recruits were wounded. The third, a combat veteran nearing his end of service, went home in a box. Brutal lesson learned: Complacency kills.

They were now circling over Kuwait City. Reid took a few shots with his phone, snapping photos of the city and the surrounding desert. As soon as they landed, he texted his family in Wyoming. It would probably be the last time he'd have cell service for the next eight or nine months, not that the phone would do any good anyway. It was a huge mistake to take any electronics into the desert. They were usually trashed by dust and sand within two weeks. If he couldn't find a way to store it, he'd have to throw it away. For now, he could at least share a few photos.

He then sent a one-liner to Haley. Still thinking about u Haley Cooper...Reid. He might be out of sight, but he refused to be out of mind. Moments later, she surprised him by replying with her email address.

—◦◦◦—

After disembarking, they assembled for a briefing. The entire battalion was gathered under a scorching desert sun, battle guidons barely flickering in a scarcely perceptible breeze. Though nighttime temps would be close to freezing, days were hot as hell, 110 degrees without counting the slow-cooker effect of body armor. Standing stone-faced in rigid lines, the companies faced one another in formation as their stoic colonel made his motivational address.

"You are marines. You protect innocent lives. You stand for the universal cause of freedom and fight to keep our country from further threat. You are United

States Marines. The world's finest warriors. The most feared fighting machines. This is a moment you will remember for the rest of your lives. The time you carved a place in history with the entire world watching. You are marines," he reiterated. "*Never* forget it."

After being muzzled and chained for months, the Devil Dogs were about to be unleashed.

The next hours were spent with individual commanders reviewing the battle plan, breaking it down by company, platoon, and individual squads. Dust choked their throats as Reid and Garcia grabbed their gear and trekked toward the lines of armored Humvees and 7-Tons lining the periphery of the airfield. With weapons shouldered, the "Balls of the Corps" piled into their respective transport vehicles.

Within hours of their arrival, the miles-long convoy pulled out onto the highway headed for FOB Volturno, two miles outside Fallujah—the hottest zone in Iraq. The marines grew quieter and more reflective the closer they approached the Abdaly checkpoint separating the two countries. There were a number of changes since his last deployment. Hundreds of soldiers, low-flying helicopters, and a new barrier comprised of electrified fencing and razor wire, reinforced by a fifteen-by-fifteen-foot trench.

A short time after crossing into al-Anbar, a storm of screaming rockets and mortar fire commenced. Reid's gaze flickered to the blanch-faced, wide-eyed "boots." Although they'd had plenty of live-fire exercises at home, this was the real deal. Several mortars hit nearby, rocking the vehicles and quaking the earth.

Garcia snagged his gaze. "Ali Baba's hospitality

committee." A wide smirk stretched across Garcia's mouth. "Welcome back to hell, *esé*."

Reid regarded the craters, careful to keep his tone bland. "At least their aim hasn't improved."

"Time to embrace the suck, *hombres*," Garcia quipped to his comrades. "For the next eight months, this is about as good as it gets."

On the heels of the attack came the familiar drone of an AC-130 Ghostrider circling overhead.

Garcia pointed to the sky. "I'm getting a hard-on now. I love that fucking plane."

More earthquakes echoed in the distance—the Ghostrider's reciprocation.

By nightfall, mortars and missiles were raining down like a meteor shower, with hellfire rockets lighting up the nighttime skies like shooting stars.

—∿∿—

Dear Haley,

> *This is my first real letter to you. I may not get another chance for a while. Hell, I may not get another chance, period. Truth be told, I don't even know if I'll send it. Although I prefer to live by the adage that if you can't say something positive, it's best to say nothing, there aren't a whole lot of rainbows in the middle of a shit storm. And that's what we're up against. The grunts we came to replace greeted us with a nod and the thousand-mile stare. No words were exchanged. None were needed. We all know what we're facing.*

Every morning begins a new game of Russian roulette as we sidestep IEDs, dodge RPGs, rockets, mortars, and sniper fire, taking every minute as it comes, knowing nothing over here can ever be taken for granted. My first thought every morning is only to make it through the coming day, and my last, at night, is a prayer of gratitude that I'm still alive. At the end of each day, I can only marvel at the beauty of sunsets that are some of the most spectacular I have ever seen. Watching them is an evening ritual.

Reid paused to read the message, realizing it was far too raw and real. Did she ever think about him? He didn't know. Did she care? He didn't know that either. Maybe he never would.

With a shake of his head, he deleted the text of the email, attached a photo of a breathtaking desert sunset, and hit Send.

Chapter 5

San Jacinto, California

HALEY MUMBLED A CURSE AND INSERTED HER EARBUDS. She wished her grandpa would swallow his pride and get hearing aids. He loved watching shoot-'em-ups, but the explosive bursts from the TV always broke her concentration. With a sigh she turned up the volume on her iPod, hoping to drown out the blare of the TV with the more soothing sounds of Evanescence. She'd barely returned to her notes when Yolanda barged into her room, an annoying habit formed from twelve years as best friends and neighbors.

"Oh my God, Haley! Have you been watching the news?"

"No." Haley yanked out the earbuds and threw her notebook down in disgust. "I've been *trying* to study for exams. What has you in such a tizzy?"

Yolanda grabbed her arm and dragged her into the living room where Gramps lay snoring in his La-Z-Boy.

"Do you see that?" Yolanda jabbed a finger at the TV. "It's happening right now, and Rafi and Reid are over there!"

Haley's pulse quickened at the images of a full-blown military assault. Only weeks ago, Reid had sent her a selfie of him and Garcia both sporting ridiculous-looking moustaches that all the marines had been ordered to grow, ostensibly to improve cultural relations. By the state of things, the mustache mission had failed.

Amid Yolanda's near-hysteria, Haley willed herself to sound calm. "They knew what they were getting into, Yo," she argued. "It *is* a war, and they volunteered for it."

"You are like ice! How can you be so heartless?"

"I'm not heartless. I just see the other side. We're invaders. Of course they're going to fight back. Wouldn't you if someone invaded us?"

"I don't care about the politics. I only care about our *people* over there." Yolanda sniffed. "Is that what you have against Reid? You think he and Rafi *want* to hurt people?"

"No, but I think they're misguided. War is never the answer," Haley insisted.

"You really think so?" Her friend scowled. "It's that university crap, isn't it?"

"C'mon, Yolanda. Don't be angry just because I have a different viewpoint."

Yolanda threw her hands up. "It's like I don't even know you anymore. Having a degree doesn't make you smarter than the rest of the world."

"No, but it makes one more aware. More enlightened."

"*Enlightened?* So you think I'm ignorant because I want to be a pastry chef?"

"Of course not! Everyone should do what makes them happy…as long as it doesn't hurt anyone else."

"We can't expect to go through life without ever hurting anyone, Haley. It's going to happen whether we intend to or not. Did you know Rafi went to college?"

"He did?"

"Yeah. Three years at UCLA on a full scholarship but he quit to join the Marines."

"Why would he do *that*?" Haley asked.

"He said college bored him, and he couldn't stand the thought of wearing a suit and working a desk. That kind of life doesn't fit everyone. He joined the Marines because he wants to protect people. I really *liked* Rafael." Yolanda's eyes misted. "There was *something* with him. I thought maybe when he gets back…" Her lips quivered. "*If* he comes back…"

"They'll get through this, Yo." Haley wrapped her arms around her best friend. "He'll come home." But even as she comforted Yolanda, her thoughts filled with Reid. It was true that she didn't believe in the war, but that didn't mean she didn't care about Reid.

Later, after Yolanda left, Haley opened her books again but still couldn't concentrate. His jacket still hung in her closet. She pulled it off the hanger and put it on, shutting her eyes and breathing hints of leather and male musk. His scent evoked the memory of the night he'd driven her home and initiated stirrings of unsated lust deep in her belly.

She didn't understand why he'd held back that night. She also didn't know why she'd hung on to his jacket. She could have mailed it back to base long ago but hadn't been able to bring herself to part with it. Maybe just smelling him made her believe he'd stay alive?

She still couldn't understand her powerful attraction to him. It was as if they were the north and south poles of a magnet—and just as drawn to each other.

She'd tried to put him out of mind, but every week or two a random message appeared in her inbox.

Sometimes it was just a captioned photograph, like the one of him and Garcia fishing at Lake Baharia, a place the Marines had nicknamed Dreamland. Sometimes he only sent a short line meant to make her chuckle. The emails were never very long or overly personal, but just enough to keep him in her thoughts. She supposed it was his way of laying a quiet siege.

Still unable to study, she scrolled through the half dozen emails she hadn't been able to delete.

———∿∿———

Temperature topped 120 today. With flak & helmet on a sauna would have been cooler. Our mission is to win Fallujah peacefully, but the prospect is less than optimistic. Thinking about you, Haley Cooper. —Reid

Peacemaking with tanks and rifles seems contradictory to me. Thx for the pictures. The mustache doesn't work for you. Looks more like a caterpillar on your face. —Haley

Spent two days building a soccer field for the Iraqi kids only to have the insurgents destroy it. It's an uphill battle at best. Still thinking about you, Haley Cooper. —Reid

I've been accepted to UC Davis. Heading to Sacramento in a few weeks, so I won't be here when you return. Should I send your jacket to Camp Pendleton? —Haley

Negative, Haley Cooper. Will collect it in person... along with something else I promised myself. —Reid

In your dreams, Marine. —Haley

Every single night, sweetheart. —Reid

—⁓—

Over time she'd come to look forward to his messages.
The last email had been a photo of a desert sunset with no
message attached. Her chest tightened. That was almost
three weeks ago. She hadn't heard from him since.

Chapter 6

Camp Pendleton, Southern California coast

GARCIA WAS SACKED OUT ON HIS RACK WATCHING Reid pack. "You going back to Bum Fuck for the holidays?"

"Yeah. I haven't been to Wyoming in over two years."

When their time had come up, he and Garcia hadn't balked about staying on, but following back-to-back tours and all the post-deployment bullshit, he now had an eighteen-month-long promise to keep to himself.

"'Sides," he added, "seventeen hours alone in my truck is better therapy than any of that mandatory decompression the government provides."

"You need a hand with anything?"

"Nope." Reid slung his duffel over his shoulder. "Got it covered."

Garcia cocked a brow. "You're gonna drive to Wyoming dressed like that?"

"You got a problem with it?" Reid challenged. Although he rarely wore his dress uniform, he was proud of the fresh stripes he'd earned and the gold chevron that marked his promotion. He was pulling out all the stops. Few women could resist a U.S. Marine in dress blues. He hoped Haley Cooper didn't prove immune.

"No man." Garcia chuckled. "I guess you're taking lessons from me now…along with a detour."

Garcia was right on both accounts, but Reid refused to comment and headed out the door. Although his final destination was Wyoming, a stop in San Jacinto wouldn't be out of his way. He hadn't heard from Haley in months, but his combat duties hadn't allowed email access. He'd debated calling her first, but then decided the element of surprise might work in his favor. In all likelihood she was involved with someone else by now, but, one way or another, he was determined to find out.

Reid threw his gear in the truck and hit the highway bearing east. An hour later, he pulled onto a street lined with rows of small stucco houses. They looked much alike, but he remembered which was hers. Recon was a big part of his job.

He parked in the drive and climbed out of his truck, taking a moment to straighten his uniform. By the time he approached the front door his palms were sweating. He could run without a thought straight into AK-47 fire, but the thought of seeing Haley made him sweat? *Fuck that*.

He cursed himself and wiped his palms before ringing the bell, waiting in a parade stance, psyching himself up to engage. His mission was to win her over by any means, fair or foul. He was even ready to throw her over his shoulder, if it came down to it.

To his disappointment, it wasn't Haley who answered, but an elderly gentleman surrounded by a choir of barking dogs.

"Hush now!" He stifled the canine chorus. Straightening, he slowly assessed Reid from the mirrorlike gleam of his black shoes to his snowy white cap. "Can I help you, young man?"

Reid slowly released his breath. "Yes, sir, I'm looking for Haley Cooper."

"Are you now?" One bushy brow rose over a pair of sharp gray eyes. "Are you a friend of my granddaughter?"

"You might say that, sir. We have a long-standing acquaintance."

"And you're a *marine*?"

"Yes, sir. Staff Sergeant Reid Everett, Third Battalion First Marines out of Camp Pendleton." Reid relaxed his stance and offered his hand.

"I'm Bill Cooper, Haley's grandpa," the older man replied, closing his hand over Reid's. He glanced past Reid to his black truck parked in the driveway. "I remember that truck. Were you the one who drove her home when she went out dancing with Yolanda?"

"Yes, sir. We met that night at the Temecula Stampede. She cleaned my clock at the pool table. I'm guessing you taught her that jump shot?"

"As a matter of fact, I did." The old man chuckled.

"Is Haley at home?" Reid asked.

"No, I'm afraid she's not. Why don't you come on in, Staff Sergeant Everett. You drove all the way out here. Let's at least get acquainted. Do you like apple pie?"

Reid grinned. "Yes, sir. It's my favorite."

"Good." Bill opened the door in invitation. "My wife just made a couple of 'em. Come on inside and have a slice."

"Thank you, sir. I'd love some." He was disappointed not to see Haley, but recognized an intel opportunity when he saw it. Reid removed his cap and followed, only to be assaulted by a pack of aggressively friendly dogs.

"Down!" Bill commanded. "Please pardon my grand-daughter's motley crew of misbehaving mutts."

"They don't bother me." Reid squatted on his heels to scratch their heads, giving each its due. They were some of the strangest looking mongrels he'd ever seen, but all responded with wagging tails and lolling tongues.

"Ugly bunch, aren't they?" Bill remarked. "Haley has a habit of collecting the ones no one else wants."

Reid stored that new Haley insight as he stood. The house was small but neat and filled with the mouth-watering aroma of cinnamon and spice. He felt a momentary pang of homesickness. His mother and sisters loved to bake.

"Put on some coffee, love of my life. We have a guest. My wife, Dorothy," Bill introduced the petite woman with a slightly faded version of Haley's green eyes.

"Reid Everett." He once more extended his hand. It completely enveloped hers.

She regarded Reid with as much curiosity as her husband had. "You're a friend of Haley's?"

"Yes, ma'am," Reid replied. "Do you expect her back anytime soon?"

"No, I'm afraid not. She's gone to Alaska."

"*Alaska?*" Reid repeated. "I thought she was at UC Davis." He'd been prepared to drive to Sacramento if necessary, but Alaska? "What is she doing there?"

"She's taken the semester off to participate in some wolf study," Dorothy replied.

"A wolf study? I thought she was going to be a veterinarian."

"Sit down, please," Dorothy urged and turned her attention to the coffeemaker. "Do you like cheese or ice cream on your pie?" she asked.

"No thank you, ma'am, just plain."

"How about your coffee?"

"Black. Just having it in liquid form will be a luxury."

Dorothy gave him a quizzical look. "I don't understand."

"In the field, we had packets of instant coffee in the MREs but often had to swallow it down dry." He shrugged. "You learn to make due."

"Haley changed majors late last year," Bill finally answered. "She started thinking about it after a summer internship at that wolf place over in Julian. Now she wants to work for one of those wildlife conservation groups."

"She went to Alaska to assist one of her professors." Dorothy placed a cup of steaming coffee and a huge hunk of pie in front of Reid before joining him and her husband at the kitchen table. "He's the one who encouraged her to swap majors, but we're still hoping she'll change her mind."

Reid digested that tidbit as he took a bite of pie. Was she involved with this guy? The pie was delicious, but his thoughts left a bitter taste in his mouth.

"She never mentioned any involvement with a marine," Dorothy said.

"No. I don't suppose she would have since we weren't technically *involved*."

Dorothy's tiny hand rested on his. Her gaze softened. "I'm surprised Haley would have led you astray. She detests the military. Always has."

"I gathered that," Reid replied. "It's an unfair prejudice."

"She has good reasons," Bill argued.

"Does she? She told me her father was a marine. I'd like to understand the circumstances."

Dorothy sighed. "Yes. He was a marine, but we never met him. Don't even know his full name. He got our Beth pregnant and shipped out. She was only eighteen and not ready for a child. She wanted to abort. We talked her out of it. She had Haley, and we filed for legal guardianship."

"Where's her mother now?" Reid asked.

"Up in Seattle. She's married with four kids. Beth tried to get Haley back about ten years ago, but Haley won't have anything to do with her."

Reid shook his head. "That's got to be a real tough situation for all of you."

"It has been." Dorothy's eyes misted. "We love them both, but Haley needed us more."

"Everyone needs someone in their corner," Reid said.

"We just want her to be happy," Dorothy said. "She loves animals. Always has…sometimes I think more than she likes people."

"That's often a matter of trust," Reid said. "Animals love unconditionally. People don't."

"True enough," Bill admitted. "Haley's never gotten over her mother's abandonment, and I think we've spoiled her in our attempt to make up for it. I admit we've never taken to her politics, but we've always tried to stand behind her."

"She's lucky to have you." Reid said.

"What about your family, Reid?" Dorothy asked.

"How did they feel about you joining the military, with all that's happening?"

"My mom tried to talk me out of it, but my ol' man is from the school of tough love. When I told him my plans, he said the best gift a father could give his son on his eighteenth birthday was a suitcase." Reid chuckled. "We come from a long line of military men. There've been soldiers, sailors, and marines in the family for five generations."

"Where are you from, Reid?" Dorothy asked.

"Wyoming. My family runs a hunting outfit in Dubois."

"Hunting?" She gave him a look of surprise. "Does Haley know this?"

"Yes, ma'am." He grinned. "It was one of several controversial topics we've discussed. As a matter of fact, I'm going home for Thanksgiving. I came in hope of persuading her to drive out there with me."

"If you know how she feels about the military and hunting, why Haley?" Dorothy asked.

He shook his head. "I can't rightly answer that. Wish I could. There's just something there."

The older couple exchanged a look he couldn't interpret.

Reid stood. "Thanks so much for the pie, Miz Cooper. It was a real treat."

"Just a moment, Sergeant—"

"Reid," he corrected her.

"Reid, there's a jacket in Haley's closet. Is it yours?"

"It is," he said, "But I'll come back for it when she's here. Do you expect her home for Christmas?"

"We'd hoped so, but she hasn't committed yet," Dorothy answered.

"Maybe I'll try and talk her into it."

"Good luck," Bill said. "She's a very stubborn girl, especially when she sets her sights on something."

Reid grinned. "Me too. So I s'pose that's one thing more we have in common. Thanks again. It was a pleasure meeting you both."

Reid had planned only to spend Thanksgiving at home, but now, unless Haley decided to return, he'd probably stay in Wyoming until after Christmas. He wasn't certain how to proceed with her after that. Maybe he should just abandon his Haley campaign? He quickly discarded that defeatist strategy. Her grandparents weren't very encouraging, given their obvious differences, but they didn't actively discourage him either. He wasn't ready to concede, not yet anyway. Not until he saw her again. The Marine Corps' campaign in al-Anbar had been based on patient and persistent presence. Reid's personal campaign would be no different. Today he'd made inroads by forging a connection with her family. He left with the satisfaction that he'd at least won *them* over to his side.

Chapter 7

WHAT THE HELL WAS SHE THINKING? HERE SHE WAS, A Southern California girl, marching in circles and waving a severed wolf paw in the ass-freezing cold. She'd planned to return home before the first snowfall, but the death of several of their study subjects, under the guise of predator control, had changed everything. Chased to exhaustion by hunters with high-powered rifles in low-flying aircraft, the animals had had no chance of escape. And now the governor was preparing to take this travesty to a whole new level by offering a bounty for wolf kills—a hundred fifty dollars for a left forepaw and hundreds more for a full pelt.

Haley had stayed on to join the confederation of wildlife activists who gathered at the state capital. They'd stood vigil outside the Department of Fish and Game, offering the same wolf hunters two hundred dollars for the paws that they now used as a visual symbol of the slaughter. But after weeks of protests, the governor still refused to meet them or to be interviewed. Adding insult to injury, the media had paid the protest minimal attention.

"How are you holding up?" Jeffrey appeared by her side bearing an encouraging smile and a steaming cup of coffee.

She needed both. Her frustration was growing, along with her fear of losing her fingers and toes to frostbite. She chided herself that the fight against aerial gunning was far more important than her discomfort. And she was incredibly lucky to be working with someone like Jeffrey Greene. The association with him would surely open new doors to her.

"N-not v-very well, I'm afraid," Haley answered through chattering teeth. "The only people who seem to care are the ones marching with us."

"The people here aren't apathetic," Jeffrey argued. "But they're feeling defeated. Alaska has already voted this issue down twice, only to be overridden. If the hunting lobbyists had their way, they'd turn Alaska into a giant game park. That's why we have to stop this now."

"How? We don't have money or legislative support."

"Perhaps not here, but we have other options. We have a strong conservation base in California *and* sympathetic legislators. All we need to do is prove we have public support and money, and new federal legislation will follow."

"But how can we do that when we can't even get any local news coverage?"

"We have to find a way to get *national* attention. All we need to do is capture this brutality on video and show the world the ugly truth. The documentary *Wolves and the Wolf Men* led to the Federal Airborne Hunting Act in the seventies." Jeffrey's jaw was set with determination. "It worked once before. It'll work again."

"That sounds easier said than done," Haley replied. "I can't imagine any hunters are going to invite us to go along for the ride."

"We'll just hire a pilot and follow them with a film crew. As long as we don't interfere, we're still operating inside the law."

"But how do you expect to even find these hunters? They don't exactly advertise their activities."

Jeffrey eyed her slowly up and down. "I won't. *You* will."

"A Berserker, two Arctic Devils, and three Duck Farts." Haley rolled her eyes as she called out the order to the bartender.

She'd thought her waitressing days were over when she'd left San Jacinto, but here she was, dressed as a nineteenth-century saloon girl in a smoke-filled bar in the middle of nowhere. She could barely breathe from all the cigars and cigarettes. At almost eight bucks a pack in Alaska, you'd think people would give it up.

Her mission hadn't proven as difficult as she'd first thought. The Hole in the Wall Saloon catered to the beer-swilling, Duck Fart–shooting, big-money hunters from the Lower 48 who'd drop seven to ten grand without batting an eye just for a chance at big game.

Although winter days in Alaska were short and unbearably cold, the darkness and frigid temperatures didn't keep people from the bars. If anything, it seemed to foster social drinking, and drinking encouraged talk. Over the past weeks she'd compiled an entire notepad filled with places, dates, and times. It was only a matter of weeks before the days would be long enough for these would-be wolf hunters to take to the skies.

While Haley gathered information, Jeffrey had returned to California to hire a film crew. With several California legislators friendly to conservation, all they needed was video evidence to garner legislative support. Although she'd hoped to be home for Christmas, and missed her grandparents and the California sun, she told herself that her future required sacrificing certain creature comforts for the greater good.

Haley filled three frosty mugs from the tap while the bartender topped the trio of shooters with Crown Royal. "Thanks, Mike." She offered a smile, adjusted her corset, and then scooped up the tray. She delivered the drinks with a forced smile, endured a lewd joke and a slap on the ass, and then moved on to bus the next table.

She was on her break when her phone vibrated. Her pulse sped. Jeffrey said he'd try to return to spend Christmas with her. Maybe she wouldn't be alone for the holidays after all.

Her heart sank when she didn't recognize the number. She debated whether to answer, but it was a California area code. Her next thought was for her grandparents. Maybe something had happened? "Hello?" she answered tentatively, half-braced for bad news.

"Merry Christmas," replied a deep, velvety baritone.

Was her imagination playing tricks? It couldn't be *him* after all this time.

"Who is this?" she asked.

"It's Reid."

"Reid?" she repeated dumbly. "You're back? You're safe?"

"Yeah. Just arrived in Wyoming, actually."

"So you're spending Christmas with your family? I'm glad."

"Thanks. I took a detour to San Jacinto hoping to convince you to come with me."

"You did?"

"Yeah. I thought you might like to see Wyoming. I also hoped we could make up for some lost time. I've waited a long time, Haley... I've been looking forward to seeing you again."

She swallowed hard. What could she say to that? She'd been so busy that Reid had hardly entered her thoughts. She hadn't heard from him in months and had thought herself long over her infatuation until she'd heard his voice again. The timbre alone awakened something she'd nearly forgotten.

"I met your grandparents," he continued. "I like them... I think they liked me, too."

"They would," she replied dryly. "Gramps and I aren't exactly politically aligned."

Reid chuckled. "No wonder he and I hit it off. Personal politics aside, it's clear that they love you very much. They miss you too."

His words made her heart ache for home. "I love and miss them too."

"But you're not coming home for the holidays?"

"No. I can't. What I'm doing here is too important." She saw no point in divulging more to someone who had at least one foot in the enemy camp.

A brief silence followed. "I thought you'd set your sights on vet school. Seems you've veered pretty far from that plan."

"Maybe not as far as you think," she said. "I'm still helping animals, just wild ones now instead of pets."

"How is it going?" he asked. "Do you like it there?"

"Well enough, I suppose, but not enough to stay permanently, if that's what you're asking."

"So you plan to come back?"

"Eventually, yes."

"I want to see you."

"But why?" she asked.

"Do I need a reason? I just do. Why did you reply to my emails?"

"I don't know." She twirled a lock of hair. "It just seemed rude to ignore them under the circumstances."

"It's more than that," he insisted.

"Look, Reid. I'm truly glad that you're home safe, but there's no point in us seeing each other."

"Why not?"

"It doesn't make any sense when you'll just be leaving again."

"But not for another six months. Why can't we just see where it goes in the meantime?"

"Because this is crazy. We hardly know each other. We met only once almost two years ago."

"Nineteen months," he corrected. "But who's counting?"

"That's my point," she argued. "And we've not seen each other since."

"That's what I want to rectify. I want us to get to know each other. We need some time together just to talk. Come to Wyoming and spend Christmas with me."

"I can't, Reid. Even if I wanted to. I have a job here and responsibilities. They're all counting on me. But even if I could, this thing between us can't go anywhere. I'm too busy to get involved with anyone at this point in my life. I have plans that are going to require all my time and energy."

"I can respect that," he said. "My job is a big strain on my resources too."

"Yes," she said. "I imagine it is."

"But you still shouldn't be alone for Christmas, Haley. We have plenty of wolves out here too. I'll even drive you out to Yellowstone to see them. Say the word and I'll buy your ticket."

For a few crazy seconds she actually considered it, but then reason returned. "No, Reid. I can't."

"It's your boss, right? That professor guy? He won't let you leave?"

"It's not that, exactly."

"Is he there with you?"

"No," she replied. "He went back to California."

"And left you alone in Alaska?"

"He had important business to take care of."

"Are you involved with him?"

"That's none of your business," she snapped.

Although shared politics and common values had originally brought them together, Jeffrey had recently hinted about taking their relationship in a more personal direction. She'd thought about it a lot lately.

"That's answer enough," Reid said. "He's not the one for you. He's a jackass."

"How the hell would you know that? You've never even met him."

"He left you there alone. That says everything. He's not right for you. When do you come home?" he asked.

"I don't know for certain. It'll still be a couple of months yet. Probably early April," she answered his question without knowing why.

"Good. I'll still be around." She could almost hear the smile in his voice. "I'll be waiting for you, Haley Cooper."

"Good-bye, Reid." Haley ended the call feeling dazed and confused.

His doggedness was flattering. No one had ever shown that kind of interest in her before, but she resented how his words had roused her own feelings of self-pity and loneliness. She also hated that he made her feel unsure of Jeffrey, a man who'd offered nothing but encouragement and support. Reid, on the other hand, made her question almost everything she believed in.

She still couldn't deny her attraction to Reid, but it could never be enough to overcome their incompatibility. Nevertheless, late that night, in the darkest and loneliest hours, it wasn't thoughts of Jeffrey, but a tall cowboy with sky-blue eyes that heated her body and haunted her dreams.

Dubois, Wyoming, the same night

Reid had stepped outside to escape the sudden crushing sensation in his chest. He'd never suffered claustrophobia before, but the music, the laughter, the smells, and the questions he wasn't ready to answer were like sensory overload. His family all just carried on like normal, but he couldn't. He almost wished he hadn't come home. It was just too much, too soon after his deployment.

He sucked in a breath, filling his lungs with frosty air and then shut his eyes in a silent prayer for all the guys who'd never see another Christmas. Bravo company had arrived in Kuwait with 185 men; a quarter of them would never return to their families. His platoon had been among those hit the hardest. They'd accomplished their mission but had paid a heavy price in blood.

He took a long swig of his beer.

A moment later he'd dialed his phone. He hadn't even thought about it. He'd just wanted to hear *her* voice. The conversation was short, even a bit terse. He'd felt her resistance about seeing him again, but in the end she hadn't actually said no. He pocketed his phone with a smile.

"Hey you! The party's inside." Tonya sat down beside him, drink in hand. She rested the other one on his thigh. Her touch and voice were light, as if testing the waters.

He tensed slightly but couldn't think of a tactful way to get away from her.

"Who was that on the phone?" she asked.

"A friend." He decided just to play it cool. Tonya wasn't dumb. She'd eventually get the hint.

Her black brows arched, but she didn't press that line of questioning. Instead, she tilted her head skyward and released a long sigh. "I love the cold weather, don't you? It lights up the night. The sky seems darker, and the stars more intense. And I love the snow too, walking in it, skiing on it, and even catching the flakes on my tongue. Did you miss it much, Reid?"

"Yes, I did. I hate the desert."

"Then why did you go? Your family's outfitting

business is doing well. Better than well. There's a whole new lot of oil barons coming in from the Dakotas."

"I'm doing what I was called to do. If you don't understand that by now, you never will."

She shrugged. "I was hoping you'd be back for Christmas. We really need to talk, Reid."

"That so? Then why didn't you just *text* me?"

"Ouch." She winced. "I'm sorry about that. More than I can say, Reid, but I just didn't know how else to break it off. I was afraid that if I called you, I wouldn't be able to do it, and that wouldn't have been fair to either of us."

"At least it was clean. I'll give you that much," he replied with a dry laugh.

Although it had hurt like hell when she'd dumped him, he was over it now. Over *her*. Utterly and completely. He resented that his well-meaning but misguided sister had invited his ex for the Christmas Eve family gathering. Then again, he should have expected it, given that Krista had set them up to begin with. She and Tonya had been best friends forever. It was only natural that she'd want to see them reconcile, but he had no interest whatsoever in resurrecting the dead relationship.

"It was a mistake," she insisted. "I realize that now. I was lonely and resentful, Reid. At least I was honest about it. I didn't cheat on you."

"You think *I* wasn't lonely?" he countered.

"But it was *your* decision to leave. I had no part in it, and then you went and signed on for another four years."

"I did it because we're not done over there yet," he said. "Would you turn over a half-broke colt for use on the trails?"

"Of course not. I'd finish the job."

"Same here. I'm damn well going to finish what I signed on to do."

"But you extended your time without even discussing it with me. Of course I was angry. Did you expect me to wait forever?"

"No. That's why I bought a ring."

"A ring?" Her brown eyes widened. She visibly swallowed. "You did? When?"

"A few weeks before your text. I was going to surprise you on my next leave." He shrugged. "Look, there's no point in rehashing it all."

"But I think there is. Do you have any idea what it's like watching the news and hearing about all those guys getting blown to pieces? That's what I was afraid of. You risk life and limb with every deployment. I wanted *all* of you, Reid, not some lesser, broken version."

"So you'd just scratch that line that says 'in sickness and in health'?"

"Don't twist my meaning, Reid. Maybe I was being selfish, but I still want you. Can't we just start over?" She set down her glass of wine on the porch rail and turned to face him, running both hands up his thighs, before settling on his lap, arms twined around his neck. "It was really good between us once, wasn't it?"

"Maybe once, but that's in the past now, Ton." He lifted her back onto her feet. "You're the one who broke it off. Not me."

"But here we are, both still free, aren't we?"

He didn't answer. Yeah, technically he was free, and she was still the same Tonya, but the attraction he'd felt was gone. Dead as dirt.

She glanced at the phone in his hand. "Or was that more than just a *friend*?"

"Not yet," he replied. "But I have hope."

"Really?" Her lips curved into the slow, sexy smile that had once dazzled him but now had little effect. "Then so do I."

Chapter 8

HALEY HAD BARELY DROPPED HER DUFFEL AND backpack before her grandma folded her in a smothering hug. "Sweetheart! We're so glad you're finally back!"

"I'm glad to be home too, Grams, but it's only for a couple of weeks. I've enrolled for the summer semester to try and make up for the nine months I spent in Alaska."

"But weren't you working on research while you were there?"

"Yes," she said. "And I'll get some special credit for it, but I still have another year to finish my undergrad degree. The good news is I've just been offered a position with the Wolf Recovery Alliance. They're studying wolves in all the national parks."

"So this is a *paid* position?" Gramps asked.

She pursed her lips. "Well…not exactly. It's still voluntary, but there is a stipend. What matters is how it'll look on my CV. I'm certain it will help get me into the master's program at Montana State."

He eyed her skeptically. "Sweetheart, while I fully understand a young person's yen for adventure, are you really certain this is the career direction you wish to take?"

"Yes," she insisted. Her work with the wolves had given her a feeling of purpose she'd never known before.

"I've never been more certain of anything. You have no idea what it's like to be out there in the wild. Wolves are unlike any other beings, Gramps. They're affectionate, monogamous in their mating, and will die to protect their pack. They even mourn the loss of their loved ones. In some ways, I almost think they're superior to us."

"We appreciate your passion, Haley," Grams interjected. "But perhaps you could work with wild animals in a more *practical* setting? How about in a zoo? They hire veterinarians, don't they? All those creatures need care, and San Diego has a lovely zoo."

"But they're captive, Grams, don't you see? Sure, they get food and medical care, but so do people in prison. It's a miserable life for them. How could I ever be part of that?"

"But *you* could have a normal life," her grandmother suggested with a look of concern.

"It's *my* life, isn't it? Shouldn't I be allowed to decide? And what's normal anyway, Grams? Maybe the wilderness is not what *you* would want, but living close to nature *is* normal for thousands of people."

"You want to be one of them? With no electricity? No plumbing?" Gramps shook his head. "Why on earth would anyone want to go back to the Stone Age?"

"Maybe technology hasn't advanced society as much as you think it has. Our lives are so rushed that no one takes time out to care about anything or anyone anymore. That's what impressed me most about the wolves, how they look after one another."

"So you're saying you want to give up your car, laptop, and iPhone?" Gramps asked. "All for the betterment of society, of course."

Haley flushed. "That's not fair, Gramps. You know I need those things. How can I finish school otherwise?"

"But sweetheart, you just said…"

"You're missing my whole point!"

"Then maybe you can explain it to me a little better?"

Haley exhaled a big sigh. "I'm just saying I want to make a positive impact in the world."

"That's admirable, Haley," Grams interjected. "But perhaps you should take some time to think all this through. There are many careers that could give you a similar feeling of satisfaction. How about something in medicine? Nurses make a difference every day."

"The universities are full of nursing students," Haley argued. "But how many people are fighting to save the environment? Our wildlife? You can't even begin to understand the magnitude of the issues until you've seen them with your own eyes. That's why we're making a documentary—to *show* the world what's really happening."

"Haley," her grandpa began, "you know we love you and have always encouraged you to follow your dreams, but this time—"

She shook her head. "I love you too, Gramps, and know you only want the best for me, but I'm not a child anymore. This is what I want for my life. You'll see. It's not a mistake. I'll make you proud. I promise."

On that note, Haley hauled her gear to her bedroom and began unpacking. She was home at last, but felt almost as if she was a stranger in the house she'd grown up in.

She opened her closet to find Reid's jacket still hanging there. She was suddenly reminded of his Christmas

Eve phone call, almost four months ago. He hadn't called her since. She wondered if he'd finally given up. She pulled the jacket from the hanger, wondering if she should just send it back to him. Something dropped from the pocket, landing at her feet. A Leatherman utility knife? She'd bought a similar one while in Alaska. Haley picked it up and shoved it back into the pocket only to encounter something else. Paper, but smoother, stiffer.

A photograph? She retrieved it slowly, with a slight stab of guilt.

It was a picture of Reid with his arms around a tall, slender brunette. They were staring into each other's eyes as if in a prelude to a kiss. Her brows met and chest tightened as she flipped the picture over.

A night I'll always remember. Tonya.

She stared at the note through burning eyes. She didn't know why Reid's deceit hurt so much. Maybe because she'd begun to trust him. She should have been relieved to discover his true colors, but felt only anger and a profound and aching disappointment.

She'd *wanted* to believe he was different, but this just proved he wasn't truly the man she'd thought he was… had secretly hoped he was. "Reid Everett. You are just another lying, cheating son of a bitch."

She should have known better. He was a marine, after all.

———

The next day, Haley stopped at The SJ Café on her way home from the post office, seating herself in Yolanda's section.

"Haley!" Yolanda's face lit up the moment she

emerged from the kitchen. She dropped off her order, whipped off her apron, and sat down across from Haley. "When did you get home?"

"Day before yesterday."

Yolanda's smile faded. "And you didn't phone me?"

"I'm sorry. It's just been so hectic."

Apart from a couple of postcards, she hadn't been in touch with her best friend in months. Part of it was her lack of cell service, but that didn't excuse her for not calling once she'd returned home. It just seemed awkward all of a sudden, as if they'd drifted further and further apart.

"I understand." Yolanda's hurt expression said she really didn't. "How was Alaska?"

"It was incredible," Haley gushed. "Where else can you find polar bears, wolves, and humpback whales?"

"I don't know, but I can't say I've ever looked for any of them before. The pelicans and sea lions at the La Jolla marina are enough wildlife for me. I can't believe you stayed up there all winter."

"Me either actually, but it was really important. Jeffrey thinks we'll be able to get new conservation legislation passed."

Yolanda arched a brow. "*Jeffrey?* Since when are you on a first name basis with your professors?"

Haley's face heated. "I'm not his student anymore. Not in the technical sense anyway. I'm his research assistant now. We've grown pretty close over the past few months."

"Really? *How* close?" Yolanda pressed.

"Not like *that*...well, not yet anyway."

"But you're thinking about it?"

"Maybe," Haley confessed. She was comfortable with Jeffrey. They understood each other. Wasn't that the best foundation for a relationship?

"What's he like?" Yolanda asked.

"Intelligent. Articulate." Haley began ticking off her mentor's qualities.

"Is he good-looking?" Yolanda asked.

"Yeah, I suppose he's easy enough on the eyes."

"Does he make you laugh?"

Haley had to think about that one. "No, not really. He's more serious. Focused. Intense."

"Intensity is good and focus is even better at the right time…and in the right place." Yolanda grinned. "But you're too serious. You need a man with a sense of humor to balance you."

"I'm not sold on the theory that opposites make good relationships," Haley argued, thinking immediately of lying, cheating Reid Everett. "Mutual goals and compatibility make a whole lot more sense to me."

Yolanda rolled her eyes. "Sure, if you like predictable and boring…"

"I only said I'm *thinking* about it. I'm not ready to jump into anything with anyone right now. I'm just glad to be home for a while. I loved the adventure of Alaska, but I missed the California sun."

"Then let's go to the beach," Yolanda suggested. "It's been ages since I've been. Do you remember the summer I took you out to Black's Beach?"

Haley groaned. "How can I ever forget when you didn't warn me it was clothing-optional."

Yolanda laughed. "I wish I'd had a camera when we ran into that group playing *desnudo* volleyball. The look on your face was priceless." She burst into another ripple of mirth.

"There were far too many jiggly parts for my taste." Haley shuddered. "Why is it that the last people you'd ever want to see naked are always the first to take off their clothes?"

"Let's do it again," Yolanda said. "It would be just like old times."

"No, thank you!" Haley shook her head. "I had nightmares for months. Besides, I have too much work to catch up on."

"Work? Don't you ever take a break? All you ever think about anymore is work and books. You haven't been yourself since you went off to that school."

Haley shrugged. "I just have a lot on my mind."

"Then your mind needs to take a vacation. C'mon, *chica*," Yolanda cajoled. "You've been gone for months. Let's drive out to Coronado Island. Just for half a day. We can have lunch and walk the beach."

"I really can't," Haley insisted. She had a pile of journal articles to catch up on as well as work on one of Jeffrey's projects. He was brilliant, but horribly disorganized. She'd begun reordering all of his notes from Alaska. It would take weeks. The very idea incited a headache. She massaged her temples. On second thought, maybe she *should* take a short break.

Yolanda shook her head with a sigh. "You know what they say about too much work and no play, *chica*…"

"Okay. I'll go." Haley huffed. "Are you free tomorrow?"

"I *can* be," Yolanda said. "They owe me a day off after I pulled two extra shifts last week."

"Can we head out early? Maybe around nine? We could walk the beach first and then have an early lunch. That way I can still get some work done when I get back."

Yolanda's brows met in a frown. "Why don't you just bring it all with you?"

"You know, I hadn't even thought of that," Haley replied.

"*Dios mio*, Haley! Have you even forgotten sarcasm? I wasn't serious." She cursed under her breath. It was between lunch and dinner and the place was nearly empty. Nevertheless, the manager flashed them the evil eye. "Got to get back to work now. Are you going to order anything?"

"Yeah, I'll take the veggie pita and a mineral water."

"Got it. I'll pick you up tomorrow at nine, but plan to make a *whole* day of it."

———~~~———

Reid stared blankly at the package postmarked San Jacinto. He didn't have to open it to know what it was. Why had she returned it? The message was clear. She wanted to break it off completely. Did it really matter? It wasn't like they'd even been dating. He still hardly knew her.

Hell yeah, it did. Maybe it was pure ego, but he couldn't accept defeat. He'd never failed at anything before, at least not anything he'd ever set his mind on. And he wanted her.

It was time to change tactics. His notion of wearing down her resistance with patience and persistence had blown up in his face. He'd held back with Haley when he should have acted. He wouldn't make that mistake again. If she wanted to break it off, fine, but she'd have to tell him to his face.

"You still seeing Yolanda?" Reid asked Garcia between shots on the rifle range. Scout snipers had been the Marine Corps' greatest asset in Fallujah. They went almost daily to keep their skills sharp.

"Yeah," his buddy confessed, looking almost embarrassed. "I backed off for a while. You know, it seemed to be getting too intense, but now we're back on again. I don't know what it is with her." Garcia shook his head.

Reid popped off a shot and then paused, eyeing Garcia again over his sights. "Think you could set something up?"

"You don't take no for an answer, do you, *esé*?" Garcia chuckled. "It seems to me she doesn't want anything more to do with you."

"Maybe. Maybe not." Reid shrugged one shoulder. "I'm thinking the latter, but then again, I've always been a stubborn shit. You gonna make that call?"

"Yeah, I'll make the call. Just don't blame me when she hands your balls back to you."

Chapter 9

SURPRISINGLY, YOLANDA WAS RIGHT ON TIME. "Do you want to drive all the way or park at the bay and take the ferry over to Coronado?" she asked.

"Let's drive," Haley replied. "I hate lines and crowds." She'd always despised being confined but had noticed it a lot more since coming home. California seemed so much more congested after the wide-open spaces of Alaska.

They took Yolanda's VW convertible, driving with the top down, the radio blaring, and the wind whipping their hair. Haley leaned back, relishing the combined sensations of warm sun and cool breeze. The day was picture perfect, clear and cloudless, casting rays of light rippling over the frigid waters of San Diego Bay. The bay was dotted with sails and kayaks as they drove over Coronado Bridge.

Traffic into San Diego was surprisingly light but became heavier once they crossed the bridge, and then came to a virtual standstill once they hit Ocean Boulevard toward Central Beach. With its silvery sand and backdrop of majestic mansions, there couldn't be much greater contrast after living for months in the Arctic wilderness.

After driving up and down the street several times, they finally found a parking spot. Haley shaded her eyes and gazed out at the pristine beach while Yolanda unloaded a couple of folding beach chairs and a small cooler.

"If you're hungry, I packed a few snacks, but save your appetite for dinner. We have an early reservation at Candelas."

"Sounds great to me," Haley replied. Candelas on the Bay was a local favorite offering a unique fusion of Mexican and French cuisine and breathtaking views of the San Diego skyline. "You know, I'm really glad you talked me into this."

"Me too, *chica*." Yolanda's mouth curved into a wistful smile. "Who knows if we'll ever get another chance to do this kind of thing again?"

"Probably not for a while," Haley agreed.

"You aren't coming back after you graduate, are you?"

"I don't know where I'll end up, but probably not here." She laid her hand over Yolanda's. "But we'll still keep in touch wherever I end up."

"Sure we will." Yolanda didn't meet Haley's gaze. "There's a perfect spot for us." She pointed down the beach, and they walked past a cluster of small dunes where they set up their chairs. They stripped down to bikini bottoms but left their shirts on. Although it was a gorgeous day, it was still a bit early in the season for sunbathing.

"I'm dying for a run," Haley said, already kicking off her shoes. She couldn't wait to bury her toes in the soft, powdery sand. "Wanna go with me?"

Yolanda shook her head with a laugh. "You know how I hate to sweat. Besides, this body was not designed for *that* kind of physical exertion." She waved Haley on. "You go ahead. I'll be right here."

Haley headed down to the waterline where the mile and a half of packed sand offered the perfect surface. She hadn't run on the beach in forever. It was another simple pleasure she'd missed. She started at a fast jog, but, invigorated by the ebb and flow of the Pacific waters blasting her feet and ankles, quickly sped to a sprint.

Panting from her run, Haley returned to her original spot where she waved to Yolanda. Throwing trepidation to the wind, she tore off her shirt and dove into the frigid surf, emerging a few moments later with a shriek of laughter that died on her lips the second her gaze met a pair of sky-blue eyes.

Reid had always preferred the mountains to the ocean, but then again, there weren't many beaches in Wyoming. On top of that, he'd experienced about as much sand as he could stomach after three tours on the Arabian Peninsula, but Garcia had insisted the beach was the best place to meet up with Yolanda and Haley. He'd agreed with little enthusiasm—until spying a mermaid, in all of her golden-skinned glory, emerging from the water.

Dripping wet in her tiny turquoise bikini, Haley blasted the breath from his lungs. This new version of her obliterated all lingering memory of the girl in the demure yellow sundress at the Temecula Stampede.

She halted in front of him with a glare. "Reid? What are *you* doing here?"

"It's a gorgeous day." He gazed up at the sky. "Do I need another reason?"

"Are you trying to claim this is just a coincidence? You aren't even dressed for this. Who wears jeans and boots to the beach?"

"It's not coincidental at all," Reid said. "I wanted to see you and asked Garcia to set something up."

Her gaze swept past him to where Garcia and Yolanda lounged together. She'd wondered about Yolanda and Rafael, but had never asked if they were still seeing each other. She'd wring Yolanda's neck for this.

"You didn't have the balls to just call me yourself?"

"Would you have come?"

"Nope." She shook her head. "Absolutely not."

"That's what I thought when I got your package. Why did you send it back when I told you I'd come for it?"

"I didn't want to see you again." Her bluntness was like a blow to the gut.

"I don't get it. You answered all my emails. Why the sudden turnabout? Are you involved with someone?"

"Maybe." She tore her gaze away with a guilty look to focus on a group of squealing kids on boogie boards. She continued to avoid his gaze as she tied her wet hair into a knot on top of her head.

"That's not an answer. Either you are or you aren't. Which is it?"

"It means I'm *thinking* about seeing someone."

"But you aren't yet. That means I still have a chance," Reid said.

"I t-told you before, I'm not into m-marines."

Her lips were blue-tinged and her teeth chattered. His gaze dropped a tad lower to her beaded nipples and his prick swelled. He whipped off his T-shirt and offered it to her. "So you keep saying, but you *are* into me."

"You conceited j-jackass! J-just because I l-let you k-kiss me once?"

"It was more than once and more than just a kiss." He grinned back. "And for the record, I'm very much into you, too."

Her eyes drifted over his bare torso, lingering for several seconds. When he caught her staring, she snatched his shirt from his hands. The shirt swallowed her delectable body, covering her to the knees. He almost wished he'd let her shiver instead.

After a moment she broke the silence. "You want to know why I returned your jacket? I'll tell you why. I found a picture in your pocket, Reid. A picture of you with another woman. It was inscribed on the back. *A night I'll always remember. Tonya.* Wanna explain that?"

He exhaled in exasperation. "That's an old picture. Taken three years ago at my brother's last wedding. Tonya's the ex I already told you about. It was over between us before I ever met you."

"Then why do you still have the picture?"

He rubbed the back of his neck. "To be honest, I had forgotten all about it. I can't even remember the last time I wore that jacket."

"Why should I believe you?"

He cupped her chin, forcing her to meet his gaze. "Because I'm telling you the truth. Look, Haley, I can understand your caution, given your history, but I've done nothing to deserve your mistrust."

"What do you mean *given my history*?"

"C'mon. Let's walk. We've got a lot to talk about." He kicked off his boots, leaving them in the sand, and then pressed a hand lightly to her back. She balked at first but then gave in, reluctantly matching his steps. "When I met your grandparents, they explained a few things to me."

She halted, digging her heels into the sand. "What *kind* of things?"

"Haley kind of things." He guided her back into motion down the beach toward the red roofs of the Hotel del Coronado. "They told me about your mother and father."

"I don't *have* a father," she protested.

"Sure you do. Have you ever tried to get in touch with him?"

"No!" she snapped. "Why should I? He's never tried to contact *me*."

"There's two sides to every story, Haley. Maybe you should hear his."

"You're justifying what he did?"

"No," he said firmly. "I'm not justifying anything at all. I just believe in hearing both sides before passing judgment on anyone."

She snorted. "I suppose it only makes sense when you're as much of a dog as he was."

He grasped her tiny shoulders and spun her around. "What the hell is *that* supposed to mean? I told you the night we met that I've only been with two women in my life and that number hasn't changed. I don't sleep around, Haley. I'm *not* a liar, and I *don't* cheat."

"You really expect me to believe that?"

He watched doubt and uncertainty warring in her eyes. "You can believe me or not, but it's still the truth."

She didn't comment but began walking again. Minutes later she asked, "If that's so, then why did you and Tonya split up?"

"I didn't mess around on her if that's what you're thinking. She broke it off with me. She said she didn't want to wait."

"Oh." Her shoulders relaxed. "I suppose I can understand that. Waiting has to be very hard. I think it would take a very strong person to cope with that... I can't imagine dealing with all the stress and uncertainties of a loved one in such a dangerous situation."

"So you don't think *you* could do it?"

She cocked her head, as if considering the question. "I don't know. I'd like to think so, but it wouldn't be easy."

"A lot of worthwhile things don't come easy," Reid answered. "Like you, Haley Cooper. You give 'difficult' a whole new meaning. I know it's hard for you, but I'm asking for your trust."

She spun on him, hands on hips. "Why? What am I to you, Reid? What's the big appeal here? I'm not getting it. Is it just the challenge?"

"Maybe that's part of it," he confessed. "But it's a lot more than that, and I'm pretty sure you feel it too."

She shook her head. "Don't even try to go there now, cowboy. You passed me up when you had your chance."

"I had a real good reason for waiting. The timing wasn't right for either of us. But I've thought about this... about you... for a long damned time, so don't take it as lack of interest on my part."

"Well, there's none left on mine." She jutted her chin defiantly but then licked her lips. "I told you then that it was a one-shot deal."

"Is that so?" he asked. Vulnerable one moment, bold the next. Haley was a bundle of contradictions. Whether it was conscious or not, she'd issued a challenge and an invitation at the same time. He would have been tempted by either one, but the combination was damn near irresistible.

This was *supposed* to have been a girls' day out, time alone with her best friend. Not a walk down the beach with an incredibly hot, half-naked marine. What the hell was she thinking? In truth, she'd stopped thinking the moment he'd stripped to the waist.

Her gaze rested at eye level on the USMC tat of an eagle stretching out its talons above his heart. His well-developed pecs, broad shoulders, and rippling abs made her mouth water. She couldn't deny his physical appeal. Everything about Reid attracted her at the basest level, but she was above all that primal lust. Wasn't she? She prided herself on her intellect and self-control, but just being with Reid seemed to bring out all these dormant animal instincts, every one of which craved to be satisfied.

He stepped in closer, intentionally invading her personal space, and then his mouth came crushing down on hers. He suddenly swept her up into his arms and waded, jeans and all, into the surf. She screamed as the icy waves blasted over them, but he muffled the sound with his glorious mouth. Within seconds, the heat of lust displaced the cold, her protests forgotten with the invasion of his hot tongue.

He gripped her ass and she moaned, wrapping her legs around his waist, seeking his hardness to ease her ache.

"I want you, Haley," he groaned. "Come with me."

"Here?" she asked.

"No," he chuckled. "That's not quite what I meant. I have a room. A bed. I want to take you there. Will you go with me?" His gaze met hers with an intensity that made her shiver. "I held back the last time and regretted it the whole time I was away. I don't believe in living with those kinds of regrets anymore. Life is too damned short."

Seconds ticked by. Her mind whirred with irresolution.

She wasn't ready for a relationship, but she still wanted him. Reid excited her in a way she'd never experienced with anyone else. They were still nearly strangers, but seemed to connect on a level that she didn't understand. Maybe it was only lust, but what did it matter? She desired him too. She *needed* to feel passion at least once in her life.

He kissed her again, teasing her with promises of things to come.

She kissed him back, sucking his lower lip between hers, releasing it slowly, thrilling at the flare of his pupils. "Yes, Reid," she replied in a husky whisper. "That's one thing we finally agree on. Life *is* too short for regrets."

Chapter 10

REID CARRIED HER BACK TO SHORE, EASING HER DOWN his body and over his erection with a groan. Her legs went to jelly the moment her feet hit the sand. She immediately felt the loss of his hardness. His heat.

He grabbed his boots and then took her hand. Even in his wet jeans, Haley could barely keep up with his long strides. His jaw was tight, his expression purposeful as he dragged her through the hotel lobby, leaving a trail of water in their wake.

Finding the elevator empty, he didn't hesitate to drop his boots and pull her back into his arms. His kiss was deep, passionate, and still tasted of Pacific salt. It grew more urgent, and so did she. Haley trembled against him, but her shivers had nothing to do with the air-conditioning blasting arctic air on her wet skin. She was a huge bundle of nerves. She'd never done anything like this. But why Reid? Why now? She didn't try to kid herself that it was anything more than raw attraction. How could it be anything else?

Her legs were still rubbery, and her mind reeling from his kisses when the doors dinged open. He released her with reluctance and led her down a long hallway, stopping only long enough to fish a key card out of his back pocket. He'd booked a room before finding her? She tried not to think too much about the significance of that.

The door clicked open. They stepped inside. Haley caught her breath.

He hadn't skimped on either the hotel or the room. It was large and well appointed with a gorgeous view and a king-sized bed. Her heart raced. She glanced back at the door, briefly considering retreat. If she was going to back down, the time was now.

"Second thoughts?" He read her mind. "I want you, Haley. You know that, but the decision is still yours, not mine." He kissed her gently, his tongue coaxing her mouth, evaporating her doubts with tender persuasion.

No regrets. She once more murmured her new mantra to herself.

"Good." Taking her hand, he led her into a marble-tiled bathroom with a huge Jacuzzi tub and a walk-in tile shower enclosure. He turned on the shower tap. "Get in."

"You expect me to just strip here in front of you in broad daylight?"

"Sand is abrasive to delicate places. You're covered with it...not to mention the vegetation." He plucked a piece of seaweed from her hair, dangled it before her eyes, and then tossed it into the trash. "But if it's an issue of modesty, you can stay in your suit...for now. As for me, I'm not about to shower in my clothes. I need to get these damned wet jeans off. Now. Would it offend your delicate sensibilities to see me naked?"

"Of course not. I mean we came here to...to..."

"Can't even say it?" he teased.

She blushed. She wanted to see him...to touch

him…but shyness and feelings of ineptitude made her hesitate. She marshalled her nerve. "Do you…er…need some help?"

"I sure wouldn't refuse it." He'd already worked the button free.

She moved in, taking hold of his zipper with one hand, and cupping him with the other. Even through wet denim, the feel of him surprised her. Her hands shook so much she couldn't lower his fly.

He seized her hand in guttural tones. "On second thought… It'll be a hell of a lot easier to get them off without a hard-on."

"That quick?" she asked.

"Oh yeah." He gave a dry laugh. "All you have to do is *look* south to get me hard." He peeled down his jeans. The thwack of wet denim hitting the floor followed. His erection sprang out. Bigger than she'd expected. *Much* bigger.

Although she wasn't a virgin, her experience was limited to her first and only boyfriend, Kevin. The "big event" had taken place on a beach blanket with a bottle of Riunite Lambrusco. After emptying the bottle together, he'd pulled her down onto the blanket. The kissing and petting had been pleasant enough, but what followed was mildly painful. It was ten minutes of frantic thrusting on his part while she bit her lip, waiting for him to be done. Their few repeat encounters were only marginally better. He'd eventually broken up with her, calling her cold and sexless.

For months Haley tortured herself, wondering what she'd done wrong. She'd eventually concluded that he was right. She just wasn't a sexual person. After that, she'd been in no great hurry for any further "sexploration." Until now. Looking at Reid, she was beginning to understand what was missing the first time around.

He took her hand, closing her fingers around his erection. It was huge, hot, and pulsing. She wondered with a mix of eagerness and trepidation how it would feel inside her.

"Reid?"

"What, sweetheart?"

Her gaze darted back to his face. "Are you *normal* size? I mean, you seem so much bigger than…" *Kevin*.

"*You* do that to me," he replied in husky tones. "And I warn you not to look at me like that again unless you're prepared for some serious repercussions."

Unable to help herself, she eyed him once more and gave him a soft squeeze.

He grabbed her wrists with a groan, pinning them overhead and plastering her body against the tile wall. "I'll be damned if I can figure you out. Meek one minute and bold as brass the next? Do you like tempting the devil, Haley?"

"I don't know," she breathed. "I guess I'm just curious. This is all new territory for me."

"New *how*?" His gaze narrowed. "You're not saying you're a—"

"No." She shook her head in denial. "I'm not a virgin, but I've never done this kind of thing before. I mean, you and me. This hotel room. All of it."

"Me either," he said. "Don't think this is routine."

"But you got the room," she argued.

"Because I believe in being prepared."

"Me too," she said. "I'm also a believer in positive thinking…in envisioning a desired outcome to help make it happen," she nervously rambled.

"Oh yeah? I think I've got that one nailed. I've been envisioning various outcomes to this particular scenario for a long time."

He still held her pinned. What was next?

"Have you ever thought about me, Haley? About this? About us?"

"Yes," she confessed. "Sometimes… But it doesn't *mean* anything. It's only—"

He cupped her nape, pulling her into a kiss that made her head spin.

"Lust," she finished, gasping for air. "Nothing more."

"Sure there's more." He grinned. "But lust is real good…for starters."

His gaze drifted over her breasts and down the length of her body, his hungry eyes devouring her whole. "Your turn to get naked. I need to see the rest of you."

Her breath hitched as he reached behind her to the tie of her top.

One sharp tug and it dropped to the floor.

His pupils darkened. "I need to touch you."

She still held her breath at the first teasing caress of his fingers along the outside of her breasts, releasing it in a long, slow gush as he cupped one in his big, warm hand.

"Smell you."

He nuzzled all the way up her neck, eliciting ripples of pleasure deep in her belly.

"Taste you." His tongue traced the shell of her ear.

He lingered at the hollow place behind it, his breath hot and moist. "I've thought about that last one the most, Haley, licking you all over…going down on you."

"You like that kind of thing?"

"Hell yeah. Don't you?"

She shut her eyes on an incoherent moan, squeezing them even tighter as he released her hands to peel down her bottoms. Her breath was coming shorter. "I don't know. I never did before, but everything feels so different now."

"Different? How?" He wedged a hard thigh between hers, applying the perfect pressure to make her whimper with need. His mouth melded with hers again in a longer, deeper kiss.

"Like that, Reid. I don't understand what you do to me. I've never felt like this before."

"How about that shower now?" he suggested, low and husky.

He drew her into the tile enclosure, blasting them both with steamy water. He spun her around, her back against his chest. "Take your hair down."

He ripped open the bar of soap, lathering her breasts as she fumbled with her wet and tangled hair. His hands were strong, callused, and skillful. "Here. Soap yourself." He handed her the bar and then grabbed the tiny bottle of shampoo. Next thing she knew, his fingers were buried in her hair, massaging into her scalp. She leaned into him with a little moan of pleasure.

"You like that?" His voice was warm and velvety in her ear.

"God, yes. How did you know?"

"I was raised to pay attention to the little things. A smart man does, especially where women are concerned. Tip your head back."

She arched her spine and shut her eyes against the blast of water and simultaneous sensation of his mouth suckling her nipple. "Too hard to resist," he murmured. "Fucking perfect."

He squeezed her breasts together and then moved on to the other side. She dropped her hands to his head, holding him as he suckled harder. He released her with a pop, then moved behind her again, his chest forming a wall of muscle at her back.

She sucked in another breath, basking in the sensual onslaught of his erection pressing hard and hot against her back, the coarse hair of his thighs lightly abrading her butt cheeks. He had the soap in hand, gliding it up her thighs. He slid his slick fingers slowly down the cleft of her ass and slipped between her legs. "Spread them."

His mouth came down on her shoulder, gently sucking and biting as he explored her folds. She cried out, her inner walls contracting in rhythm with his exploring fingers.

"God," he groaned. "You're so damned tight. Do you have any idea how much I want you?"

"Then quit playing around, Reid," she gasped. She'd *never* been so turned on, so cranked up, so ready. Yet he continued to ratchet her need until she thought she'd snap. She needed him inside her. Now. "It's past time to put your money where your mouth is."

"You got that all in reverse, sweetheart." He cut off the water and backed her slowly to the wall, his lips curving into a dangerous smile. "It's time to put my mouth where your honey is."

Reid sank to his knees, plying open kisses over her belly, then licking around her navel. Haley dropped her head back against the tiles, her body quivering and her mind racing as he worked his way slowly and methodically southward. Every touch, every stroke of his tongue blinded her with pleasure. How the hell did he know so much?

He drew one leg of her legs over his broad shoulder. Her hands came down to his head, holding him tight as he kissed, licked, and tongued her into a state of mindlessness. She stifled a sob of frustration. Responding to her cue, he sucked her clit.

Her climax swelled, crested, and then broke free, washing over her in a series of waves that left her whimpering and weak-kneed. Only his hands anchoring her hips kept her from melting into a puddle on the shower floor.

―――

Reid gazed up at her with a poorly suppressed smirk. He wiped her juices from his mouth and kissed her inner thigh before sliding it down from his shoulder. He'd wanted to do that to her since the night they'd met…and so damn much more.

Her lids flickered open. "What about you? Don't you want—"

"I want all right." But he still held himself in check. "There're a few things I promised myself first. *That* was only one of them." He yanked down a couple of towels and proceeded to rub her dry.

Her gaze widened. "There's more?"

"Oh yeah. I've got a whole laundry list."

He dropped the towel, grasped her at the waist, and

hoisted her onto the vanity top. He parted and stepped between her knees. He was still rock hard and she was still wet. Her essence teased his nostrils, further testing his restraint. It would be so easy. All he had to do was position himself and thrust into her, but he suppressed the urge.

"You want to do it here? Like this?" She leaned back, regarding him with her forehead wrinkled as he reached for the hair dryer. "Are you some kind of frustrated beautician or is this a weird fetish thing?"

"It's your hair," he answered. It was as long and thick as he'd imagined it. He'd dreamed for months of surrounding himself with it as he buried himself in her. "I want to see it down and dry. I want it to curtain my face, to see it shimmering down your back, kissing your ass while you ride me. *Those* are the things I've fantasized about. What I promised myself."

He flipped on the hair dryer, burying his fingers in her silky strands.

"Knock yourself out then, Warren Beatty."

"Huh?" He drew back with a quizzical look.

She blew out an exasperated breath. "I should have known better. The reference is from an iconic '70s film called *Shampoo*."

"You like old movies?"

"I grew up with them. My grandparents are always watching the TNT classics." The grooves between her brows deepened. "You've *fantasized* about me?"

"I told you a man's got to have something to look forward to out in the desert for months on end. I was looking forward to you."

"Why *me*?" she asked. "Surely there are lots of other women…"

He shrugged. "Hell if I know. But I didn't care about any others. You're the one I wanted. I've given up trying to figure it out."

His attraction was beyond his comprehension. He'd wanted her from the moment she'd slapped her twenty on the pool table. He'd known that night that sooner or later they were going to happen. He loved her hair, her gorgeous green eyes, her smell, her taste. The way she'd looked when she came. The way she looked now. All soft and satisfied with her arousal still scenting the air. *Fuck.* That last thought almost broke him.

"Well, now you have me. What are you waiting for?" Once more she challenged him, shattering what little remained of his self-restraint.

"Good enough." He slammed down the dryer. Her eyes widened as he jerked her hips to the edge of the vanity, then gripped the underside of her thighs to wrap her legs around his waist. She entwined her arms around his neck and writhed against him. He shuddered at the welcoming warmth of her soft, wet flesh. He'd waited all this time to feel her melting beneath him. He ground his teeth against the urge to pound into her.

"You know this doesn't really mean anything, right?" she said. "We're just satisfying curiosity and animal instinct. That's all."

"That's what you think, eh?"

"Yes," she insisted.

"Then you think too damned much." His mouth claimed hers in a hungry kiss, their lips melding, breaths mingling, and tongues twining. The kiss grew fiercer, hotter. Tearing his mouth from hers, Reid cleared the vanity as he groped for his wallet.

"Looking for this?" She held up the wet leather.

He shook it open, scattering the contents over the vanity, snatched up the foil wrapper, and tore it open with his teeth. Barely skirting the razor's edge of self-control, Reid gloved himself and penetrated her in a single, slow thrust that seated him to the hilt.

He shut his eyes on a groan. *Shit. It's been so goddamn long.*

"You okay?" she asked in a breathless whisper.

"That's supposed to be my question."

"I'm very much okay." She squirmed against him again, her walls squeezing him, inciting blinding spasms.

His pulse roared. "Bed. Now."

Reid cupped her soft, sweet ass in his hands, and carried her into the next room, where they toppled together onto the bed. It was a far cry from the slow and deliberate seduction he'd planned, but the instant he'd breached her, all of his well-formed fantasies had gone out the fucking window.

Bodies entwined, he rolled her beneath him, claiming her mouth once more. His mind blurred to all but the sensation of deep, drugging kisses. The rhythmic thrust and retreat as he moved inside her. Their tangling tongues. The slick friction of his body sliding in and out of hers. The erotic scents of mutual arousal. Her soft sounds of pleasure. The short, sharp, breaths and mingled moans that pierced the air. The slap of flesh as he plunged in and out of her.

Holy shit. Had it ever felt *this* good?

His body screamed for release. His lungs burned and balls ached with the effort of holding himself in check, but he'd sworn to take his time. To make a lasting impression. To brand her as his, body and soul.

Haley's senses were drowning in Reid as he filled her over and over in a ceaseless cadence of deep and shallow thrusts. She'd never felt anything like this, had never even dreamed such deep and profound pleasure could exist—but it still wasn't enough. She needed so much more.

She reached out blindly, clasping his firm buttocks in both hands, urging his pistoning hips harder, faster, but he still refused to give her the release she demanded. Instead, he teased and tormented, bringing her to the brink of climax, only to ease her back again. The denial made her want to scream and sob and claw. "Please, Reid," she gasped. The words were barely out of her throat before she found herself on top of him, staring down into intense blue eyes.

"You want it? Take it," he growled. "Ride me."

"I don't know how," she said.

"Shut your eyes." She felt his hands on her hips. "You're in control—position, angle, pace. It's all yours. Take it."

Her eyes fluttered open. "But what about you?"

"Don't worry about me, sweetheart. I'll get mine, but right now I want to just lie back and enjoy the show."

Reid continued to confuse her. Only a moment ago she'd thought of him as the warrior out to claim his spoils, but now? He gazed up at her through heavy lids with a heart-stopping half smile lingering on his lips. He made her feel like the most desirable woman in the world.

Hands braced on his pecs, she leaned forward to kiss

him. Raising his head from the pillow, he met her halfway. He seemed to be doing a lot of that. She'd underestimated him in so many ways. "Stay just like that," he murmured once their mouths parted. "Just think about what feels good and do it."

She shut her eyes on a moan as he cupped and suckled her breasts. While he licked and sucked, she began moving, experimentally at first, until finding a position that took him deep. Once she found her tempo, he thrust his hips in counterpoint. Her walls tightened. Her body tensed. Her breath came faster. Their climax hit simultaneously, a scorching explosion of heat, light, and sensation that left them both panting.

He rolled her beside him, where they lay together in a spent tangle of limbs. Haley felt as if she'd had an out of body experience and even now still floated on air. Staring at him in incredulity, she suddenly erupted in a paroxysm of laughter that sent tears streaming down her cheeks.

He frowned back. "What's so damned funny?"

"You. Me." She gasped between uncontrollable bursts of mirth. "I had no idea it could be like this, Reid. I didn't know *anything*."

He'd given her much more than an earth-shattering orgasm. He'd gifted her with her own sexuality. And she'd never be the same.

Chapter 11

MUSIC STARTLED HALEY AWAKE. *I NEVER DREAMED THAT you'd be mine. But here we are, we're here tonight… Singing Amen, I, I'm alive…* Nickelback's "If Everyone Cared" seemed a poignant anthem for Reid's ringtone.

"Just ignore it," Reid mumbled, his hot, moist breath fanning the back of her neck. He'd penetrated her from behind the last time, and his hard body still cocooned hers. Although half asleep, he was growing hard again.

"It's yours, not mine," she said.

Reid groaned. The mattress shifted. He rolled over and reached for his phone, stopping the song mid-chorus. "Hello," he answered sharply. "Krista?" His tone registered surprise.

Her chest constricted. Who was Krista?

"What's up, little sister?"

His sister. She exhaled in relief. He'd mentioned he had three of them. He'd also explained the photo, so why did she instantly think the worst? She supposed old habits were hard to break. Trust didn't come easy to her, and she was feeling especially vulnerable right now. She'd given him her body, and she feared her heart was perilously close to following suit.

He padded to the other side of the room. Her eyes tracked leisurely over his sculpted body, lingering on his taut ass. Desire flickered to life inside her. They'd made love three times. How could she still feel it? It seemed her plan to get all that suppressed lust out of her system had failed. Dismally. She really should get up and give him some privacy, but his demeanor set her on alert.

"You're coming here? Now? Of course I'm happy. It's just a bit unexpected. Why didn't you let me know sooner? Tonya's with you?"

Tonya? That was his ex's name, the brunette from the picture. She sat up, crossing her arms over her chest as her head filled with visions of Reid doing the same things to *her* that they'd done. Her stomach tightened. It was completely irrational, but she couldn't ignore the stab of jealousy.

"No, I don't. Wait—" He covered the receiver and exhaled a soft curse. "Hey, Tonya." He met Haley's resentful stare with a helpless look. "Please, give me a chance to explain," he whispered to her, and then spoke back into the phone. "No, Ton, I was talking to someone else. No, I'm not on base, but this really isn't a good time. Can I call you back in a few?" He went to the bedside table and took up a pad and pen. "Where are you? South Utah? And you're staying in Anaheim? That's about eight hours away from you." He scribbled a few notes. "Sure, I'll come up. It's only about an hour north of here. I gotta go now. Tell Krista I'll get back to her in a little bit, okay? Bye, Ton." Reid ended the call. "That was—"

"Your *ex*?" Haley supplied, a knot choking her throat.

"Yeah," he confessed. "She's with my little sister, Krista. They're on their way here. Not *here* precisely." He rubbed his neck, visibly flustered. "I mean to California. I'm sorry, Haley. I'd wanted to spend my free days with you, but now I have to go meet my sister.

I had no idea she was coming. Krista's never traveled this far from home before."

"I'm sure she'll be very happy to see you."

"Yeah. Me too. We're pretty tight. My whole family is."

"I'll call Yolanda and see if she's ready to go."

His gaze widened. "You're leaving? Now?"

"Yeah." Common sense told her it was past time to make a strategic retreat. "Yolanda and I were supposed to go to dinner together. What time is it anyway?"

It was impossible to tell. The room was dark. They'd drawn the drapes for privacy. She rose from the bed with the sheet wrapped around and dug her phone out of her purse. She quickly scanned her messages. There were three texts from Yolanda. The first was a reminder of their dinner reservation. The second informed her she'd missed dinner, but Yolanda had taken Garcia instead. The third message said she was worried and to call ASAP. She noted the time. That was an hour ago. She felt a sharp stab of guilt. She was a horrible friend.

Reid sat on the bed and pulled her onto his lap. She tried to get up but he held her tight. "Come back to bed with me."

"No, Reid," she said, forcing out her reply. She wished she could stay with him forever, but it was over. It had to be. It was far better to suffer a little bit of hurt right now than a whole lot more later on. "I have to go now. We had a good time, but now it's out of our systems, right?"

"Is it?" He brushed a stray lock of hair from her face, then his fingers grazed her cheek. "I don't think so. Not by a long shot. I like being with you, Haley, and whether you're ready to admit it or not, I think you feel the same way. I'm not ready for it to be over."

"Look, you got what you wanted. I don't resent that. But what more did you expect from me?"

A better question might have been what *she'd* expected. She'd been a fool to think she could be sexually intimate with him and not become emotionally engaged. But she didn't need entanglements. Not at this point in her life.

"You think all I wanted was a fuck? Is *that* what you really believe?"

"I don't know what you wanted, but there's no sense in continuing this. You're leaving again soon and so am I. It can't go anywhere."

"I know our circumstances make this difficult," he said, "but I'd like to try and make it work."

"But aren't you leaving for Anaheim tonight?"

"No. They'll be getting in late. We'll drive up first thing in the morning."

"*We?*"

"Yeah. Come with me, Haley. I'd like you to meet her."

She shook her head. "No, I'm not comfortable with that. You haven't seen your sister in months. I'd only feel like an interloper."

"It's not like that with my family. People are different in Wyoming. Maybe it's because we're in the least-populated state, but we're more open, more welcoming to outsiders. You'll see. You'll like Krista. I promise."

"It's not my liking *her* that's the issue. Did you forget that she's bringing her best friend, who just happens to be your ex-girlfriend? No thank you, Reid."

"If the idea of Tonya bothers you, we'll invite Garcia and Yolanda to come along."

"But I don't have any clothes with me," she continued to protest.

"Easy fix," he countered. "There's a boutique in the hotel. I'll buy you something."

Before she could formulate another argument, he picked up the phone and hit the redial button.

"Hey, Sis. Sorry I was tied up when you called. No, it wasn't anything I couldn't handle." His gaze darted back to Haley. Her chest ached every time he looked at her like he was looking at her now. "I'll drive up to Anaheim in the morning to show you the sights. I'll be bringing a couple of friends with me. You remember Garcia, right? He'll probably be coming. The other's Haley. You'll like her too, Krista." He paused. "Yeah, I said *her*. We'll see you around eight." He ended the call with a wrinkle furrowing his brows.

"She doesn't want to meet me, does she?"

"She didn't say that." Yet his frown lingered.

"But she implied it."

"You have to understand that Krista's a determined matchmaker, but I'll set her straight."

"I'm not about to come between you and your sister, Reid."

He shrugged. "She'll get over it."

"I don't want her to *get over it*."

"Trust me. It'll be fine."

Trust me. He had no idea how hard that was. The only people she'd ever truly trusted were Grams, Gramps, and Yolanda. Her instincts told her not to go with him, but she was as reluctant to end their time together as he was, just for different reasons. For her, this was not a beginning of something but the end. She'd already come to that resolution. When it was over, it would truly be over, but that didn't mean she had to be in a hurry about it.

"All right, Reid," she blurted, contrary to all reason. "If Garcia and Yolanda agree, I'll go with you."

"Good decision." The wrinkle instantly smoothed from his brow. "I'll call Garcia while you text Yolanda that you're staying the night with me."

Her stomach leaped. "No. I can't."

"Just one night, Haley," he coaxed. "What difference can a few more hours make?"

Soft and seductive, his lips met hers.

She still gripped the sheet. He peeled it away and eased her back onto the bed. She forgot all about leaving the moment his lips grazed her shoulders. His tongue was magic, inciting shivers of pleasure as he licked and nuzzled his way up her neck.

What difference? All the difference in the world.

Hours later, Haley stirred out of a sex-induced coma to find herself alone in the bed.

"Reid?"

She padded to the bathroom, but he wasn't there either. Had he left without her after all? She experienced a brief moment of panic until noticing that all of his things were still in the room. He'd mentioned buying her some clothes last night. Maybe he'd gone out to get something?

She stepped into the bathroom for a quick shower,

and then shrugged into one of the complimentary robes hanging in the closet. A few minutes later, a soft knock sounded on the door. She opened it to find Yolanda with a shopping bag in one hand, a Starbucks latte in the other, a sparkle in her black eyes, and a wide grin stretching her face.

"Having fun, *chica*?" She pushed into the room without giving Haley a chance to respond. "I admit you surprised me when you disappeared with Reid. But I'm glad you and he are hitting it off. I was wondering when you'd finally find someone."

"It's not like that, Yo. We're just having some fun. Isn't that what you're always hounding me about?"

"Yeah, I do, but we both know you're not that type. Here, take this one." She offered Haley a coffee. "It has a shot of espresso. You look like you need it more than me."

"I am pretty wiped out," Haley confessed.

"Me too." Yolanda yawned and stretched, adding with a chuckle, "Marines have endurance."

Haley flushed.

"The bag is also for you." Yolanda took a sip of her drink and nudged it toward Haley with her foot. "Reid asked me to pick up a few things for you. I bought you some undies—the sexy, lacy kind." She winked. "Also a pair of capris and a belly top."

"Thanks, Yo. I owe you. Where is Reid now?"

"He and Garcia went for a run on the beach. Even in their downtime these guys never stop—not that I'm complaining. I prefer a man with stamina." She plopped herself on the sofa. "All right, Haley, time to dish. How was he?"

Her face heated.

"C'mon," Yolanda pressed. "I've shared every little detail whenever you've asked me."

"I've *never* asked."

"But I told you anyway, didn't I? That's what best friends are for. Now dish."

"It was…good."

Yolanda rolled her eyes.

"*Really* good."

Yolanda pursed her lips and tapped her foot. "That's not enough for me."

"All right!" Haley threw her hands up. "It was great! Earth-shattering! Are you happy now?"

"Hardly, but at least it's a start. You are far too uptight about sex."

Haley ground her teeth. "I'm not uptight. I just don't like to talk about *it*, okay?"

"*It?* Can't you even say the word?"

"Of course I can," she huffed.

"How about 'orgasm'?"

"Yes. I can say *orgasm*." She averted her gaze. "Just not in public."

Yolanda was undaunted. "Did you have one? Does he know how to use his mouth on your *coño*?"

"God, yes," Haley gushed, then looked away in embarrassment.

Her best friend chuckled. "Then he made you come?"

"Uh-huh. Several times."

"Oh yeah?" Yolanda grinned. "Now, it's getting good. How about with his—" She arched a brow.

"No." Haley shook her head. "We're not going there. I'm not going to describe his anatomy to you."

Yolanda smirked. "You got it bad for him, don't you?"

"No, I don't. It's just a fling. That's all," she said, still trying to convince herself.

"Then why are we going to meet his sister?"

"Because he invited us, and I thought it would be fun. I haven't been to Disney since I was a kid."

"But you hate crowds and never go on the rides."

"Only because I don't like those crazy ones you always want to go on. I'm afraid of heights. A lot of people are," she added defensively. "But you're right. Maybe we shouldn't go. I'm starting to think this is a bad idea."

"Oh, no you don't." Yolanda laid a hand on her arm. "I'm not going to let you back out just because you're getting cold feet."

"I don't have cold feet. I just have more important things to do than cavorting at an amusement park."

"He scares you, doesn't he?"

Haley scowled. "What do you mean?"

Yolanda's gaze held hers. "I mean, you really like him and don't know how to deal with it."

"There are a few things I like *about* him," Haley hedged. "But I'm not in any danger of falling in love, if that's what you think."

"Why?" Yolanda asked. "Because he doesn't fit your ideal?"

Haley laughed. "Reid? Not at all. He's about as far from my ideal as I can imagine."

Reid was far more complex than she'd ever imagined. It would be all too easy to lose herself in a man like that, but logic insisted that he was all wrong. Totally wrong for her.

"Why? Because he's a marine and not some university geek? When did you become such a snob?"

"I'm not. But maybe if Reid was in school we'd at least have something to talk about."

"First off, men aren't good talkers, Haley. Save the talking for your girlfriends. Men excel at other things."

Haley heaved an exasperated sigh. "You're missing my point. I'm saying we have nothing to build a relationship on."

Yolanda cast a slow gaze over the rumpled bed. "Several orgasms in one night? It seems to me you have more than enough. And you're still here, aren't you?"

"We're all entitled to a few stupid mistakes, aren't we? It's not like I plan on making a habit of it…of him."

"Don't underestimate him, *chica*." Yolanda grinned knowingly. "I think your cowboy has very different ideas."

Chapter 12

FIGURING REID WOULD WANT TO SPEND THE remainder of the weekend with his sister, Haley insisted on driving separately to Anaheim. She still had serious qualms about meeting his ex-girlfriend, but curiosity about Reid ate at her. She wondered what he was like with Krista and the rest of his family. She knew so little about him and couldn't help wanting to know more.

When she and Yolanda pulled into the Hilton, he and Garcia were just climbing out of Reid's truck. By the time she and Yolanda parked, two young women had appeared. The first, a curvy redhead, threw herself into Reid's arms with a squeal.

"*That* must be Krista," Haley remarked. Reid's grin was blazing white as he spun his sister in the air, completely indifferent to passersby. Haley's chest squeezed at the happy reunion. She'd always dreamed of that kind of family.

"Yeah?" Yolanda elbowed her in the ribs. "And who's the *muchacha morena* making sheep's eyes at my Rafi?"

Haley covertly eyed the second girl, who slouched against the truck beside Garcia. Long, straight, blue-black hair hung over her shoulders and tight jeans and cowboy boots showcased lean legs, making Haley self-conscious of her barely-over-five-foot frame. She wore a straw hat that shadowed the upper half of her face, but revealed an indulgent smile on full lips as she watched the brother–sister reunion. *Tonya*.

"You can relax, Yo," Haley said. "I don't think she's after Rafael. That's Reid's ex-girlfriend."

"Really?" Yolanda's gaze narrowed in speculation. "Is she Latina?"

"I don't know. Reid never said."

When Tonya tipped her hat back and looked Haley's way, her Native American heritage was clear. She gave a half nod as if in recognition, then her gaze swept slowly over Haley as if sizing her up. She murmured something to Garcia, pushed off the truck, and approached with lithe, confident strides.

She extended her hand with a smile. "Hi. I'm Tonya Rivers, a close friend of Krista…and Reid." Haley noted the emphasis on the last two words. Tonya was staking her claim.

"Nice to meet you, Tonya." Haley accepted her hand. Tonya's grip was surprisingly firm, more like a man's than a woman's and nearly as callused. But aside from her brusque manner, there was nothing remotely masculine about her. Their eyes locked for a long moment. Hers were black as agate under finely arched brows. With sculpted features and flawless mocha skin, she was a stunning woman. "I'm Haley, and this is my best friend, Yolanda."

Before introductions were completed, Garcia and Reid appeared beside them. Reid was still beaming and holding his little sister in his arms. He tossed her once more in the air before setting her back on her feet. "Krista, Tonya"—Reid nodded to the latter—"I'd like you to meet Haley and Yolanda."

"As usual, we're one step ahead of you, Reid," Tonya replied with a smirk. "The three of us have already introduced ourselves."

Haley watched Krista with bated breath. Her eyes sparkled and face glowed, but both faded as her gaze darted between Tonya, Reid, and Haley. Haley forced a smile and stepped forward. "Nice to meet you, Krista. How was your trip?"

"Not too bad," Krista replied. "But then again, Ton here did most of the driving. We dropped off some horses at a dude outfit in Utah, unhooked the trailer, and then drove straight here."

"Horses?" Haley asked.

"Tonya's family breeds and trains them, and leases them out to dude ranches and outfitters," Reid explained. "She also works part time with Krista as a wrangler on our ranch."

"You have a ranch? I thought your family ran a hunting business?"

"We do," he replied. "But we also keep about eighty head of horses and a bunch of mules for hunting, packing, and for guests who just want to ride the trails. It's not a big spread by any means, but we do keep our own stock. Krista and Tonya mostly take care of that side of the operation. How is the horse business these days?" Reid asked Tonya.

"We're doing okay," she replied. "Thanks mostly to Keith."

"So he's still doing his dog and pony show?"

"Yup." She grinned, her teeth blazing white against her tanned skin. "He's even hawking calendars now, and just put out one of those big coffee table books. He's quite a commodity these days. Last I heard, he'd even been approached by some big-name film producer."

Reid turned to Haley and Yolanda. "Keith is Tonya's cousin and one of those so-called horse whisperers—"

"He prefers the title Equine Behaviorist," Tonya corrected.

Reid made a scoffing sound.

"He's also incredibly hot," Krista interjected.

"Keith?" Tonya made a face. "You think my cousin's hot?"

"Heck yeah! Who wouldn't?" Krista said. "How else could he travel around the country trailed by a bunch of horse-loving groupies?"

"I s'pose you're right," Tonya admitted. "There are certainly a bunch of women who can't seem to get enough of him, especially the Europeans. He's booked for a big summer tour over there next year. Six countries I think."

"Unbelievable." Reid shook his head with a chuckle. "Got to give the guy credit for making the most of his assets."

They all laughed.

Haley shifted in place, feeling increasingly awkward. "Is this your first visit to California?" She directed the lame-sounding question to Krista. She'd never been good at small talk and still didn't know what to make of Tonya. She didn't feel overt hostility from her, but certainly didn't feel warmth either.

"Yeah, it is," Krista replied. "I'm really excited to see the sights. Maybe it sounds silly, but I've wanted to go to Disney since I was a little kid. I was a hopeless Disney Princess addict and still have the entire collection of dolls."

"Except Pocahontas," Tonya said. "You gave her to me."

Krista grinned. "She was always my favorite, but I thought she looked just like you."

"The weather looks great for a day in the park," Haley chimed in, feeling even more like a fifth wheel.

"It does," Tonya agreed and then turned her attention to Reid. Haley noted how her gaze worked him slowly up and down. "You're looking well, Reid. I think this California sun agrees with you."

He shrugged. "The winters are a damn lot easier here than in Wyoming."

"That's for sure," Krista laughed. "We're still wading through several feet of snow back home. That's probably what's put the bow hunters off. We didn't have any booked until the end of the month, so it seemed a great time to come out here."

"You hunt with bows?" Haley asked.

"Yeah," Krista replied. "We usually get a couple dozen bow hunters every spring and fall that want to bag a bear."

"That's barbaric!" Haley laid a hand on Reid's arm. "Did you hunt bears with a bow and arrow?"

"Only black bears," he clarified. "Grizzlies are still endangered, although they've more than recovered and need to be delisted. They're actually booming in the areas around Yellowstone and Grand Teton and encroaching on populated areas. They need to be managed."

She scowled. "Managed or *murdered*?"

"C'mon, Haley. We've already been down this road. Do you really think a griz is going to stay within the park just because we say pretty please?"

Although they'd come to a truce of sorts, his mocking remark was stark proof that their differences remained. "There must be another way."

"Like what?" Krista laughed. "Telling all the hikers to carry pepper spray and wear bear bells?"

Tonya chimed in, "Do you know how we tell the difference between black bear and grizzly bear scat back in Wyoming? Black bear droppings have berries and the Grizzly bear droppings contain little bells and smell like pepper."

Everyone laughed but Haley. Her eyes burned, but she refused to show her embarrassment. Surprisingly, Krista was the one to break the building tension.

"Don't worry too much about the bears," Krista said. "They have little cause for fear. Most of the hunters are rich guys from back east who would probably piss themselves if they actually saw one. The majority of them come back empty-handed since Reid's been gone. For the most part, they're happy holing up at the lodge, drinking and *talking* about hunting. It's really just a testosterone-laced version of a hen party."

"Are you a hunting guide too?" Haley asked.

Krista shook her head. "Nope. Although I can shoot as good as any of them, and better than most, guiding is still a male-dominated realm. Tonya and I manage the horses. Mom cooks, and my father and brothers lead the hunts. Our family's been doing it for three generations. Does anyone want to come inside for a beer? We picked up a cooler full last night."

"I'll take one," Garcia eagerly replied.

Glancing at Tonya, Yolanda latched on to his arm. "Make that two."

Reid made to follow while Haley dragged her heels, still hurt by Reid and Tonya's combined mockery. She wished she hadn't come. She'd even begun to think Reid had forgotten her existence until he looked back over his shoulder. "You comin' inside?"

"I'm not thirsty," she sulked.

"What's wrong?"

Annoyed by his ridicule, Haley jutted her chin. "I'll tell you what's wrong. You just stood there while your ex-girlfriend made fun of me. You even laughed, Reid!"

"Because it was a *joke*. C'mon," he coaxed. "You need to lighten up a little."

"Lighten up?" She jerked back. "It's hard for me to meet strangers to begin with. I told you I wasn't comfortable coming here, but I did because *you* asked me to."

"I know that, and I'm sorry if the joke offended you. It really wasn't personal."

She appreciated his apology, but it still wasn't enough to vanquish her insecurity. "How serious was it, Reid?"

"What?" he answered blankly.

"You and Tonya. I can understand your sister coming out here, but why would Tonya join her if it was finished between you?"

"Because she's my sister's best friend. It's nothing more than that."

"How serious *was* it?" she persisted. She didn't know why it mattered. Irrational maybe, but she couldn't deny the sick churning in her gut.

"Serious enough, I suppose. We were almost engaged."

"*Engaged*," she repeated. "You gave her a ring?"

"No. It didn't get *quite* that far."

"How far?"

He scrubbed his face. "It's ancient history, Haley. It's done."

"So you claim, but I get quite another impression from her."

"I told her clearly at Christmas that I'm not interested in picking it back up with her."

She searched his eyes for any sign of deceit, but his gaze remained steady. "Well *clearly* she didn't accept that if she's come all the way out here from Wyoming. And now you plan to *entertain* her?" Haley planted her hands on her hips.

"How can I avoid it?"

"I'm starting to think this whole thing between us was a huge mistake."

"C'mon, sweetheart," he cajoled. "There's no reason to be jealous."

"Jealous?" Her brows met in a glower. "You think I'm *jealous*?"

He chuckled. "I'm a bit flattered by it, actually, but Tonya's arrival doesn't mean anything. You're the only one I want. Understand?" He tilted his face to kiss her, but she turned away.

She despised this feeling of insecurity that squeezed her chest and resented him for being the cause of it. "You're right, Reid," she snapped. "It *doesn't* matter because *this*"—she gestured between them—"doesn't mean anything. I admit we have powerful chemistry, but it's bound to wear off sooner or later—"

"Wear off? I don't think you mean that. There's something more here, Haley, and it's not going to just *wear off*. You know it as well as I do. You just don't want to admit it because it doesn't fit into your master plan."

He was right that she wasn't ready to admit it, even to herself.

"I *do* have plans, Reid," she argued. "Big plans that require me to maintain focus. I can't afford distractions. And you qualify as a huge distraction. On top of that, our lives are on completely divergent paths."

"You haven't even given this a chance. That's all I'm asking. I want us to spend some time together and see where it goes. Please let's just give it a little more time before you decide to jump ship." He grasped her chin, holding her gaze. "Just a chance."

His calm and confident reassurance made her *want* to believe in him, to trust him.

"Okay," she replied softly. She couldn't believe how easily he'd defused her, but Reid always seemed to have that effect on her.

"Good." His lips met hers, soft and tender, as if sealing a pact. He released her with a smile, then planted another kiss on the tip of her nose before pressing a hand into the small of her back. "C'mon, let's go join the others inside."

They hung out in Krista and Tonya's room for an hour or so before heading over to the amusement park. Feeling out of place even with Yolanda's presence, Haley's anxiety only increased upon entering the amusement park. She hated loud noises and crowds. That's why she'd adapted so easily to the isolation of Alaska.

"Look at that, Tonya!" Krista shrieked. "I've never been on one that tall before. How big is it anyway?"

Haley's stomach dropped when she pointed to the gigantic Ferris wheel soaring high above Paradise Pier.

Reid stared up at the structure. "It's got to be well over a hundred feet. I went on it once. It's a special design that allows the gondola cars to slide out on a track as it moves. It offers an incredible view of the park."

"Forget all the parades and kiddie stuff." Krista yanked his arm. "Let's go!"

They'd no sooner started across the park toward Paradise Pier when Tonya pointed to Haley's worst nightmare, the California Screamin' roller coaster. "Check that one out, Krista! I love roller coasters."

Haley's heart leaped up into her throat. Why the hell had she ever come here? *Reid*. She reminded herself she'd done it for him. And now he was bounding toward the Ferris wheel almost as eagerly as his sister.

"I can't do it, Yo." Haley clutched Yolanda's arm. "You know how much I hate heights."

"Sure you can, *chica*," Yolanda said. "It'll be fun."

"You don't understand," Haley ground through her teeth. "I *really*, *really* can't do it."

"But it's perfectly safe," Yolanda reassured. "If it bothers you, just close your eyes."

She shut them on a curse. "God help me."

Her knees weakened as their turn came to fill the six-passenger gondola. Garcia and Yolanda entered first. Reid stepped back to let Tonya and Krista follow. Tonya was visibly disappointed when he gestured to Haley. She gulped a huge breath as she eyed the metal cage but still couldn't seem to get enough air into her lungs.

"Are you all right?" Reid asked, plainly concerned. "You look like a ghost. Do you want to sit this one out?"

Her gaze darted back to the car. Krista, Garcia, and Yolanda occupied one side and Tonya sat alone on the other. She slid over to make room for Reid. *Oh, you'd like that, wouldn't you, Tonya?*

"I'm fine," Haley replied tight-lipped, trying to choke down her terror. She sucked in another breath and entered the cage, taking the seat beside Tonya.

Reid entered last. He reached for her hand. "I didn't know you were afraid of heights."

"There's a lot you don't know about me, but I'll be fine," she insisted with a forced smile. "I'm just not a big fan of amusement park rides."

"You could have told me. I'd have stayed behind with you."

"You really would have?" she asked in surprise.

"Sure." He gave her clammy hand a reassuring squeeze as the wheel slowly began its ascent. Her grip on Reid's hand tightened as the gondola rose. Her stomach clenched and head reeled as it began to rock. Halfway up, she squeezed her eyes shut, but it only emphasized the sickening, swinging sensation. The wheel paused for another stomach-lurching second as they reached the top.

"Ooh! Look at that incredible view!" Krista crooned.

"This is so cool!" Tonya exclaimed. "I can't believe how high up we are."

Haley stole a peek through her lashes just as the car slid forward to pitch way out over the lagoon. Suspended over a hundred feet above the ground, she broke into a cold sweat. An insuppressible wave of nausea followed. "Oh my God. I think I'm going to hurl!"

—∿∿—

"It's all right, *chica*," Yolanda consoled as Haley rinsed her mouth for the fourth time. "Lots of people get sick on rides."

"Please, just take me home now," Haley begged. The Mickey's Fun Wheel ride would go down in the "annals of Haley" as the most humiliating ten minutes of her life. "I don't think I can ever look any of them in the face again." *Especially Reid.*

"He's waiting for you outside," Yolanda said.

"I don't want to see him."

"Don't be silly. You can't hide in here forever."

"You want to bet on that?" Haley mumbled, running her fingers through her sweat-dampened hair. She pinched her pale cheeks hoping for color, but still looked like death warmed over. "Is there a back way out of here?"

Yolanda sighed. "C'mon, *chica*, you've already kept the poor guy waiting for twenty minutes."

"Good. Maybe he gave up and left."

"I doubt that. He was truly worried about you, you know."

"What about the others?"

"Rafi took Tonya and Krista on the roller coaster."

"Thank God for small favors," Haley mumbled.

"Just talk to him, Haley, and then if you still want to leave, I'll take you home."

With a groan of defeat, she reluctantly trudged out behind Yolanda.

Sure enough, Reid was waiting as she emerged from the restroom. He was propped against the wall with booted ankles crossed, looking as if he hadn't a care in the world. She noticed with a new wave of embarrassment that he wore a Mickey Mouse T-shirt.

His gaze met hers, and his expression instantly softened. "You okay?"

Her face flamed. She wished she could just slither away unnoticed. "No." She shook her head. "I'm absolutely not okay. I just want to forget this day ever happened."

"It's really no big deal," he said.

"I puked all over you, Reid. How is that not a big deal?"

He shrugged. "I've had worse."

She let that one go. Some things were better unasked. "Please tell your sister that I'm sorry I ruined everything. I'm going to go home now."

He pushed off the wall. "I'll take you."

She shook her head. "No. You came here to see Krista. Yolanda will drive me."

"Krista will understand."

"No, Reid. I've already done enough to spoil everyone's day. I just need to be alone."

"Okay. If that's what you want, I can respect that. When can I see you again?"

She snorted. "You're kidding, right?"

"No. Not kidding."

Yolanda's gaze darted from one to the other. "I'm going to go get a lemonade. Either of you want anything?"

"No thanks," Haley and Reid replied almost in unison, neither taking their eyes off the other.

"Be back in a few then." Yolanda slipped off toward the drink kiosk.

"You should go find your sister," Haley said.

"Is that what you want?"

"Yes."

"Then I'll call you tomorrow," he said.

"No."

"The day after?"

She averted her eyes, making every effort just to breathe. "You need to spend time with your sister. Krista is only staying for a week, and I'm leaving soon."

"Then I'll take some leave and drive up to Sacramento with you."

"No, Reid," she answered softly. "There's no point in continuing this. It would be a wasted effort for both of us to invest any more time in this...this..." She waved her hand. "Whatever it is."

He grasped her shoulders, but she avoided his eyes. "I get that you're embarrassed about what happened, Haley. But that's no reason to give me the brush-off."

"It's more than embarrassment," she insisted. "Don't you see this is impossible? I'm a bookish, acrophobic, pacifistic vegetarian, and you're a bow-hunting, roller-coaster-riding cowboy carnivore. I don't fit into your world. I knew that the minute I saw you with Krista and Tonya. You all belong together. *We* don't. We'll just end up hating each other in the end. Can't you see that?"

"No, I don't. I only *see* you."

"Why are you making this so difficult?" she asked in a strangled voice.

"Because you're making a mistake."

"No. I'm not," she insisted. "Starting this was the mistake. What more do you need me to say?"

His hands tightened almost painfully on her shoulders.

"What more do I need? Tell me flat out that you don't want me, Haley."

She stared into intense, infinitely blue eyes. "I don't want you," she blurted, almost choking on the words.

He flinched. She had to look away. "You really mean that?" He drew her closer, his gaze searching her face. "Are you sayin' you feel *nothing* for me after last night?"

Please don't kiss me. Please don't kiss me. I'll become a blubbering fool if you kiss me.

"This has been way too much too soon for me. I'm not ready for what you want. I told you, I have plans for my life. I'm sorry, Reid."

"If that's how you feel, I guess there's nothing more to say." He gave a fatalistic shrug and eased his grip. "I'll walk you back to the hotel."

"No, please don't." She swallowed hard. Her throat felt like sandpaper. "Let's just part ways here. It'll be easier."

"If that's really the way you want it." He hesitated and then his hands dropped lifelessly to his sides. "Good-bye then, Haley Cooper."

"Good-bye, Reid," she answered back almost inaudibly, her eyes blurring as she watched him turn and walk away.

"Where's Reid?" Yolanda returned, drink in hand.

"Gone," she whispered.

"Gone where, *chica*?" she asked.

"Gone, as in I sent him away." Haley stifled the sob that rose up in her throat, but try as she might, she couldn't suppress the moist heat that began trickling down her face.

Yolanda's eyes widened. "Why? When I left I thought for sure you were going to work it out."

"Never, Yo." She sniffed. "It's impossible." She spun away, fiercely palming her eyes. "C'mon. Let's go. I don't have time for this emotional crap."

———

Reid caught up with Garcia, Tonya, and Krista standing in line for a second ride on the roller coaster. They smiled and waved. He grimaced. Hanging out at an amusement park was no longer very amusing. He didn't understand why things had gone south when only hours ago she'd lain beneath him so warm and soft and beautiful, her body welcoming and sweet. He knew she'd lied to him about her feelings. She couldn't have given herself to him if she felt nothing. She wasn't the type, but he'd overestimated his success. She'd given him her body but still withheld her trust and her heart.

"So where's your friend?" Krista asked.

"Her name's Haley," Reid snapped.

"Poor thing," Krista remarked. "I never saw anyone puke on a Ferris wheel before."

"She doesn't like amusement park rides," Reid said.

"Then why'd she come?" Krista asked.

"Because I pressured her to." With as long as it had taken to wear her down, he should have known better. Like a dumbass, he'd pushed her too hard. Now she didn't want to see him again.

"Why would you do that?" Krista countered.

"Because I wanted you to meet her."

Krista's gaze narrowed. "Then it's *serious*?"

"I thought it could be." *Now I'll never know.* Haley was such a fascinating contradiction. Smart and sexy, yet shy and insecure. But brave, too. She took risks, faced her fears. She'd proven that on the ride today. If only she'd take the same risk with him.

Krista shook her head. "She doesn't suit you at all, Reid. She's too uptight. Takes herself way too seriously."

"Why would you say that? You don't know anything about her."

"To start with," Krista challenged, "she has no sense of humor."

"Only because she felt like we made her the butt of the jokes," he defended.

He never should have brought her to meet Tonya and Krista. He'd done it because he didn't want to lose any time with her. It was a selfish, dickhead move. Now he'd lost *her*.

"I know *you*, big brother. She's not right at all." Krista laid a hand on his arm. "Trust me on this. Women have intuition, especially about other women. Tonya knows she screwed up, Reid. You should give her another chance." Although engaged in conversation with Garcia, Reid noticed that Tonya slanted them curious glances.

"She's the one who called it quits. Not me. And now I've moved on."

"But—"

Reid raised a silencing hand. "While I appreciate your sisterly concern, my love life is off limits. I don't want or need your meddling in it. I can fuck it up perfectly well all by myself."

—∼∼∼—

Haley began packing her things almost as soon as she got home.

"You're leaving already?" her grandmother asked.

"I thought you were going to be home for at least another week."

"I was," Haley said, sniffling, "but now I'm not. I really need to go back to school. I have a lot of work to catch up on."

"Did you and *Yolanda* have a nice time at the beach?"

"Yes. It was real nice," Haley replied woodenly.

"He seems like a decent young man. Attractive too," Grams remarked with a knowing look. "Want to tell me about it?"

"How did you know?" Haley asked.

"You don't get to be my age without learning what heartbreak looks like. Besides, I've experienced it firsthand."

"You have?"

"Yes. Your grandpa wasn't my first love, sweetheart."

"He wasn't?"

"No." She shook her head with a wistful smile. "There was one before him. His name was Brian. We were high school sweethearts."

"What happened?"

"I waited for him to graduate college, expecting we'd marry, but he wasn't ready to settle down. Brian was an idealist who wanted to join the Peace Corps. Kennedy was president. It was a very popular thing to do back then. He went to Africa without making me any promises. I suppose I could have gone with him, but I was a traditional girl. Like most young women in the early sixties, I'd expected to marry and make babies."

"Do you regret not going?"

"No, sweetheart." Grams shook her head. "I like my creature comforts too much and didn't have any grand ideas about changing the world. He did. Our relationship had run its course. At the time I was heartsick, but in the end, I realized we didn't suit. Later, I met your grandpa."

"Do you ever think about Brian?"

"On occasion I do, but Bill and I have been happily married for forty-nine years. Although he wasn't my first love, he'll certainly be my last. I don't think it's the same with you and Reid as it was with me and Brian, Haley."

"How can you say that? It's all wrong with Reid and me. *He's* all wrong." Haley dropped her bag on the floor and threw herself into her grandmother's arms.

"I disagree, sweetheart." Grams stroked her hair. "Maybe you have different beliefs about things, but seems to me that you and he are more alike than you think. You are obviously both strong-minded idealists. I think maybe you even want the same things, but just have a different way of going about it."

"I believe what I believe, Grams. I want to be with someone who respects my opinions, not someone who wants to change me. I'm not about to let myself become anyone else's shadow."

"A man like Reid is certainly the type who's continually going to challenge your way of thinking. It would take a strong woman to hold her own with that kind of man."

"But I don't *want* that type of relationship, Grams. We'd only end up fighting all the time." Maybe Grams was right, but Reid wouldn't just change her world, he'd *become* her world. If she let herself fall any further, she feared she'd lose it all. She'd lose *herself* in Reid Everett. Perhaps it was plain cowardice on her part, but she wasn't willing to risk everything she'd worked so hard for. She couldn't take that chance.

"Maybe so." Grams smiled. "But making up can be a heck of a lot of fun."

"Grams!" Haley protested.

"It's true! Make-up sex is the best kind. They've done surveys on *Oprah*." She paused. "Do you really think you only want someone who agrees with you all the time?"

"Well, no...but we have to at least have *some* common ground."

"Perhaps you and Reid truly aren't suited. Then again, maybe you just aren't ready for someone like him yet. Perhaps one day you will be."

"I know Reid's not the right one for me, Grams. Time won't make any difference," she insisted with forced conviction.

"Can I share one last pearl of grandmotherly wisdom?"

"Sure, Grams."

"Your grandfather and I want you to achieve your goals, Haley, but not at the expense of your long-term happiness. It's great that you have ambitions, but remember, that doctoral degree you covet won't keep you warm at night. A good man is a whole lot more satisfying than a thermal blanket and a vibrator."

"Grams! I can't believe you just said that!"

Her grandmother replied with a wink. "I may be old, sweetheart, but I'm not dead yet."

Chapter 13

Northern California

WITH DAMP PALMS AND A DRY THROAT, DR. HALEY Cooper stepped up to the podium. She always felt jittery prior to any public address, but tonight hundreds of people with very large bank accounts had turned out for the fund-raiser. She glanced nervously at Jeffrey sitting to her right, who nodded back at her with a reassuring smile. After five years of working together, he knew as well as she did that her passion would soon overcome her nervous qualms. She took a quick sip of water and then stepped up to the mic.

"Ladies, gentlemen, and esteemed colleagues," she began with a tentative smile. "We have gathered together this evening as guardians of one of the most unfairly maligned of all living creatures."

She signaled her assistant to begin the slide show.

"Once roaming North America from the Arctic tundra to Mexico, the gray wolf was ruthlessly and deliberately eradicated from the western United States. It has taken almost twenty years since their reintroduction to the Northern Rockies for wolves to recover. Their renewed presence has helped to restore ecological balance and even boosted the regional economies in several of these western states. But now, it seems our labor is about to be undone."

She paused and let her gaze work the tables, seeking out and acknowledging every nod.

"Although a dozen conservation groups joined forces in the fight, our recent legal challenges to the delisting of wolves have been overruled. Our injunction to block hunting was also denied. Since the federal government removed the gray wolf as an endangered species, open season on wolves has already begun. Idaho has not only extended their wolf-hunting season, but it is now even considering aerial hunting as a means of predator control. We don't need a crystal ball to know where all this will lead."

She gave the nod and the film clip began.

Haley watched the horrified expressions as the screen behind her flashed vivid images of the brutal and bloody aerial wolf hunt they'd captured on film five years earlier. The clip ended with snow stained red with blood, the grisly aftermath of the kill. She consoled herself that the wolves' deaths had not been in vain. The footage had gone viral on YouTube and the donations had flooded their offices.

"This inhumane practice must be stopped. Last year alone, dozens of collared wolves surrounding the national parks were senselessly slaughtered under the guise of *wolf management*, with no regard to the individuals wearing radio collars, animals crucial to our long-term studies of this fascinating species."

She continued, her throat thick with emotion. "Hunters in the west claim that the wolves are depleting the native elk populations. Ranchers maintain their livestock is at risk, but these claims have no basis in fact. Nevertheless, both of these groups have powerful lobbyists in Washington, whereas the animals have no voice…but ours.

"We are gathered this evening in support of the proposed Protect America's Wildlife Act, sponsored by our own Senator Feinstein. If passed, this legislation would effectively close the loopholes in the existing Airborne Hunting Act. It will protect America's wolves from all such barbaric practices. Unless we act quickly and decisively, we will soon face a second eradication of wolves."

Haley's gaze skirted once more over the tables. Many of the donors were already reaching for their checkbooks. "While this is certain to be a long and costly battle, with your generous and ongoing support, we will ultimately prevail. Thank you."

"You were fabulous tonight," Jeffrey gushed, handing Haley a glass of champagne. "I knew even when you were a student that you'd become a great asset. No one can charm the purses and checkbooks like Dr. Haley Cooper."

"Thank you," she said, adding with a sigh, "But I'm glad it's done. How much do you think we raised?"

He smiled over his drink. "By my estimate, at least five hundred grand."

Haley beamed. "That's twice what we'd hoped for. It's more than enough to fund all the radio collars for my mating pairs study."

Jeffrey's smile faded. "Sorry to burst your bubble, but that project's going to have to go on the back burner."

"Again?" He heart dropped with disappointment. "Why?"

"Because we need all the money for our attorneys and the media campaign."

"But we just raised half a mil," she protested. "Can't I at least have a small percentage of that to buy the collars?"

"Sorry." He shook his head. "Half a mil might sound like a lot, but it's only a drop in the bucket. We spent twice that in Idaho, Montana, Washington, Oregon, and Utah and still lost. We'll need to tap into all of our resources if we're going to prevent delisting in Wyoming."

"I see. But it seems to me that our chances are slim no matter how much we spend. The wolf population has more than recovered. You know it's only a matter of time before they allow hunting. Why not simply concentrate our efforts on protecting the packs in Yellowstone and Grand Teton? It's where most of our study subjects are anyway."

Jeffrey's lipped thinned. "That would be to admit defeat."

"But we're swimming against a riptide here, Jeffrey."

"The decisions can be reversed," he insisted. "We can't give up until we get new legislation passed."

"I don't agree, Jeffrey. I think we're just wasting money that could be put to a much better purpose." Although he'd been her mentor for the past six years, they didn't always see eye to eye. He was far too involved in politics for her liking, using his research to support lobbies and lawsuits, while she cared more about the animals themselves. "And while we're on the subject, I should tell you that I'm *thinking* very hard about accepting a job in Wyoming."

"What?" His gaze narrowed. "This is the first you've said about it. Why haven't you mentioned it before?"

"When have I had a chance? We've hardly seen each other in months." She often wished they had more time together, but field research and various projects often kept them apart.

"I promise to make it up to you," he said. "We'll go away together once my current project is done."

"You've said that before, but it never happens. Something always seems to come up." She paused. "Jeffrey, what's going on with us?"

"What do you mean?" he asked.

"It just feels like we're drifting apart."

She'd told herself for years that romance held little importance in the great scheme of things. They had the kind of relationship she'd always *thought* she wanted, one founded on friendship, mutual respect, and common goals, but lately it seemed much more like a business partnership than a romantic relationship. She wondered about his recent lack of interest in sex. Was he involved with someone else? Was that why they'd spent so little time together lately?

He shrugged. "We're both busy. Sometimes the greater good requires personal sacrifices, but I promise to take some time off once I'm finished with the Denali project."

"How is it coming?" she asked.

"Better now that I have a new assistant."

"You hired someone?" She struggled to digest that news. "You didn't even tell me you were considering a new assistant." She wondered who it was. It was strange he hadn't mentioned it before.

"It's no biggie, Haley." Jeffrey shrugged it off without elaboration.

"Are you coming over tonight?" she asked.

"I figured you'd be too tired," he answered. "I know *I* am. This kind of schmoozy thing always wipes me out." Odd. That wasn't like Jeffrey at all. He loved attention in any form.

"Oh. Okay. I understand." She struggled to mask her disappointment. She'd hoped to celebrate their success together. After nearly three months of celibacy, she was wound tight with sexual tension.

"So, what's this job you're considering?" he asked, oblivious to her thoughts.

"U.S. Fish and Wildlife is forming a task force to review and monitor wolf management in the northern Rockies. I got a call from a recruiter about it a few weeks ago."

"And you're actually considering it?" Jeffrey regarded her with incredulity. "Let me get this straight. You're going to leave your position with this organization and abandon a possible tenure track at the university?"

"Is there a reason I shouldn't?"

She held her breath, waiting but knowing he'd never express the words she needed to hear. Jeffrey supported and encouraged her work and appreciated her intellect and dedication, but it wasn't enough anymore.

"What about us?" he finally asked.

Her gaze sought his. "Is there really any *us*?" Although they had a tacit understanding about exclusivity, he'd made no move toward any kind of permanent commitment. And though she'd hinted several times about moving in together, he'd always hedged about that too.

His brows met in a scowl. "You know how I feel about marriage."

"But I want a family, Jeffrey."

"The world is already overpopulated," he argued.

"And many countries have taken measures to control it. One child, Jeffrey. That's all I want." In almost five years together she and Jeffrey had never had unprotected sex. Not once. He was obsessive about it. For the longest time she'd secretly hoped he'd come around about the idea of kids, but he still hadn't. She, on the other hand, had begun thinking about it. A lot.

"If you feel that strongly, why don't you just adopt a kid?"

"On my own?"

"Why not?" His nonchalance made her heart drop.

"Because I'd want my child to have a normal family—a mother *and* a father. We aren't going anywhere, Jeffrey. We want different things now." She wanted a family, but once more he balked at the very idea. It was past time to reevaluate her future.

"So you're really going to leave?"

"Yes." She exhaled slowly, almost in relief. Perhaps a new job in a new place really was the answer, and eventually a new relationship might follow. She'd held on too long. He didn't love her any more than she loved him. It was time to move on.

"I didn't think at first that I'd take the job," she said, "but I can't just sit by and watch from a distance while all we've worked for comes undone. And I'm tired of all the politics, Jeffrey. I want to do something for the greater good. You can wage your war in the courtrooms, but I'm taking mine back to the field."

Chapter 14

Whiskey Mountain, Wyoming backcountry

"GODDAMMIT, SLOW DOWN! I NEED TO CATCH MY WIND. The air's so thin up here I can hardly breathe."

Reid ground his teeth. *It would probably help if you dropped about eighty pounds.*

In their brochure, Everett's Extreme Expeditions cautioned potential clients about the need for physical conditioning prior to a backcountry trek, but some folks seemed to think money took care of everything. This one was worse than most.

Frank Barstow had expected not just a private guide, but a personal pack mule. *Reid.* He'd been carrying almost all the gear since they'd left their lakeside base camp. Apparently, Barstow didn't know the unspoken law among all outdoorsmen—you pack your own shit or you leave it behind.

They'd ridden the horses as far as they could, but that was about five miles back. The rest of the way was wild and rugged terrain, only accessible by foot. It was also all uphill, which made it the perfect habitat for the country's largest wild herd of bighorn sheep.

"I dropped almost ten grand on this hunting trip," Barstow continued to grouse. "We've been hiking this goddamned wilderness for the better part of a week, and I haven't seen a single elk to show for all that."

"You'll get your elk just like you got your bighorn sheep," Reid promised. "Or I'll refund half your money."

Jared would shit a brick if he heard *that* promise, but Reid was damned tired of rich assholes who treated hunting guides like lesser beings. He'd been home three months, but he was wrong to think he'd be able to slip right back into his old life. They all expected it though. He was resentful about playing babysitter to begin with, but it was only getting harder to keep his mouth shut and temper in check—especially with Barstow.

He was a big man with a ginger-colored beard who reminded Reid all too much of a certain Austin Powers' henchman with the same initials. He'd told Reid to call him FB, but Reid secretly thought of him as "Fat Bastard" ever since.

Reid dropped his pack and pulled out two water bottles, offering one to FB who waved it aside with a grunt, only to pull out a flask of Scotch instead. The guy drank like a fish. Reid hoped the man wouldn't have a coronary before the trip was over. He didn't know how the hell he'd get FB back down the mountain if he did.

"We've got about another half mile and then we'll make camp up on that ridge." Reid pointed up ahead. "There's a gorge down below where the elk come for water. We *might* catch some of them at dusk, but the best time is gonna be right before sunup."

That was the second problem. Fat Bastard liked to eat *and* sleep. While Reid was used to hitting the trail with a thermos of instant coffee and a wad of beef jerky in his pack, FB refused to budge before breakfast. Eggs— sunny-side up with no brown around the edges. That's right. He was camp cook now too. Went along with the private guide gig.

Two more days, he reminded himself, and then he'd take a few off. Maybe get away for some badly needed R & R. Tonya was slowly wearing him down to go away with her to Chico Hot Springs. He'd avoided giving her any answer for as long as he could. He was still trying to get his head straight.

He didn't love her. Didn't know if he ever could, but she was an old friend of the family, a decent companion, and keen to get back together. They had a lot in common, and he was damned tired of being alone. He was on the wrong side of thirty now and wanting to settle down. Hell, the way things were going, he'd probably be digging out her old engagement ring before year's end. That was a dangerous thought.

"You rested?" he prodded FB. "We don't have much daylight. Maybe another hour or two, and we still need to set up camp. If we move it along, we can try and spot some of those elk."

It took nearly an act of God to get FB moving before sunup, but by the time its rays were melting the shadows, they were in position overlooking the river below. Reid peered through his glasses into the tree line. Just as he'd hoped, several elk were emerging to drink.

"You're in luck, Barstow." He handed him the field glasses. "There's a six-point bull down there with your name on it."

"Where? I don't see it."

"There. About ten yards into the tree line. You'd best get that twenty-pound cannon of yours ready." Reid hoped to hell the guy knew how to fire the thing. "You sure you don't want to shoot mine?" He offered his .300 Winchester.

"I know what I'm doing," FB growled. "I bought this baby specifically for big game."

"Maybe so, but if you're not careful, the recoil from that fifty cal will take your head off."

At any closer range, the rifle would also destroy any chance of claiming the elk as a trophy, but they were at least four hundred yards out. FB fancied himself an expert marksman. He'd literally bought lock, stock, and barrel into the new cult of distance shooting. It was also why he'd forked over ten grand to hire a guide who was a former marine scout sniper. Reid's reputation was a mixed blessing.

FB handed Reid his field glasses, raised his rifle, and peered through the scope just as the bull emerged into the clearing followed by a small herd of cows.

"Don't take the shot until he's completely in the clear, nothing within 15 meters on either side of him," Reid instructed the hunter and then called off some adjustments. The elk raised its head and bugled, a sound that not only attracted elk cows, but gave every big game hunter an instant hard-on. "Got him sighted?" Reid asked.

FB grunted. The bull stood stock-still, in a broadside stance—a perfect kill shot.

"All right now. Take a deep breath, exhale slowly, and then fire," Reid advised.

"Holy shit! Look at that!" In the instant FB would have pulled the trigger, the bull spun around to face one of the biggest wolves Reid had ever seen. A second and third wolf emerged and slowly circled, flanking the bull who now had the river at its back and almost nowhere to run.

"Don't shoot," Reid said. "You've lost your chance."

"Fuck that! If I can't have my elk, I'll take the wolf."

"The hell you will," Reid growled. "Wolves are endangered in Wyoming."

"Then I'll pay the fucking fine. I'm taking down that wolf."

Should he disarm him? His job was not only to keep the client safe, but also to ensure no laws were broken during the hunt. But Reid hesitated too long. The rifle exploded and kicked back straight back into FB's face. He screamed and threw the gun down, blood streaming down his face.

Ignoring the hunter, Reid snatched up the field glasses, hoping the stupid son of a bitch had missed. The herd had bolted, but the first wolf was down, bleeding heavily and struggling to recover its feet. It was then Reid noticed the animal's radio collar. *Shit*.

The other two wolves were circling, teeth bared. *Double shit*.

They wouldn't miss a meal after all. They were ruthless killers that way, even to their own kind. In seconds they'd rip their injured pack mate to shreds. With no other choice but a mercy kill, Reid quickly chambered a round and took his shot.

~~~

Haley had been scanning the GPS reports all morning, correlating every collared wolf with its last tracked position on her digital map. She did this daily, notifying wildlife services whenever a wolf encroached on areas occupied by grazing livestock. It was a tedious task but necessary to protect both wolves and cattle. She also hoped her efforts would help to build a better rapport with the ranching community, not that she'd expected much progress on *that* front.

She paused with a frown when she came to number 442, the main breeding female she'd studied for her doctoral dissertation. She shoved the report aside to pull out the one from the day before that showed 442 deep in the Whiskey Mountains. Impossible! Although a wolf on the hunt could easily cover fifty miles in a day, there was no way in hell she'd traveled into the city of Jackson.

Haley's throat tightened. The positioning signal could mean only one thing—Cinderella was dead.

----~~~----

With only seventy-two hours to report the wolf incident, Reid drove into Jackson. He'd already filed the compulsory report to the Board of Outfitters in Cheyenne. Although an investigation would still follow, the board had assured Reid that the hunter would be charged, but there wouldn't be any upshot for Reid's mercy kill. He knew the board had gone easy on him due to his family's upstanding reputation, but he still had to turn in the collar to Wyoming Game and Fish.

"Ah, Reid! I'd heard you were back." Jim Banks, the regional chief of WGF, extended his hand with a smile. "I'm glad to see you home safe."

"You might not be so happy to see me once you know why I'm here," Reid replied.

"And why's that?"

Reid held up the radio collar. "An overzealous trophy hunter. I've already made my report to the Board of Outfitters."

"I see." Jim accepted the collar with a grimace. "Unfortunately, I'm not handling wolves anymore. We have a new federal liaison who's overseeing wolf management. C'mon. Let me introduce you to her."

Reid didn't relish meeting the new liaison with news of a dead wolf, but he figured the circumstances were best explained in person. There was no honest way around it. Jim continued with a few more trite remarks as he led Reid down a short hallway of offices.

They stopped at the last door where a tiny blonde sat behind a desk frowning over a stack of papers. Jim knocked. She looked up. Her gaze flickered from Jim to Reid and then stuck. Her eyes widened and her smile froze.

Holy shit. It couldn't be.

Reid's chest seized as his gaze honed in on a face he'd never forgotten. And one he'd never expected to see again. She was five years older now, wore her hair differently, and hid her pretty green eyes behind ugly glasses, but he'd recognize her anywhere.

"Reid." Jim's voice jarred him out of his shock. "I'd like to introduce Dr. Haley Cooper. Dr. Cooper, this is Reid Everett. His family runs one of the oldest backcountry hunting outfits in the region."

––––––––

Oh my God. It's him. I can't breathe.

Recognition simultaneously numbed her mind and struck her dumb. What were the chances of running into Reid Everett after all this time? She'd never even considered the possibility when she'd accepted the job.

Haley cleared her throat, but her voice still emerged as a barely audible croak. "Mr. Everett and I are already acquainted. We met several years ago in California."

Reid raised a brow. "So you haven't forgotten?"

"No," she said. "I haven't forgotten." Although she'd done her best to, his image had never faded in her mind. It was still there as crystal clear as it had been at their parting. But *this* man, the one who seemed to use up all the air in her office, was so changed that she might not have known him without the introduction.

His hair was longer and lighter, and his face was leaner, the angles sharper. There was a hardness to his mouth, and gone was the hint of humor from his blue eyes. He'd always dwarfed her, but now seemed so much bigger. But it wasn't just his appearance, there was something different in his whole demeanor, an edge that he'd never had before.

"What a coincidence," Jim remarked, oblivious to the tension that charged the air. "Since you know each other, perhaps Reid here would like to orient you to the region in my place? Dr. Cooper has yet to get the lay of the land," he explained to Reid, who still hadn't even blinked.

"There's really no need," she blurted. "I know the area quite well already. I spent two years in Yosemite and Grand Teton National Parks when I was working on my dissertation."

"Maybe you know the geography," Jim countered, "but you don't know the people. The ranchers and out-fitters here are a close-knit community. The Everetts know them all. I can't think of anyone better suited to be your guide." He chuckled. "No pun intended."

"I'd be pleased to show Dr. Cooper around," Reid replied in a soft, deep baritone that sent ripples over her skin.

"Another time, maybe," she replied tightly. "I have a lot to do. I'm really swamped."

"Then I'm sorry to add to your burden," Jim said.

"What do you mean?" Even as she asked, her gaze tracked to the radio collar in his hands. "Oh my God! What happened?"

"Reid here can fill you in. No doubt the two of you have a lot of catching up to do anyway. Guess I'll leave you to your business now. Good to see you again, Reid." Jim laid the collar on her desk, tipped his hat, and left.

Haley stared helplessly after him, struggling to maintain her equilibrium and silently cursing him for leaving her alone with Reid. First, she'd received the shock of seeing him again, and now had a dead study subject to deal with? And not just any subject. She picked up the collar, tracing the number with her fingers, shutting her eyes on a whisper. "Cinderella."

Reid's brows pulled together. "Come again?"

"This collar belongs...*belonged*...to 442 F. I was part of the team who captured and collared her as a pup. We called her Cinderella."

"Unusual name for a wolf," he remarked. "I could see maybe Red Riding Hood, but Cinderella?"

"She was an unusual specimen, an underling who rose to become the alpha female of one of the largest and most powerful wolf packs in the Tetons. Thousands of wolf-watchers loved her. *National Geographic* even made a documentary about her. She did so many things wolves *don't* do. I built my entire doctoral dissertation around her."

"I'm sorry for your loss," he said softly.

Haley stared at the GPS collar fighting back tears. "You couldn't possibly understand."

"Why would you say that?" Reid propped a hip on the edge of her desk. "Do you think I don't care about animals just because I hunt? You couldn't be more wrong, Dr. Cooper. I happen to love all animals and have a special regard for wolves and bears and big cats. But I also adhere to the belief that apex predators need to be kept in check for their own safety, as well as humans'."

"By killing them, Reid?" she snapped. He was so different. They both were. But some things hadn't changed. They were still opposite poles of the magnet.

"Sometimes. But only when the numbers require it. Hunting itself isn't evil. It's humane if done responsibly. In the end, I think you and I both want the same thing—for people and wildlife to coexist. We just go about it in different ways."

"This wolf was central to the project I'm working on," she continued tersely. "She's part of the reason I came here. I had hoped for several more years to study her." She looked up at Reid with a sick churning in her gut. "Wait a minute. What do *you* have to do with all this?"

"I'm the one who turned the collar in."

"You were there?"

"Yes. I was there."

She fired off the next question before even taking a breath. "What happened to her?"

He doffed his hat and raked a hand through his

hair with a heavy sigh. "She was shot during an elk expedition."

"Shot? But it's *illegal* to hunt wolves in Wyoming. In fact, it's a felony. The ESA is very specific about this. It prohibits harassing, harming, pursuing, hunting, shooting, wounding, killing, trapping, capturing, or collecting any listed species. I promise you, if this was a willful rather than accidental kill, *someone's* gonna pay."

Reid met her gaze levelly. "I'm well aware of all that. It's my job to make sure those kind of things don't happen."

"Then how the hell was she shot? What *exactly* happened on this elk hunt?"

Reid scrubbed his face, visibly agitated. "I'd like to say it was an accident, but it wasn't. I was hired as a private guide by someone who should never have been allowed a hunting license."

"Then why did you take the job?"

"Because he *paid me*. It's how I make my living. Lots of people come to Wyoming to hunt. It's impossible to screen every prospective client. I do my best to keep all my clients safe and to uphold the game laws, but this was beyond my control. By the time I realized he was going to shoot it was too late to stop him. Believe me, if I'd had any clue something like this was gonna happen, I would have refused the job."

"Really." She pursed her mouth in disbelief.

"Yeah. *Really*. I uphold the game laws, Dr. Cooper. I've already made my full report to the Board of Outfitters."

She pushed out of her chair to stand eye to eye with him. "This won't go unanswered."

"I can understand why you're upset, but please try to put it in perspective. She was a wild animal and shit like this sometimes happens. Hell, more wolves are killed by each other every year than by man."

"But this shouldn't have happened at all. I'm requesting a full inquiry."

"I told you the Board of Outfitters is already handling it," Reid assured her.

"I don't care. I'll still be doing my *own* investigation. I have questions, Reid, and until those are answered to my complete satisfaction, I'm recommending the suspension of your license."

"What? You're putting both my reputation and my livelihood on the line here! We were friends once, Haley. Hell, we were even lovers. Don't you think I deserve a little more courtesy?"

She clenched her teeth. "Our past has no bearing on this whatsoever. If this event goes unanswered, it'll be open season on all wolves in Wyoming. I'm not about to let that happen."

Her position required her to maintain neutrality, but he was clearly in the enemy camp. She could never allow him a pass due to their former relationship.

"I don't appreciate your insinuations, *Dr. Cooper*. No one is trying to hide anything. I told you I made a full report."

"Then you have nothing to fear from an inquiry. If there was no wrongdoing there's no cause for concern. The suspension will be lifted."

"How long? We have groups booked for the entire elk season."

"I guess your family will have to make due without

you for a few weeks. Just be thankful they don't shut the whole operation down."

"They or *you*?" He stood, towering a full foot over her with eyes as frosty as snow-covered peaks. He snatched up his hat and shoved it on his head, turning for the door with long, angry strides. Halfway there, he stopped, facing her one last time. "I guess that tour I promised you is off. I'll see you next at your damned *inquisition*."

———

Half an hour later, Reid threw a leg over the saddle that served as a barstool at the Million Dollar Cowboy.

"How'd it go?" Jared asked.

Reid ignored the question to order a double bourbon with a beer chaser.

"That bad, eh?" his brother smirked.

"You keep up with all the political bullshit. What the hell is this Rocky Mountain Wolf Management Task Force anyway?" Reid asked. "Why doesn't the WGF handle the wolves like they do all the other wildlife issues?"

"It's too controversial. You know as well as I do that the tree huggers are looking for any excuse to delay delisting those sonsofbitches."

"Maybe... Probably," Reid amended.

Jared continued, "This task force is *supposed to be* an independent review board, but I've been checking on their new appointee. Independent, my ass. Did you know Dr. Cooper worked for one of the very same groups that sued the state last year? They won. Now we've got a new plan to manage wolves, and they don't like this one either." He shook his head and took a swig of beer. "So how'd it go with Dr. Haley Wolf Lover anyway? I'm guessing by your expression she broke your balls."

"Yeah. You might say that." Reid downed his bourbon in one long, burning swallow. He set the glass down with a sigh. "She's going to have my license suspended while she investigates."

"Fuck that!" Jared protested.

"I don't see a hell of a lot we can do about it if she's the one calling the shots. Why didn't you give me a heads up about her anyway? Had I known it was her…" He could only hope she'd see reason once she got over her initial shock.

"Maybe you can make this whole wolf-kill business go away. You should take one for the team, Reid. Buy her a steak dinner and nail her." Twice-divorced, Jared was the man-whore of the family. He raised the long neck to his lips with a wink.

"She doesn't eat steak."

"A vegetarian? That figures. Then make it a fucking tofu burger. You're missing my point. You can make this easier on yourself by making it *hard* in her. Do her justice, and she'll forgive and forget quickly enough. A good dinner and a better fuck have always worked for me."

"Don't talk about her like that, Jared."

His brother's gaze narrowed. "Why so defensive?"

"I know her."

"How?"

"She's from San Jacinto, not far from Camp Pendleton."

"Did you *do* her?"

"That's none of your fucking business, Jared, and not even remotely related to this conversation."

"Guess I got my answer." Jared smirked. "But you're wrong, little brother. It's entirely relevant because it puts you in a unique position to find out what she's *really* doing here."

"This is bullshit. If you want to know something, just ask her. I'm not going to act as your spy."

Jared's mouth compressed. "Maybe you don't realize what's really on the line here. The ranchers. The hunting outfits. Our business. *Your* livelihood. We're all hurting, and it isn't going to get any better until we can control the vermin that caused this problem."

To Jared, the only good wolf was a dead one.

"So, what's the real deal with you and her anyway? I admit she isn't bad on the eyes, but once she opens her mouth…" He shuddered.

"There's not much to tell. We met at a dance club before my third deployment. We saw each other for a little while, but that was a long time ago." He upended his bottle.

"Are you going to see her again?"

"Hell if I know. We didn't exactly reunite on the most auspicious terms."

When he'd seen her, at first he'd hoped… He shook his head. Hell, he didn't even know what he'd hoped, but the Cinderella incident had set them back not just three steps, but three miles.

"So what's going on between you and Tonya these days?" Jared suddenly asked.

"I dunno," Reid answered noncommittally. He wondered what was behind all his brother's questions. He and Jared had never been close and were certainly not confidants. At times like this, Reid missed Garcia. Not that Raf wouldn't have jerked his chain exactly the same way, but somehow it was easier to take this kinda shit from his marine buddy than from his older brother. "Why so interested?" he asked Jared. "You lookin' to make Tonya ex-wife number three?"

Jared's gaze darkened. "Mebbe."

Holy shit. Reid tipped his hat back and stared at his brother as if seeing him for the first time. "You and Tonya?" He didn't know what exactly clued him in, but suddenly it all made sense. "When, Jared? Answer me that. Are you the reason she called it off with me? I deserve to know."

"I s'pose you do. It was New Year's Eve. You were gone… Tonya was depressed and lonely… I was on the rebound after the split with Rita…"

"You low-crawling bastard!"

"Look, Reid. It was *after* she broke it off with you. We were both drunk or it never would have happened. Then again, you left without putting a ring on her finger."

Reid gave an incredulous laugh. "Are you trying to say it's *my* fault? Shit. I can't fucking believe this."

"I ain't saying nothing of the kind," Jared replied. "But it's all water under the bridge now, and she regrets it. Not because it wasn't good," he added, too damn quickly. "But it's never happened between us since."

"But you want her?"

"Mebbe," Jared repeated. "I've been waiting to see if you'd pick it back up with her. I'd step aside if you still wanted her, but it seems to me you're in no big hurry to rush her down the aisle."

Reid wanted to tear his brother's head off, but more for the act of betrayal than any true feeling of jealousy. He took a breath and then another swig of beer, willing away his impulse to pound Jared into dust. Somehow he'd always known there was someone else. She hadn't exactly lied, but she hadn't told him the whole truth either. Even if it really was *after* she broke with him, and she really was sorry, he'd never be able trust her again.

So much for digging out that engagement ring. Maybe he should go pawn it instead. Hell, if the investigation didn't move in his favor, he might need the money for legal fees.

Chapter 15

Wyoming Outfitters Convention

THE ANNUAL OUTFITTERS CONVENTION WAS AN OLD tradition that broke up the long winter. Part business and part social, the event brought out everyone involved in hunting and dude ranching. Reid had always looked forward to it, but so much had changed in his eight-year absence. He was surprised to learn how many outfits had shut their doors. In a state so dependent on tourism, the downward economy had hit everyone hard, but it seemed the outfitters had taken the brunt of the blow.

He stared unseeingly as the state wildlife biologist droned on about moose parasites. He was restless, and his mind was wandering. Another biologist was scheduled to speak on the new mule deer initiative. Both would present their charts and graphs depicting the declining populations and hypothesize about all the probable causes—none of which included wolves.

They all tried to skirt around the whole predator controversy. It was too hot to touch without getting burned. How long would the tension continue to build before something or someone lit the fuse? He'd had enough of this kind of bullshit in the Marines—problems and solutions as plain as day to the grunts in the field but seemingly invisible or maybe just ignored by the bureaucrats.

He didn't know how much longer he could sit there.

He was antsy as hell. His palms were sweating, and the walls starting to close in. Ready to crawl out of his skin, Reid mumbled an excuse to his father and brother, grabbed his hat and coat, and made a swift exit.

Striding out of the ballroom, he made for the first exterior door leading out to a terrace. Reid paced the length of it several times before stopping to suck in a lungful of air so cold that it burned. A shiver erupting over him brought him back to earth and spurred him to drag his jacket over his arms and shoulders, but he didn't zip it. He loved the cold after having spent so much time in the blistering heat of the desert. He tried not to think about those years too much, but they were never completely out of mind. He didn't know how long he'd stood there with his gaze fixed sightlessly on the mountains, lost in his thoughts.

He turned at the creak of the terrace doors opening behind him. "Reid?"

He was stunned to see *her*.

She took a few tentative steps towards him. "I thought that was you out here."

"Dr. Cooper." He tipped his hat. "You're about the last person I expected to see here."

"Haley, please," she said. "I'm here because Jim asked me to do a presentation on wolf recovery. He thought it would serve as a good introduction for me."

"Good luck with that," he remarked dryly. He'd perused the program earlier but hadn't paid attention to the various presenters' names. He probably would have left had he known she was here.

"I was hoping you'd be here," she said.

"Oh yeah? And why's that?"

"You never gave me a chance to talk to you after the hearing last week."

He responded with a derisive laugh. "I didn't think there was a whole lot left to say after you laid your laundry list of crimes at my feet."

"You *lied* to me, Reid. The necropsy and forensics reports confirmed the cause of death as a thirty caliber round through the heart. Your client carried a fifty caliber BMG. *You* own a .300 Winchester. You told me she was killed by a hunter, but *you're* the one who shot my wolf!"

"Hold it right there. I've *never* lied to you. I told you it *happened* on an elk hunt. All the details were in the report I made to the Board of Outfitters. The hunter took the first shot and only wounded it, so I had to finish the job. I never denied that, but it was a mercy killing. She was surrounded by two of her pack mates who were ready to rip her to shreds. If you'd taken the trouble to read the report *first*, you could have saved yourself a lot of trouble. Instead, you chose to assume the worst of me."

She ran her tongue nervously over her lips. "I didn't read it first because I didn't want to be biased. I needed to examine the facts for myself. It's my job, Reid. I have to be neutral."

"You didn't have to suspend my license," he countered. "What happened to innocent until proven guilty?"

"Perhaps I was a bit overzealous," she said. "I'm sorry for making it more difficult than it had to be. My only excuse is that I'm feeling overwhelmed and defensive. I didn't expect it to be like this."

"Like what?"

"So hostile."

"Hate to say it, but it'll probably get a whole lot worse before it gets any better."

"That's why I came to the convention. Jim said my job would be a lot easier if I could gain the outfitters' cooperation, but I don't know how to go about that. I'm worried that I've already burned my bridges."

Reid considered her for a long moment. She seemed sincerely contrite and looked so small and alone. He was exactly the connection she needed to mend fences with the hunters and ranchers—especially after what had happened. He reminded himself he'd already been burned by her once, but he still couldn't find it in himself to walk away. "I offered to show you around a few weeks ago. The offer stands."

Her eyes grew wide. "Really? I—I don't know what to say."

"Say yes to dinner," he blurted without thinking.

"I'm not very hungry," she replied.

"Well, I suspect that's likely to change, given that it's barely lunchtime yet."

"Oh yeah. I guess you're right."

"Meet you in the bar at six?" he suggested.

"Six," she repeated dumbly. "All right. Please excuse me. I have notes to review." She spun toward the door as if making an escape.

He watched her departure, willing his pulse to slow down. He'd rattled her good, but damned if she hadn't done the same to him. He'd understood her anger about the wolf. He'd seen the pain in her eyes when she'd spoken about her. The wolves were like family to her, or maybe a substitute for the family she'd always craved.

At one time he'd wanted to be the man to give her what she needed, but she hadn't been ready. A lot of things had changed since then.

He could have just ignored her and walked away. Probably should have. By her reaction, she might have been happier had he done so, but he wasn't about to let Haley Cooper off the hook so easily. *Not this time.*

Dinner? Alone with him? After what she'd done? Why had he asked her? His invitation had thrown her completely off balance. She'd accepted, but what the hell was she going to do now? What was going on in his head? She hadn't a clue.

She checked the time. It was almost noon. She was supposed to meet her fellow biologists for lunch, but here she was holed up in her room, pacing the floor. She'd come to Wyoming for a fresh start, but Reid's appearance complicated everything. He'd always challenged her thinking, and once more he had her feeling unsure of herself. *Get it together, Haley. You've dealt with the unexpected before.* And deal with it she would, just not without preparation.

Snatching her phone out of her purse, she sent a quick text to beg off from lunch, using a headache as a viable, albeit not very creative, excuse.

After that, she kicked off her four-inch heels and massaged her aching feet. Although she loved heels for the height advantage they gave her, she mostly lived in jeans and hiking boots. She almost never dressed up, except for fund-raisers and speaking engagements. She shed her business suit, one of only three she owned. She also owned the same number of little black dresses that she reserved for the aforementioned occasions…and *maybe* dinners with ex-flames.

She drew a hot bath with the intention of reviewing her lecture notes while soaking in the tub. There was nothing better than a hot bath to relax the mind and body. Well, *almost* nothing, but the best thing hadn't been on her menu in months. She wondered if she hadn't already gone so long without sex if she would have been as susceptible to Reid. If she was going to be running into him regularly, maybe it was time to invest in something with batteries?

Her phone rang just as she shut off the tap. Her gaze darted longingly from the steamy tub back to the phone where caller ID showed Jeffrey's face. She hadn't heard from him in weeks. She chewed her lip and then snatched it up. "Hi, Jeffrey."

"Hi yourself. Haven't heard from you. How are you settling in?" he asked.

"Not so great, I'm afraid. I've only been here a few weeks and have already had a nasty confrontation with one of the outfitters over a wolf kill." She'd never told Jeffrey about Reid. There was little point in bringing up their past relationship.

"What kind of confrontation?" An edge of worry had crept into his voice.

"I had the guide's license temporarily suspended while I initiated an investigation, but he wasn't completely at fault. The situation hasn't endeared me to the outfitters, but at least he and I seem to have arrived at a truce." She hoped so anyway. "On top of that, I'm at the Outfitters Convention now to speak about wolf recovery."

"You're kidding, right? You're surrounded by a

bunch of redneck hunters and ranchers with guns? You shouldn't take them on alone."

She gave a dry laugh. "You're overreacting. This is the perfect opportunity to present our side."

"I don't think so," he argued. "It could get really ugly before all is said and done, especially once they realize you're in a position of influence."

She thought of Reid. He'd already connected those dots. "You fret too much, Jeffrey. I appreciate your call, but I have to get ready now. The gun-toting rednecks are waiting to string me up."

"Ha. Ha. You shouldn't take my warning so lightly. This issue is a social and political quagmire, and you're about to march right into the middle of it."

"I can take care of myself," she assured.

"I hope you don't discover differently. Call me if you need anything. I can be on the first plane."

"Thanks. I appreciate your offer of moral support, but there's really no need for concern."

"Of course I'm concerned," he said. "I still care about you, you know."

"I know. But not enough," she said sadly. "Good-bye, Jeffrey."

"Bye."

Haley hung up, undressed, and sank into the now-tepid tub. But instead of reviewing her notes, she tossed them aside to mull over the awkward situation she found herself in. Although she still felt a bit melancholy about ending the relationship with Jeffrey, she couldn't regret leaving California. Coming to Wyoming had renewed her sense of purpose, but seeing Reid again filled her with so many contradicting emotions.

So much had changed over the years, but the attraction between them remained. It simmered beneath the surface even during their moments of hostility. Now Reid had offered an olive branch. She still didn't know why. Maybe she really was about to be sucked into a quagmire—just not the kind Jeffrey meant.

—∿∿—

Hours later, Haley scanned the blank faces of the few people who still occupied the room. It had been filled to capacity only minutes ago for the panel on elk management, but following her introduction, the occupants had begun slinking out, much like rats from a sinking ship. Not a good omen. "Good afternoon," she said with a nervous smile.

No one smiled back. Her stomach knotted tighter.

She cleared her throat and began again. "It's my pleasure to be here today as the new liaison from the Rocky Mountain Wolf Management Task Force. We are a team of conservation biologists and wolf specialists contracted by the U.S. Fish and Wildlife Services to review and monitor the wolf management strategies in the Rocky Mountain region." She drew another breath to recite the lecture she knew by heart. "The recovery of the gray wolf after near extinction is a true American success story—"

"If they're recovered, why the hell are they still listed as endangered in Wyoming?" a voice called out.

Haley glanced up in surprise. "Please, if you will bear with me, I think my presentation will answer most of your questions. If any remain at the end, I'll be happy to stay for an open Q and A." She glanced down at her

notes in an effort to recompose. "Since the reintroduction of the gray wolf in the mid-nineties—"

"Reintroduction my ass," someone else mumbled.

"Excuse me?" Her hands had begun to tremble.

"It wasn't a *re*introduction. The Feds imported a
whole new subspecies that are half again the size of the
plains wolf that used to be here. My granddaddy has
picture proof from the last big wolf hunt in the '20s.
They had good reason for getting rid of the ones we had,
and they weren't near the size of those sons of bitches
that you people brought down from Canada."

"On the contrary, we've been conducting ongoing
genetic studies that prove—"

"I don't care about your science. The *fact* is there
wasn't ever any plains wolf that could take down an elk
all by its lonesome. Now there're whole packs of them
that *you people* are allowing to wipe out the elk and
moose herds."

"According to our records, wolf depredations
account for only—"

"'Sides that," the old man continued, "most of the
time they only eat half of what they kill before moving
on to fresh game. Wolves are killers. It's what they do.
And they have no natural predators to control them.
Now, *we* have to suffer for it. If you don't believe me,
you need to go talk to my buddy who runs a sheep outfit
outside of Victor, Idaho. He'll set you straight real
quick, little lady. Only a few months ago two wolves
terrorized the whole herd. He lost over a hundred lambs
and fifty-seven ewes at a cost of twenty grand." The old
man shook his head and stood up. "I ain't listening to
any more of this wolf preservation bullshit."

The younger man beside him spoke. "I've got a question that's on all of our minds. What's the *real* purpose of this so-called task force?"

Haley licked her lips. "I thought I already explained that. Our purpose is to review, monitor, and provide timely updates on all wolf management activities—"

"Updates to whom? The Fed or those fanatical activists that are suing us?" He eyed her with open hostility. "The same people *you* worked for."

Haley's chest constricted. She glanced frantically around the room that was now abuzz. They did somewhat resemble the lynch gang she'd joked about. Maybe Jeffrey hadn't exaggerated so much after all.

"I believe Dr. Cooper stated she'd take questions at the *end* of her talk."

She hadn't noticed Reid's entrance until he laid a hand on her antagonist's shoulder. They stared each other down for a protracted moment. To her relief, her adversary backed down, taking his seat again with a sullen look. Reid took a place beside him and nodded to Haley to continue her lecture. The next twenty minutes passed in a blur as she mindlessly recited from her notes, her gaze remaining focused on Reid's passively reassuring face.

"In closing, thanks to the cooperative efforts of federal, state, and tribal agencies, as well as conservation groups and ecologically-minded private citizens, we have succeeded in restoring this magnificent species to most of the Northern Rockies. We now look to you, the ranchers, sportsmen, and outfitters of Wyoming, to help us build upon this success."

She paused, surveying the room, but rather than the

smiles, nods, and applause she was accustomed to, she was met with dead silence and cold, steely stares. Her smile wavered. She cleared her throat again. "Now then, does anyone have any questions?"

Arms across his chest, her former detractor maintained his icy glower. His light blue eyes reminded her all too much of Reid's. Did all Wyoming men have eyes that color?

After a moment of strained silence, Reid raised a hand. "I do. I think everyone in this room wants to know the same thing. We've already presented a wolf management plan to the Feds. What more will it take for them to delist?"

Haley replied, "While I can't answer for the federal government's final decision, the task force will review the data and look for assurances that breeding pairs and collared subjects will continue to be protected. We feel that further monitoring is needed since so many of our study subjects periodically migrate out of their protected habitats and into Wyoming."

"If that's so, what's to keep you from slapping collars on every wolf?" her first heckler asked.

"Money and manpower," she answered bluntly. "I wish we *could* monitor every wolf. We'd then be able to prove that your concerns about livestock depredation are largely unfounded, but it's just not feasible."

"And what about the declining moose and elk?" he pressed. "What's your answer to that? Our herds are a fraction of what they were ten years back."

"There are many factors for the decline of ungulates outside of predators. Namely changes in migration patterns and habitat due to expanding human interference.

I'm sorry I can't elaborate more," Haley hedged, "but I believe my colleagues who spoke earlier can better respond about the herd decline. Any *other* questions?"

Another glower from Reid silenced her two antagonists.

Haley exhaled in relief. Still shaken, she shuffled her notes while waiting for the room to disperse. When she looked up again, it was empty of everyone but Reid.

Stepping down from the podium, she laid a hand on his sleeve. "Thank you for coming to my rescue. I had no idea this would become so confrontational."

His gaze met hers. "Don't mistake my actions, Haley. What I did doesn't mean I agree with you. I'm not on your side on this issue. I just don't adhere to bullying."

"Then I appreciate your intervention all the more."

"I invited you for dinner, but perhaps you'd like to get a drink?"

"Yes," she replied shakily. "I could definitely use a drink, but could we please go somewhere beside the hotel bar? Someplace quieter maybe?"

"That leaves out the Million Dollar Cowboy," he replied. "I'm assuming all steak houses are also out, right? You still a vegetarian or have you gone full-out vegan?"

She looked abashed. "No. I'm not a vegan. I tried it for a time but I caved on dairy," she blurted with a guilty look. "And shoes."

"Shoes?" He returned a quizzical look. "'Fraid I don't follow you there."

"True veganism is a lifestyle, Reid. Vegans shun not just animals as food but animal products. I had a very hard time finding decent shoes that weren't leather. I also had a hard time giving up wool, especially while in Alaska."

He shook his head with a tsking sound. "So Dr. Haley Cooper chose personal comfort over ethics?"

"Yes," she confessed with a look that made him chuckle. "The whole truth is comfort coupled with vanity. I love high heels. When you are barely over five feet tall, you need all the extra inches you can get. But I suppose you wouldn't understand that, not being challenged for inches."

He cocked a brow.

Her face flamed. "That didn't come out right. At. All."

"Yes. I'm thankful for all my *inches*." His lips curved in a slow smile that made her insides quiver. "They help get me into those really hard-to-reach places."

She shut her eyes on a distant memory of all those thick, hard inches moving inside her. Her thighs tightened against the sudden surge of desire.

"What's the story on dairy?" Reid's question jerked her mind from the gutter.

"I made a sincere effort to fall in love with soy and tofu, but there's no comparison with real ice cream…or cheese. Not even close. One night, when I was feeling particularly blue, I was seduced back to the dairy side by a four-cheese pizza and a pint of Moose Tracks. I fell off the wagon and never got back on. There you have it. Pathetic, isn't it? I'm the Benedict Arnold of vegans."

"So pizza was your Achilles' heel?" His laugh was low and rumbly. She loved the sound. Jeffrey rarely laughed, but when he did it was nasally and grating.

"Can't blame you there," he continued. "I love pizza,

second only to a good steak. Those were two of the things I missed most in the sand pits."

"What else did you miss?" she asked.

His grin disappeared. "Ever heard of General Order Number One?"

"No. What is it?"

"The prohibition of booze and all sexual contact in a combat zone. I did seven deployments in eight years, all in combat zones. Each averaging seven months. Some longer. Fifty months of total abstinence. Four-point-one-six *years*, if you do the math."

"Oh," she said. His gaze was too intense. She had to look away. "I guess you must have been real eager to make up for all that lost time."

He shook his head slowly. "Time, once lost, can *never* be recouped."

Was there a deeper message in that? What were they doing now? He'd begun to thaw. In some ways it felt the same between them as before, as if the years had never passed, but in other ways, it was as if they were perfect strangers.

"C'mon." He pressed a hand to her back. "Let's go. I know just the place."

Reid drove her to a small Italian restaurant, hoping to get in without a reservation, but the dining room was full. "Do you serve in the bar?" he asked the maître d'.

"Yes. We offer the full menu."

"Will that suit you?" he asked Haley.

"Yes. I'm easy," she replied and then colored. "To *please*, I mean."

Another Freudian slip? She was edgy as hell, and the tension between them was only growing. She didn't hide it well. He was happy to see her squirming in her panties and feeling pretty damned smug to know she was thinking the same thoughts he was.

He'd tried to ignore it, to suppress his lingering lust, but he couldn't deny the semi he'd been sporting almost from the moment he'd seen her. They followed the maître d' into the bar where he chose a quiet corner table. A waitress appeared almost immediately to take their drink order.

"Jim Beam Black, straight up." He looked to Haley. "A *mojito*? Is that still your poison?"

"Yes," Haley said. "I'm surprised you remember."

"I never forget details." He shrugged. "Marine training." It was true, just not the whole truth. He remembered *her*. Had memorized every detail over those cumulative four-point-one-six years. He'd wanted her back then, and still wanted her now. He didn't know why, but he couldn't help himself.

The waitress left menus behind while she went to fill the drink order.

"You've changed. The glasses. The hair," he remarked. It was still the same pale blonde, but shorter, barely brushing her shoulders.

"I'm not twenty anymore," she said. "I needed a more sophisticated, less coed look. When you're as short as I am, it's hard to be taken seriously to begin with, so I cut my hair and started wearing glasses again." She slid them off her face and set them on the table. "I really only need them for reading."

Her eyes were the deep sea green he so vividly

recalled. They softened as her gaze met his. She seemed less certain of herself now. More vulnerable. Yeah, she felt it brewing too. It was only a matter of time, but if it happened again, it would have to be on his terms.

"Reid, I wanted to ask you something. Who were those two men this afternoon?"

"The ones who harassed you?" He'd hoped this wouldn't come up, but supposed it was inevitable.

"Yeah. Can you tell me anything about them?"

"The older one is a founding member of the Outfitters Association, and the younger is his son, the chairman of the Wolf Coalition."

"The group countersuing the Wolf Recovery Alliance? No wonder they were so hostile," she remarked dryly. "What are their names? I'd like to know precisely who I'm dealing with."

He heaved a sigh. "Boyd and Jared Everett."

"*Everett*."

"Yup. My father and my brother."

"So *that's* why they backed off when you intervened."

"Yes, but it was only a reprieve. They're going to win this time, Haley. All you activists can continue to fight in the courts, but you're eventually going to lose in Wyoming. It's only a matter of time. You'll never sway public opinion to your side here. Trust me on this, there's nothing you can do to stop the delisting."

"But we can certainly delay it. Our lawyers are already seeking another injunction." Haley jutted her jaw. "You aren't doing enough to protect the wolves."

"You've got to at least *try* to understand where the people here are coming from. We're traditionalists who depend too much on our lands and herds to make our living. We can't protect *your* wolves at the cost of feeding *our* families."

"You all want to cast all the blame for the herd decline on the wolves when the facts are—"

"Facts?" he repeated. "Let's just stick to bare facts, shall we? How many wolves are there in Wyoming?"

"It's hard to estimate. They move around."

"Then give me your best guess."

"Our last report stated 320 known wolves in Wyoming."

"Wasn't the recovery goal a hundred?"

"That's the *minimum* number for recovery," she insisted.

"Yet you're telling me we have over three times that number."

"But if you start killing them—"

He raised a hand. "Hold your rebuttal until you hear me out, Haley. Still sticking to *facts*, what is their primary food source?"

"Ungulates. Mostly deer, elk, occasionally moose calves."

"How many kills does a wolf need to make in a year to survive?"

She chewed her lip. "About twenty, I guess. Maybe twenty-five."

"So a wolf population of one hundred would kill about two thousand, maybe twenty-five hundred elk a year?"

"I suppose so."

"But we have over three hundred wolves killing twenty to twenty-five elk apiece. That's close to *eight thousand* elk in a single year, Haley. I'm no math genius, but it seems to me that accounts for a big chunk of the decline."

"But there are other predators and other factors than wolves," she argued.

"I don't dispute that, but those other factors only contribute further to the decreasing elk numbers, and we haven't even touched on livestock yet. You see why people are hurting? Why they're hostile? They're watching everything they've worked for all their lives go down the tubes just to satisfy the conservationists who want to watch wolf pups romp at the national parks. Problem is, the wolves don't stay in the parks."

"You're oversimplifying everything," she insisted. "The issue is much more complicated than that."

"Is it? I don't think so. Why are you really here?" he asked.

She shrugged. "It was a job."

"You already had one, didn't you? With one of those conservation groups?"

"I was an assistant professor of wildlife conservation studies at the university, and yes, I also helped fund-raise for a conservation group."

"So why are you *here*?" he repeated.

"Truth?" she asked.

"Yeah." He sat back. "Truth."

She sighed. "I was getting tired of all the politics and wanted to get back to fieldwork. All the money I've helped raise seems to be going into lawyers' pockets instead of toward what really matters. I thought this job would allow me to get back to what I love."

"But it's also landed you right smack in the middle of a minefield."

She met his eyes with a smile. "Then it's a good thing there was a marine on hand to rescue me. Why did you do it, Reid?"

"Told you. The odds were stacked against you."

"I can hold my own," she argued.

"You didn't stand a chance, sweetheart. They would have eaten you alive. When I intervened, they were barely getting warmed up."

The waitress delivered their drinks. "Ready to order?"

"I'm sorry," Haley answered. "We haven't had a chance to look at the menu yet."

"No problem. Take your time. I'll check back with you in a few."

His gaze never leaving Haley's, Reid took a long swallow, relishing the smooth bourbon burn. He wondered again why he had intervened. He'd felt compelled to protect her, and he didn't understand why. Or why he'd asked her to dinner when his instinct of self-preservation told him to steer clear of her.

She stared down into her glass, idly stirring her drink. "I don't want to talk about wolves anymore."

"All right by me," he said. "I'm game for any topic that doesn't include politics, religion, or *wolves*."

"You've changed, Reid."

"Yeah." He snorted and took another swig. "I've changed all right."

"How long have you been home?"

"Only a few months."

"Are you adapting all right? I mean, it's got to be hard, given how long you were over there."

"It's been an adjustment," he answered tersely.

"What are your plans?"

hands were trembling as she fished inside her purse. "Here. Number two nineteen." She handed him her card. "I'll just tell them I left mine in the room."

His hand came over hers, warm and firm as if meant to reassure, but the contact was like an electric jolt. "You okay?" He didn't make a move beyond touching her hand.

She looked up into his eyes with a hard swallow. "No," she murmured. "I'm not. But I *will* be." Although she quivered with trepidation, it wasn't enough to stop the train.

He gave a nod and released her hand, then unbuckled and came around to open her door. "You'd best go in alone. It's a small community. People talk."

Her legs felt like jelly as she walked to the front desk for a replacement key. She'd never been so aware of her body before. Her anticipation ratcheted up another notch with every step as she approached her room. Would he be there already or would he wait a while? She hadn't thought to ask.

She held her breath as she slid the key into the slot and opened the door, releasing a long hiss of relief when he found the room empty. She closed the door and leaned against it. She wanted this, didn't she?

Yes. She did.

She ached with physical need. She'd kept it caged far too long and was almost ready to climb out of her skin to want. But it scared the hell out of her. She didn't want him. She *needed* him.

But why was it only Reid who'd ever made her feel that way? Jeffrey had felt safe and comfortable, like a favorite pair of jeans. She'd never experience the same

"Don't have any. My life pretty much sucks right now, since I don't know what the hell I want to do with it. For now I'll just keep doing what I've always done." He gave her a narrow look. "And *try* to stay out of the politics."

"So you guide hunters?" she asked.

"It's a bit more than that. Outfitting is playing baby-sitter, game warden, and pack mule to people who *think* they want a wilderness adventure. Most of them are pretty damn clueless, hence the babysitting part. I keep them from getting lost or shooting themselves. Now that game's scarcer, we're having to trek a whole lot deeper into the backcountry, so Jared's put me in charge of Everett's *Extreme* Expeditions."

"Sounds right up your alley," she laughed.

"Yeah." He gave a dry laugh. "But the 'extreme' living is getting old too. I fantasize about getting away from it all. Just going someplace I can kick back without having to pack a mule, a tent, or a weapon."

"Like some desert island?"

"Hell no." He grimaced. "No islands. No place with sand. I've had as much of that shit as I can take."

"So where would you go?"

"Dunno. Maybe when I figure it out, I'll just go."

"Just disappear?"

"Mebbe."

She toyed with her straw again. Slanting a look through her lashes, she asked, "Are you involved with anyone, Reid?"

"No. If I was, I wouldn't be here with you."

"But it's only dinner."

"Is it?" He glanced down at her naked left hand. "What happened with your professor?"

"Work got in the way."

"He wasn't right for you. He wasn't what you need."

She gave a derisive snort. "And you think you're some kind of expert on what I *need*?"

"Yeah, when you look at me like that."

She wet her lips. "Like what?"

"Like you want me to fuck you senseless."

Her jaw dropped and her hands hit the table. "You arrogant, presumptuous son of a—"

He'd offended her with his bluntness, but he didn't care. He pushed back in his chair and eyed her levelly. It was time to cut through the bullshit. "I'm too old for games, Haley."

Her green eyes widened. "You think I'm playing *games*?"

"Don't be coy with me. I don't have the patience or temperament for it anymore. Time has become a priceless commodity to me. I've already wasted too damned much of it. If you want me, just say it."

Her mouth closed. Her gaze dropped to her hands. She looked nervous as hell. For a moment he thought she'd bolt, but she didn't.

He waited. And watched.

At last she looked up, her gaze searching his. "All right," she whispered. "I'll say it. I want you."

Chapter 16

IT HAD REQUIRED ALL HER NERVE TO VOICE IT, BUT the words were out and not to be taken back.

Reid's pupils flared, but he said nothing. Just reached for his wallet, threw a wad of bills on the table, and grabbed her by the arm.

Her body thrummed with anticipation as he guided her to his truck. She was breathless and slightly giddy, but had hardly even touched her mojito. Just the thought of being with him again did this to her.

He still didn't speak until a few minutes later, when he pulled into a shopping mart with a twenty-four-hour pharmacy. "Just need to make one quick stop."

Her gaze fixed on his ass, so perfectly defined snug denim, as he walked into the drugstore. She w to feel it in her hands while he pumped into h chided herself for being so shallow, but Reid ha brought out her baser, animalistic side.

She waited impatiently, her pulse spee walked out the door toward the truck. He c fast enough for her. He laid a small plas seat and then started the truck. Five mir were in the lodge parking lot.

"Got an extra room key?" he aske tense. She could see it in the hard li the stiffness of his movements.

"No. I've only got one, but I

passion with Jeffrey that she'd known with Reid. He'd never remotely compared, though she'd tried very hard not to. Compare, that is.

The two men were *nothing* alike, either philosophically or physically. If they were trees, Jeffrey would be a birch and Reid would be an oak, an analogy that suited their anatomical differences equally well, she thought dryly. Although she'd tried to convince herself for the longest time that she loved Jeffrey, she knew better now. If she had, she would have long forgotten Reid. But she hadn't. Would it be the same between them as it was before?

You're thinking too much. Just relax and go with it. You're a grown woman and have every right to enjoy yourself with a man. With Reid.

Should she undress? She hated to appear too eager. Then again, who was she kidding? Not Reid. He'd seen right through her, had read her every lurid thought in the bar.

With her heart racing, she kicked off her shoes but hesitated with her hands on the zipper of her skirt. Maybe he'd want to undress her? Then again, he'd probably be more than happy to get straight to the main event. *Four-point-one-six years*.

He'd done the math.

She nervously shed her skirt and blouse, but left her bra and panties on. She wished she'd worn something racier than sensible white cotton with just a bit of lace trim, but the plain packaging would have to do.

The door clicked. She inhaled a tiny gasp.

"You should use the dead bolt."

"I was expecting *you*," she said.

"I was afraid you might change your mind."

"No, Reid. I haven't changed my mind. No games, right?"

His hot gaze raked slowly up and down her body. He doffed his hat and tossed it on the chair. "You're a sight for sore eyes, Haley Cooper." His voice was low and husky, inciting tiny ripples deep inside her sex. He was in tight control, but his desire was palpable, like some powerful force that was about to unleash. He extended his hand.

She approached with an intentional slow and seductive sway of her hips, shivering again as their gazes met and held. *Oh dear God*. All the foreplay she needed was right there, reflected in his blue eyes.

～∿～

She'd surprised him, meeting him in her bra and panties, but at least her actions stated clear intent. *Thank God*.

"Take it off. All of it." Though his balls ached with anticipation, he didn't trust himself to touch her. Not yet.

She bit her lip, looking suddenly shy. All the confidence she'd greeted him with a moment ago had evaporated. He pulled her close. Locking eyes with hers, he ran his index finger slowly down the valley between her breasts. The bra had a front hook. He managed it with one hand. She trembled as it dropped to the floor.

Her breasts weren't overly full, but nicely shaped and pert as hell with pretty pink nipples standing at attention, reminding him of ripe raspberries. His mouth watered with the desire to suck them. But not yet.

His fingers tracked down the midline of her belly, over pale, smooth, satiny skin. He traced the band of her bikini panties, then hooked one side of them. Her eyes widened and breath audibly hitched as he peeled them down.

"Aren't you at least going to kiss me first?"

"Yeah," he replied with a dark laugh. "I'm going to kiss you, all right." She gave another little gasp as his knees hit the floor. "I'm going to kiss and tongue you until you scream. I'm going to brand every inch of you with my mouth, Haley, so that this time you won't forget."

"I never forgot the last time," she whispered.

The scent of her arousal washed over him in a dizzying wave, nearly knocking him on his ass. *Holy shit!* He'd never been so turned on. Grasping her hips with both hands, he made the first long, slow swipe with his tongue.

She cried out, her body quaking. She was so ready, so ripe, and he'd hardly begun.

Reid plunged his face into her mound with a moan, licking, sucking, and exploring every sweet and tangy inch of her with his hungry mouth. Her fingers clenched in his hair. He delved deeper with greedy sweeps of his tongue. She bucked her hips against his face with a whimper, urging him further into her sex. But he eased up instead, just enough to keep her on edge, sucking and swirling, teasing with flicks and darts until she rocked and moaned. He wanted to torture her with pleasure, crank her need until she couldn't take anymore.

The moment she reached that brink, when her body signaled the onset of orgasm, tensing in his hands and under his mouth, he backed off again. "Don't stop now. Please, Reid," she sobbed. "Don't. Stop."

"No need to fret, sweetheart. I'm gonna give you what you want…what we both want."

He rose and wiped her juices from his mouth with his own trembling hand before finally claiming her lips with a ravenous kiss. She met him eagerly, moaning as their tongues met and tangled, engaging in a frantic thrust and retreat. She hooked her leg over his hip, grinding herself against him with a needy sound.

Her hands moved feverishly over his chest, tearing at his shirt buttons. She moved south then, toward his crotch, fumbling for his zipper. "Please, Reid," she pleaded. "I need you inside me. You don't know how long it's been."

"I know damned well," he growled. His need was almost blinding. He could hardly think beyond it, but he still held himself in tight check. He reminded himself how it had been before. Five years ago, he'd taken it slow and easy, treating her like a skittish colt, only to have her lay waste to him. He'd tried to win her heart, only to be left with a gaping hole in his—a hole that had never quite healed. He refused to let it play out like that again.

He clasped her wrists behind her and backed her toward the bed. He'd pleasure her with his mouth. He'd screw her senseless, but no way in hell was he gonna lose himself in her again.

"Turn around," he commanded. "I want you from behind. I want to watch as I enter you. I want to see myself inside you." He bent her across the bed, shoved a pillow under her belly, and then angled her hips. She raised her ass to him in readiness and looked over her shoulder with a needy sound that was almost his undoing. He shuddered with a rampant wave of raw lust and prayed he wouldn't explode the second he penetrated her.

Too impatient even to remove his clothes, he quickly unzipped and peeled his jeans off his hips only far enough to release his throbbing dick. Fisting his length, he gloved himself in latex with his gaze locked the whole time on that sweet, beckoning ass. God, he loved the curve of it.

He shut his eyes on a hiss as he guided himself into her wetness. Circling and probing, he teased until she squirmed, rubbing herself along his length. His lungs burned with the effort of restraint, as he penetrated by slow, agonizing inches, stopping only when he was seated to the root. He exhaled in a long rush, his cock pulsing in time with his own pounding heart. He began to move, slowly and deliberately. His balls ached like hell, but he was determined not to lose it.

She rocked her hips into him with another needy cry.

"You want more?" he ground out through his teeth, still fighting the primal instinct to ram repeatedly into her.

"I love how you feel inside me, Reid. Please don't hold back. Give me all of you."

His restraint snapped. He withdrew and thrust. Hard. She met his thrust with a cry of pleasure. Squeezing her hips, he plunged in and out. Short jabs. Long stabs. Deeper. Faster. His mind locked. His vision blurred. His pulse roared as he pumped in a mad, manic frenzy.

—◊◊◊—

This Reid wasn't the warm and tender lover she remembered from so long ago, the one who'd first taught her pleasure. This version of him was more controlling and almost dangerous, and his carnal ravaging told her that the lessons were far from over. Filling and stretching her almost to capacity, he thrust with nearly brutal strokes. It was a feral, almost illicit coupling, but still not wrong. *Sweet Jesus. Anything but wrong.*

It felt so good. How his body fit hers.

The air surrounding them filled with their mingled moans, strangled gasps, and the sound of slapping flesh. Her world contracted and closed around her until nothing existed beyond the marrow-penetrating pleasure of his pistoning hips.

Her climax came hard and fast, ripping through her until she clawed the sheet and bit into the pillow to stifle her cry. His release was almost simultaneous, hitting the moment her core began squeezing him in orgasmic spasms. He muffled his own groan as he came, collapsing against her back with his sweat-coated chest, his panting breaths hot and humid on her neck. After a moment, he nipped her earlobe and withdrew.

Senseless and satiated, she rolled onto her back, watching him disappear into the bathroom. She shut her eyes on a satisfied sigh, wondering how long it would be before they could do it all over again.

Hours later, Haley shivered and grabbed for the covers, only to realize she'd never crawled beneath them. She opened her eyes to a darkened room. Had she really fallen asleep?

"Reid?" She sat up and called out to no answer.

Her gaze darted over the room. Had he left her without

a word? Her stomach tightened as her mind raced over the past few hours. Although he'd defended her earlier, he'd said he wasn't on her side. Had she been wrong to trust him? Was this whole night an act of revenge for the license suspension? Had he purposely set her up in order to destroy her reputation? Her credibility?

She clutched the sheet to her breasts as fear and shame hit her in a nauseating wave. She'd have to face them all tomorrow. Would they all know? Was he even now giving the outfitters a blow-by-blow account of how he'd done Dr. Haley Cooper? And how she'd begged him for more?

Dear God. A shower. She desperately needed a shower.

After that, she'd pack her stuff and drive back to Cheyenne. It was cowardly to slink away, but she refused to let him humiliate her in front of all her colleagues. She cursed him with angry tears streaming down her face, ferociously scrubbing her body, only to get soap in her eyes. She then cursed herself. How could she have been so naive? So stupid?

She shut off the water, grabbed a towel, and proceeded to rub her skin raw. Although cleaner, she didn't feel any better. She raked a comb through her tangles and stared at the hair dryer, remembering their first weekend at Coronado Island and his silly obsession with her hair. She'd never known anyone like him, but he was so different now. Not just older but jaded, hardened, and cynical—so different from the man she'd knowingly hurt five years ago.

Her throat went raw, and her eyes burned all over again. She plugged in the dryer, but then froze at the sound of voices coming from the bedroom. The television? But she hadn't turned it on.

Wrapping herself in a towel, Haley cracked the bathroom door and peeked out. Her heart leaped into her throat at the sight of Reid, sprawled full length on the bed, a pizza box on his lap and a beer in his hand. He was back. All her fears were unfounded. Hit by a tsunami of relief, she shut her eyes and slumped against the wall.

—◦◦◦—

Reid glanced up to find Haley standing in the doorway with arms folded. "You left without a word," she accused.

"You were sleeping, and I was starving." He flashed a grin. "Strenuous activity tends to do that to a man. I got pizza. Want some?"

Her stomach answered with an unmistakable growl.

Her gaze flickered to the box. "What kind did you get?"

"This one's everything meat."

She curled her lip.

He pointed to a second box sitting on the table. "I got you the veggie special. I thought you might be hungry too when you finally woke up."

"Thank you." She softened. "That was very thoughtful."

"There's mineral water too, unless you'd like a beer."

"Sounds great. I love beer with pizza." She grabbed a slice from the second box, a bottle of Coors, and joined him on the bed, settling back against the stack of pillows. She still wore only the towel. Not that he minded. "What are you watching?" she asked.

"*X-Men Origins: Wolverine*. It's part of a marathon." He reached for the remote to turn it off.

"Don't." She stayed his hand. "I love X-Men."

Reid did a double take. "You're kidding."

"Why so surprised?" She took a bite of pizza. "There's a lot you don't know about me."

"True enough. But I *never* would have figured you for a Marvel Comics fan."

She grinned. "What's not to love about mutants?"

He studied her for a long moment and shook his head. "Nope. I'm still not buying this, Haley."

"Why? You think girls only watch Disney movies and read Harlequin romances?"

"That's what my sisters did."

"I'm not like your sisters."

"That's for sure. All right then," he quizzed, "which is your favorite of the X-Men?"

"Mystique," she blurted without a beat. "She has way better mutant powers than any of the rest. I always wanted to be her. She's so cool."

"She's *blue*."

"But she can turn into *anyone*. I always wanted to be able to do that." She took another bite of pizza. "Shape-shifting kicks ass, Reid."

"You think so? Who did you want to turn into?"

"When I was young? Anyone but *me*," she replied softly.

He digested that tidbit.

She handed him her bottle. "Would you open this for me, please?"

He popped the top with a thumb and handed it back to her.

"I've never seen anyone do that before."

He smirked. "My mutant power. It's pretty lame."

She covered her mouth on a laugh. "So who did you wanna be?"

"I wasn't a big fan of X-Men."

"No?" She sat back and squinted at him. "Wait! I know. You're an Avenger, aren't you? Captain America, right?" She giggled. "You are *totally* Captain America, Reid. I can so picture you in his costume too. You'd look incredibly hot in it."

He gave a derisive snort. "Given a choice, I'd much rather be Cyclops so I could nail Emma Frost. For the record, you'd be smoking in *her* costume too. Gotta love all that white lingerie."

It was all too easy to imagine. She leaned forward to adjust the pillows and her towel slipped, revealing a hint of dusky areola. His prick reacted instantly. His interest in the movie quickly waning, he reached once more for the remote.

She gripped his hand. "Wait just a sec. This is the good part. Wolverine's about to make his big buck-naked escape. Do you think he used a stunt double? Or did Hugh Jackman really streak for the entire world?"

"Don't know. Don't care." Reid shrugged and clicked it off.

"A lot of them do that you know. Use body doubles. You happen to be a particularly fine specimen of *Homo sapien*. You should go to Hollywood, Reid. You could make a fortune as a booty double."

He scowled at her. "You've been ogling my *ass*?"

"Well, yeah." She grinned. "It's an exceptionally nice one. Women like butts. A lot. Did you know that? Most females are attracted to men with blue eyes and firm, shapely buttocks. So that makes you two for two."

"Do you make a habit of studying male anatomy?"

"No. But yours just happens to be very hard *not* to notice. Since we're on the subject"—she pushed the empty pizza box onto the floor and peeled away her towel—"there're parts of you that most definitely merit closer study." She straddled him and wet her lips.

Every ounce of blood rushed to his groin.

She leaned forward until her nipples brushed his chest, then moved up his neck, licking, sucking, and then biting his earlobe, sending a dizzying jolt of sensation surging through him. She reached for his belt but struggled a bit with his zipper. He was already fully erect.

"Lift your hips, Reid."

He complied with gritted teeth. He'd sworn he was going to stay in control, but he ached to be inside her mouth. He wanted it down to his marrow, but there was no way in hell he'd be able to keep it together once she wrapped her lips around him.

Shit, Everett! You are fucking screwed.

She jerked his jeans to his knees and then began working down his body with her mouth, kissing, licking, teasing, and seducing him with her lips and tongue.

He shut his eyes as his only defense, but that just seemed to magnify the sensations—her warm, wet tongue, her teeth on his nipples, his erection nestling in the valley between her breasts, her hands caressing his chest and thighs as she laved around his navel with her tongue. She moved lower until she was sprawled out over his thighs.

His anticipation ramped to a whole new level with

the moist, hot caress of her breath over his prick. He shuddered at the first warm, wet rasp of her tongue that explored his balls while she wrapped her hand around him. She slid it slowly up and down his shaft as she kissed his head and then circled her hot tongue around his glans, probing the slit and then teasing the hell out of him with flicks and darts.

He groaned and squeezed his eyes even tighter. *Don't look, asshole. If she even glances up at you while sucking you off, you're a fucking goner.*

"Tell me what you like, Reid. I want this to be good for you."

He made the fatal error of opening his eyes—straight into hers, all deep green and soft, shadowed behind the lock of pale blonde hair that had fallen in her face. He homed in on her lips, moist, swollen, and smiling shyly at him. The erotic vision squeezed all the air out of his lungs in a brutal gush. *Good?* He was already out of his fucking mind. He knew he'd last about five seconds once she started sucking. His heart slammed against his chest. He'd thought he could control this. Who was he kidding? He'd never stopped wanting her. And the more he got, the more he *wanted*. But he wanted more than animal sex.

"Come here." He reached for her.

She drew back with a taunting grin. "Nope. Not yet. It's your turn to suffer now. Turnabout is fair play, Reid."

"This isn't a contest," he said.

"Is that a complaint?" she teased. "Are you offended at the thought of being used for hot sex?"

"Not at all." His pulse raced, but he kept his tone passive. "As long as *I'm* calling the shots." He cupped her head and dragged her back up his body. Flipping her onto her back, he caged her beneath him.

"What are you doing, Reid? What are you trying to prove?"

"Why are you with me?" he demanded.

"You know why," she answered, panting beneath him.

"Is this only about sex for you?"

"If we're both getting what we want, what's wrong with that?"

"I don't know why the hell you showed up here when you did, but I'm taking it as a sign."

"A sign? What are you saying?"

"I knew what I wanted back then, and I haven't changed my mind. This is more than just a fuck to me, Haley."

Her brows pulled together in a scowl. "Do you think you *own* me just because we've slept together?"

"I don't recall any sleeping. I don't *sleep*. Haven't in years."

"You know what I meant," she snapped.

"It's real simple, Haley. I need to know if it is gonna be just you and me from here on out."

"Don't be such a caveman, Reid. It's not a crime to want to enjoy sex without any attachments."

"Not what I needed to hear." He rose from the bed, snatched up his shirt, and jerked on his jeans.

"You're leaving? Why? I don't understand this. What do you want from me?"

"Same thing I wanted five years ago—for us to be together. If you don't want it too, I'm not wasting any more time. Now I'm gonna ask you again. Why are you with me? What do you really want?" His gaze bored into hers, searching for the answer as his emotions made war inside him. He'd tried to deny it, but it was no good. He still had feelings for this perplexing woman. But he'd be damned if he'd let her tromp on his heart again.

She looked away. "I'm not ready for this kind of conversation, Reid. Why are you pushing me like this?"

"Because I've already sacrificed too much. I need to get on with my life. If you don't want to be a part of that, we're already done." He flung his arms into his shirt and stomped into his boots. "I'll pick you up in the morning. Introduce you around. You'll have an easier time of it."

"No need to trouble yourself on my behalf," she said, choking back tears.

He stiffened against the sudden urge to go back to her, to take her into his arms. Instead, he reached for his hat. "It's the least I could do to repay you for the *fuck*."

~~~

Trying to tune out her own thoughts, Haley turned on the television. The original *X-Men* was playing now. She muted the sound and stared at the screen with burning eyes, seeing nothing. She still couldn't believe he had walked out on her like that. How could he?

And why the hell *had* she taken up with him again? Was it gratitude because he'd helped her out of a fix? Or just sheer sexual frustration from months of abstinence? Maybe it was a combination of both, but if that was really all there was, why did she have this hollow ache in her chest? Once more, a night with him had turned her inside out.

She'd left California believing that a return to fieldwork was the answer, but she hadn't counted on Reid.

How could she stay here now knowing she'd continue to run into him? Sure, she could try to avoid him, but he was an area outfitter. It was inevitable that their paths would eventually cross again. Was this whole move to Wyoming a huge mistake?

Her instincts screamed to pack up and go back to California, where she could go to a restaurant and order edamame. Where she lectured for people who smiled back and wrote big checks. She wanted to return to the place where people understood her and didn't challenge her; the place where she was comfortable. Where she belonged—the place where she'd become disillusioned…complacent…and bored.

Being honest with herself, she'd felt that way for a long time. No one ever challenged her because she only mixed with people who shared her beliefs. For five years she'd surrounded herself with all the "right" people who did all the "right" things. She lived in a closed circle of intellectuals, academics, and activists, people who outwardly espoused philanthropic and humanitarian concerns. They all talked a good game about saving the world, but so much of it was hollow posturing from hypocrites who gave "green" speeches while traveling in their Gulfstream jets.

She suddenly realized the problem. She didn't really *like* them.

Although she didn't agree with Reid's convictions, she couldn't help respecting him. She admired his courage and character. He had cared enough to risk his own life for a greater cause. They were still on opposite sides of almost everything, but at least he walked his talk. How many people really did that?

Confused and growing depressed, she clicked off the television. It was time for some desperately needed perspective from the one person she could always count on. *Yolanda.*

"Haley?" Her best friend picked up on the second ring. "*Chica!* It's been so long. How are you?"

"I was hoping you'd still be up."

"Yeah, I'm still up. Motherhood is a mixed blessing."

"How is little Sergio?"

"Too much like his *papi.* They both keep me up all night. Is everything okay? It's not like you to call so late at night."

"No, Yo. Everything is not okay."

"Tell me about it, *chica.*"

"I did something incredibly impulsive and impossibly stupid… I left my job and came out to Wyoming."

"You're in *Wyoming*?" Long pause. "But I thought your future was all set. And what about your professor?"

"Jeffrey's still there."

"I thought you and he were going to move in together."

"I thought so too, but he didn't take to the notion when I brought it up. I'm really confused now, Yo. I always thought he and I would end up together, but we've been slowly drifting apart. I finally acknowledged that it was going nowhere… I wanted a new start, so here I am."

"In Wyoming."

"Yes." Haley paused, then blurted, "I ran into Reid."

"Reid? The cowboy? Oh my God! Really? Is he out of the Marines now?"

"Yeah. He's out and back home now."

"It's fate!" Yolanda declared. "It has to be."

"That's kind of what he said, but nothing has changed, Yo," Haley insisted. "I mean, I'm still me, and he's still…well…him."

"But he still does it for you?" She could hear Yolanda's smile.

"Yeah." Haley gave a dry laugh. "He does it all right. Maybe even more than ever."

"Then it *is* a second chance, Haley. If you think you want him and he still wants you, you have to stick it out and *make* it work this time."

Haley sighed. "That's what I was afraid you'd say."

"That's because I'm smart, *chica*." She paused. "You don't sound very happy about all this."

"No."

"Why not?"

"Because I've already screwed it up, maybe beyond redemption. He went all possessive on me, and I panicked. You know I don't go for that. I lashed out, and he walked out. I think I might have burned the bridge this time."

"I doubt that," Yolanda said. "He was really into you, you know. I mean how many guys would have stuck around after the incident on the Ferris wheel?"

Haley groaned. "Did you have to bring *that* up? It was only the worst moment of my life."

"Just helping you to put it all in perspective, *chica*. It's time to ask yourself what you really want from life. You've put your heart and soul into your work for too long. I know you love animals, but they can't love you back, not the way you need."

"But I'm scared, Yo. He confuses me…"

"What do you mean?"

"I don't know how to describe it. He's just so *much*." She couldn't begin to understand, let alone articulate her feelings for him.

Yolanda chuckled. "That sounds like a *good* thing."

Haley gave a huff of exasperation. "I didn't mean it *that* way…not that he's deficient in that department. What I mean is that he's so intense. He makes me feel too much."

"You're afraid of that? Of falling in love?"

"Well, yes. Of course I am. Weren't you?"

"No. Not really. I fell in love all the time. It just never lasted. But you and I are very different that way. You won't let yourself love. Why are you so scared to let go?"

"I don't know. I just can't… Maybe I'm afraid I won't be loved back. It terrifies me to take that kind of leap without knowing."

"But we can never know. You just have to have faith. You've always confronted your fears before, Haley. Reid is the only thing you ever ran away from. Maybe it's time you dealt with that. Putting all differences aside, do you think you *could* love him?"

"I don't know. What's between Reid and me is nothing like my relationship with Jeffrey."

"Did Jeffrey really balance you, Haley? Sometimes we get so lost in what we 'think' we want that we don't recognize what we actually need. I speak from experience."

"Do you still miss him?" Haley asked.

"Yeah, I do, but Rafi wasn't the right one. I thought I wanted my bad boy marine, but he loved the Corps too much. I could never compete with that. I always felt like second place."

"Any regrets?"

"No. It was great while it lasted, but now I have the real thing in my sweet, loving pastry chef. Sergio is what I really *needed*. Maybe Reid was the one for you all along. So what are you going to do?"

"I don't know yet. It all happened so fast between us. I need time to think. It feels like my brain stops functioning the minute he and I are even in the same room together. I'm done speaking at the convention. Tomorrow they have some big awards dinner for the outfitters, but I have zero interest in that. He was supposed to introduce me to some people, but I don't know if I can face him yet. Maybe I'll just check out early."

"Consider it very carefully, Haley."

"I will, Yo. I promise."

"Good. I truly want you to be happy."

"Thank you for always being there for me. I know I've been a sucky friend at times."

"Only sometimes," Yolanda laughed. "But you're you, and I wouldn't change that. Let me know how it turns out with Reid, okay?"

"I will. I'll call again soon. Kiss the baby for me."

Haley hung up feeling only marginally better.

She reminded herself that she'd made the right decision years ago to focus on her career, just as she'd promised herself, but that didn't mean she'd never experienced any "what if" moments. They still came to her at random times, along with Gram's warnings about putting her ambition before happiness. Although doubts about her decision had always lingered, she never allowed herself to dwell on them for very long. Until now.

Maybe Yolanda was partly to blame. It was hard to see her best friend married with a baby while Haley, at almost twenty-eight, had no real prospects of either.

Yolanda had voiced her own questions. Was it some kind of kismet that had brought Reid back into her life? If so, what did it mean? She'd broken up with Jeffrey because he didn't want commitment, yet was terrified to take a chance on Reid, who did? She wasn't ready to examine that too closely just yet. Not at all.

———

Reid beat himself up pretty good after leaving her last night. By the time he reached his room, he'd known she was right. He'd pushed her too hard, but he was used to being in control. For eight years, he'd taken the bull by the horns every damn day. Maybe she'd have come around if he hadn't been so heavy-handed, but damn it all, Haley seemed to balk just for the sake of balking. Now he'd come back with his tail between his legs, ready to apologize.

He knocked on her door. She didn't answer. He paced, and then knocked again, louder, drawing the attention of the housekeeper.

"She's gone."

"Huh?"

"The little blonde lady. She checked out early this morning."

"Checked out? Are you sure?"

"Yeah. She had her bags."

Fuck. Fuck. Fuck. She'd bolted. Where the hell had she gone?

He deserved the kick she'd given him in the teeth for being such a controlling ass, but he just couldn't seem to help himself. All of his life he'd attained every goal he'd ever set his eye on. Every single one.

Except her.

Reid consoled himself that he finally held one advantage—time. Rather than his enemy, it was finally on *his* side. She was working here. Circumstances would eventually throw them together again. His gut told him to back off. The next move would have to be hers.

Chapter 17

Two Rivers Ranch, Dubois, Wyoming

"Mornin', Reid." Krista glanced up in greeting as he entered the kitchen. He responded with a grunt and headed straight for the coffeepot. After pouring a cup, he snatched up a biscuit, shoving it into his mouth.

"You don't have to do that anymore you know."

"Do what?" he asked.

"Eat like it's gonna be your last meal."

He shrugged. "Eight-year-old habits are hard to break."

She buttered a biscuit, smeared it with honey, and pushed it toward him. "Sit down and enjoy them."

He picked it up and took a big bite. She was right. It was a whole lot more enjoyable to clog up his arteries. She handed him another. "Trying to fatten me up?"

"No. Just trying to be sisterly," she replied. "I can't even tell you how happy I am that you're back home. I really missed you, Reid."

He grinned. "Me too, Sis." Growing up, Krista was always the tag-along-pain-in-the-ass youngest sister, but he'd missed her a whole lot, too. "Where's everyone else?" he asked.

"Mama's supervising the spring cleaning of the guest cabins and the ol' man and Jared had some business in Cody."

"What kind of business? Did I miss anything important while I was gone?"

He'd been out on back-to-back bear hunts since the season had begun. Now that spring hunting was winding down, he'd have to switch gears and help ready the horses for summer clients.

"Yeah. Well, sort of."

Her expression alarmed him. "What's wrong, Krista?"

"Tonya and I brought in the first group of horses from the winter range yesterday."

"And?" he prompted.

"We're missing one."

"You sure?" Reid replied. "Maybe you should count again."

"I'm sure, Reid. I know every single horse out there by name."

"Which one didn't come in?"

"The old-timer, Buckshot." Krista blinked and looked away.

Shit. Reid shook his head.

"Something's happened, Reid. He would have come in with the herd. I never should have let him go out on the winter range with the rest of them."

It was rare for his tough little sister to get misty-eyed about anything, but it was even hard for Reid not to get a bit emotional over it. It seemed like the gelding had been a member of the family forever. Although he was old as dirt, he was great with kids and still sound for the shorter rides.

"Then we need to go out and look for him," he said.

"I'm worried it was wolves."

"What makes you think that? Have you seen any?"

"No, but we've seen plenty of tracks around here over the past few years. They've been gradually getting closer to the stock, but this is the first time they've actually taken a horse. That's why Jared and the old man went to Cody. They're requesting a kill permit from WGF."

"That's certainly jumping the gun. They aren't going to get anything without proof, and we haven't even found a carcass."

"The ol' man thinks Jim'll give it to him anyway."

"Then the ol' man doesn't realize there's a new sheriff in town. Jim has to answer to Haley Cooper on this, and I guarantee with my last breath that she's not going to allow any wolf kills without solid proof of depredation. You're all jumping to conclusions anyway. He might still be out there. If not, we need to at least find his remains. At that point, we'll be able to determine what happened."

"Why are you so damned quick to take *her* side on everything?"

"*Her?*" he asked. "What do you mean?"

"I mean Haley," Krista said. "I heard about what you did at the Outfitters Convention. And while we're talking about it, you've been a real bear ever since you saw her there."

"Really? I didn't realize that."

"Yeah. Really. I don't understand why you're still so hung up on her."

He scowled into his cup. "Back to that again? I thought I told you to stay out of my personal life."

"I'm just saying that *if* it ever happens to me, I hope it's at least someone I can *like*."

"That's the thing, Krista." He rubbed his neck with a sigh. "I *do* like her. She's smart and spunky and stands up for her principles. I respect that, even if I don't agree with her. Ever met someone who completely rubs you the wrong way, but you're still drawn to them anyhow?"

"No. Can't say I ever have. But I don't think I could ever be attracted to someone who's against everything I stand for. I generally tend to avoid people like that."

"Sometimes we can't help who we're attracted to, and when it happens, it's like a bad case of poison ivy. You know damned well you shouldn't scratch, that it'll make the itch a whole lot worse, but you just can't help yourself."

"Sounds real appealing." Her lips curled. "You should send that one to Hallmark, Reid. 'I love you like a virulent rash.'"

He couldn't suppress a chuckle. "Guess I'm no poet."

"But it's off again between you, right?"

"Yeah. It's off… For now."

Almost two months had gone by, and they still hadn't crossed paths again. He'd half hoped he'd accidentally run into her, but that hadn't happened. He'd even bribed Jim Banks with an expensive steak dinner a few weeks ago just to get her phone number, but he hadn't called her. Not yet. He was determined to stay the course and let her come to him.

He'd kept tabs on her though. Last he'd heard, she'd set up her home base in Jackson to pursue some independent project on the wolf packs in the Teton Pass. According to his father and brother, they were causing a heap of shit for a big sheep outfit. The last thought brought him back to the present dilemma—wolves and livestock.

Reid scarfed down another biscuit and then drained his coffee. "C'mon, little sister. Let's go look for that lost horse."

—∧∧∧—

Haley had been working out of the Jackson regional WGF office for nearly two months without incident when the first call came in from Jim Banks at the Cody office. "We've got a reported livestock depredation," Jim declared.

"Really? Where?"

"A ranch in Dubois. They're missing a horse and claim it's a wolf. They're requesting a kill permit."

"Did they locate the carcass?"

"Not yet."

"They came to you for a permit based solely on speculation?" Haley laughed outright. "Over my dead body. Have you sent anyone to investigate it yet?"

"Not yet. Care to do the honors?" Jim asked.

Haley hesitated. As the senior biologist and primary wolf researcher, she wouldn't normally be the first to go out on a preliminary investigation, but she was beginning to go a bit stir-crazy sitting in an office all day monitoring collars and writing reports.

"Actually, Jim, I'd be happy to go. Can you give me any specifics?" Jim rattled off some coordinates that Haley quickly jotted down. "Great. I'll check the grid and see if any of my monitored packs are in the vicinity. Can you give me the contact info?"

"It's Two Rivers Ranch and Outfitters," he replied.

"Two Rivers?" she repeated. "Isn't that the Everetts' place?"

"Yes. Jared and Boyd just came to see me about this."

"Do they know how long the horse has been missing?"

"No. They did a range roundup yesterday and this one didn't come in. He was the old-timer of the herd and getting lame."

"Which makes him susceptible," she remarked. "But we still aren't issuing any permits without proof. That means a carcass and a necropsy. I'll check it out and report back with my findings."

"Good morning, Reid," Tonya greeted him with a brilliant smile. "Haven't seen much of you lately."

"Nope. Haven't been around much," Reid replied, yanking his old roping saddle off the rack. He'd intentionally avoided her ever since Jared's revelation. Part of him wanted to confront her, but he hadn't known how to bring it up without creating an ugly scene, so he'd avoided it. Besides, what was the point now? They were done for good, and he still had to work with her. Sometimes it was best to let sleeping dogs lie.

"I got a big Appy mare here if you're looking for a challenge," she offered.

That caught his attention. "Do you now?"

"Yup. I brought her over for the roundup. Keith dropped her off a couple of weeks ago, asking me to put some rides on her. He was contacted by this rich German lady who wanted a gen-u-ine Indian horse."

"Let me guess, he made up some bogus bloodline that traces this mare back to Sitting Bull's stallion?"

"Not this time." Tonya laughed. "He's quit that gig. Hasn't touched a horse since that documentary destroyed his reputation. It's a shame. He really does know horses."

Reid shook his head. "So now he's got you doing *all* the work for him?"

"Pretty much." She shrugged. "I don't really care, as long as I get paid. It's a convenient arrangement."

"But he's probably only giving you half of what he's getting."

"Maybe, but he still gets more money for a horse than I ever could."

"Can't say I like how he does business," Reid remarked. "And now you want *me* to do the dirty work?"

She shrugged. "As long as the clients get well-broke horses, what does it matter who's in the saddle?"

"No reflection on you, Tonya, but it ain't honest."

She frowned. "You want to take on the Appy or not?"

"How many rides has she had?"

"Two. Popped me off both times."

"Screw that shit. I'm too old for bronc riding. Gave it up when I joined the Marines."

"Too old and decrepit, eh?" Tonya's black gaze met his in mock challenge.

"Where is she?" he demanded.

"Tied to my trailer."

Reid snatched a halter and bridle, slinging them over the saddle on his shoulder, and followed Tonya to her trailer. A big-boned leopard Appaloosa nickered at the sight of them. "How much did he sell her for?"

"Ten grand."

He whistled. "For an unregistered, unbroke horse?"

"Yup." She laughed. "It's all in the marketing. Those Germans eat up anything related to the Old West. According to Keith, they dress up in buckskin and war paint, drink firewater, and reenact our famous battles."

"The Germans playing at cowboy and Indian? You're shitting me!"

"Nope. Honest Injun," she quipped. "Keith's even thought about moving there. They idolize him."

"Then what's stopped him?"

"I think his conscience. He's changed a lot."

"That can only be for the better," Reid remarked and stepped back to look the horse over. Good conformation. And not bad-looking for the breed. None of them had much mane or tail, but this one at least had a decent head and small ears. "I'll ride her. Anything I should know?"

Tonya grinned. "You might say she's just a *tad* skittish."

"Just a tad, huh? Care to elaborate?"

"She bucks at her own shadow."

"Nothing a good long, sweaty ride won't fix. Wet saddle blankets always settle 'em in."

After months off at pasture, even the veterans in the string needed a good tune-up. As for the juniors like this one, most of them would be bombproof after a summer full of pack trips and trail rides.

He approached the horse's shoulder, running a hand down her neck and then over her back. He let her smell the blanket and then ran it over her body before placing it on her back. Her ears flickered, but she didn't otherwise react. The saddle followed.

"She's also a little cinchy," Tonya cautioned.

He didn't need the warning. He finished tacking
her up while Krista led two more horses out for her
and Tonya.

"Gonna pony any of 'em?" Reid asked.

"Not this time." Tonya shook her head. "Let's see
how Red Bird does."

Reid pulled Red Bird's head around and tested a
foot in the stirrup. She sidled. He circled and soothed
her before trying again. A moment later, he vaulted
smoothly into the saddle, his gaze intent on her flattened
ears. "Shit. She's gonna blow, ain't she."

The words had hardly left his mouth before she did
just that.

It'd been more than eight years since Reid had ridden
bucking horses, but it was something one didn't forget.
He held off the spurs, but let her have at it, encouraging her to kick and buck and wear herself out. He could
sense the turning point, the very instant she realized
she wasn't going to win. It took a bit longer than he'd
expected, but a lot of mares were feisty. It was a good
quality, if you could win them over. Finally acknowledging her defeat, the horse dropped her head with a
deep sigh.

"You ready to play nice now, Red Bird?" Reid
crooned and stroked the horse on her sweat-slickened
neck. "C'mon now. Just move your feet in the right
direction, and we'll get along just fine." He urged the
horse again and she took a tentative step. "Good girl,"
he praised her. "Now you're gettin' it."

She began walking forward calmly. Once he was
certain of her submission, he flashed a triumphant grin,
one that faded away the moment his gaze rested on the

petite blonde standing behind Tonya and Krista with her brows drawn in disapproval.

Haley? What the devil is she doing at the ranch?

—∿∿—

No one answered the door when Haley pulled into Two Rivers Ranch, so she headed out toward the corrals where she saw three people gathered. They had their backs to her, but it didn't take long to recognize Reid's tall and muscular form. She pretty much had every inch of him memorized.

She watched unnoticed while he mounted a horse and gasped when it exploded in a wild bucking fit. As a staunch animal advocate, she'd never enjoyed rodeo sports but still found herself mesmerized by the contest between horse and rider. At first she was torn between wanting Reid to get thrown and fearing he'd get hurt, but as the seconds passed into minutes, with Reid still firmly anchored in the saddle, her anxiety increased for the panting, wide-eyed horse. Should she intervene?

Stepping forward, she made herself known to the two spectators that she recognized as Krista and Tonya. "When is he going to stop?"

Krista turned around, leveling an instantaneous frown. "Haley? What brings you out here?"

"I got a call about your missing horse and came to investigate. When is he going to stop?" she asked anxiously. "That horse looks terrified."

"The horse is an Appaloosa," Tonya interjected with an impatient roll of her eyes. "She might look scared to you, but the white sclera is a trait of the breed. She doesn't *like* what's happening right now, but believe me, she's fine. She's just not used to having anything on her back that she can't readily toss." Tonya jerked her head toward the horse and rider. "She's almost ready to quit now. It won't last much longer."

Haley was almost chewing her nails by the time the horse stopped. Sweat coated the animal from nose to tail, and her sides heaved. She shook her head with a loud snort and then became perfectly calm. Reid looked up with a triumphant grin that vanished the minute his gaze met Haley's. They'd parted once more on bad terms and hadn't spoken in weeks.

Yet her pulse still sped with anticipation the second his booted feet hit the ground. He handed the reins to Tonya with a smirk. "Got her warmed up for you. See if you can stay on her this time." Haley watched the exchange with a pang of jealousy. They seemed so comfortable with each other.

Rather than opening the gate, Reid surprised her by vaulting easily over the panel, landing with a light thud almost directly in front of her. *Show-off.*

"That horse didn't look like she enjoyed the ride half as much as you did," she remarked.

Reid tipped his hat. "And a good morning to you too, *Dr. Cooper.*"

"I'm sorry, I didn't mean to be rude. It's just that—"

He raised a hand. "I'm not going to dispute you. I had a helluva time, and she fought me all the way. But I didn't hurt her."

"You exhausted her," she accused.

"No I didn't. She wore *herself* out. I never touched a spur to her."

"But—"

"At least let me finish before you jump to judgment, Haley. Just like you and me, this horse here has a *job* to do. And just like you and I would rather laze on a beach in Mexico sipping margaritas, she'd rather be grazing in a lush, green pasture. But in the end, just like you and me, she needs to earn her keep. In her case, that means wearing a saddle for a couple hours a day. In return, she gets food, shelter, and even some TLC if she's sweet enough about it. When you think it over, that's really not a bad gig. We all need to pay our own way, Haley."

She opened her mouth on instinct, but having no rebuttal, she closed it again.

"I s'pose you're here about Buckshot?"

"Buckshot?" she repeated blankly.

"The missing horse."

"Yes. I am. Don't think for one minute I'm going to allow a kill permit without proof—"

He shook his head. "There you go again. Jumping to conclusions. I already told the ol' man how it is, but you gotta remember he's been around longer than you and me, and he's set in his ways. He's used to handling things like this himself. At least he *sought* the permit."

"What are you saying?"

"That there're plenty of ranchers who would shoot first and ask questions later."

"But that's a felony!"

"You know that, and I know that, but we're on a thirty-two-hundred-acre ranch. There's no one out here to tell if he did shoot a wolf. At least give the man credit for *trying* to do the right thing."

Once more he stole the wind from her sails. "I'm trying to do the right thing too, Reid. I've come to investigate." Haley pulled a notepad from her purse. "When was the last time you saw the horse?"

"Krista?" he asked. "Do you know?"

"I generally ride out and check on the horses every few days," Krista replied. "We have them split up into two different herds and graze them on different winter ranges. Tonya and I brought the geldings in yesterday. Today we were supposed to bring in the mares, but Reid said we should go and try to find Buckshot first."

"What makes you so certain he didn't just wander off?" Haley asked.

"He was old," she replied. "Well past his wandering days. He would have come in with the rest of his buddies."

"Why do you think it was wolves?" Haley asked.

"Because we've been seeing a lot of tracks," Krista answered.

"But you said he was old. Maybe it was just natural causes. A lot of animals will go off by themselves when their time comes."

"She's got a point, Krista," Reid said. "He could have just laid down somewhere."

"Does she?" Krista jutted her chin. "There you go again, Reid."

"I don't understand," Haley said, watching brother and sister.

"It's nothing," Reid said. "Just something we discussed this morning. We're all just wasting time standing here and debating. If we want answers, we need to ride out to the range."

"If it is wolves, we need to bring the mares in," Krista argued. "We have some new foals out there that I'm worried about."

"Then why don't we kill two birds with one stone? You and Ton go out and get the mares, and Haley and I will look for Buckshot."

Haley noted the quick exchange of glances between Krista and Tonya.

"You sure about that Reid?" Tonya asked.

"Yes. We can't afford to lose any of those foals."

"You might be overlooking one thing," Krista said.

"What's that?" Reid asked.

"Dr. Cooper has to *ride*."

Reid scratched his chin. He sported an all-too-sexy amount of scruff. Even with heavy whisker shadow, he was still too damned good-looking for Haley's peace of mind. She tingled at the recollection of his bristled face between her thighs, then flushed at her dirty thoughts.

"Ever been on a horse, Haley?" he asked. "I admit it didn't even occur to me to ask you. It's kind of a given here in Wyoming. Most of us are on horses by the time we can sit up."

"I've ridden a few times before," she said, not adding that she had only been five or six and it was a pony at the county fair.

"I suppose the other choice would be to take the ATV, but you might have trouble once we hit the woods. If you don't oppose the notion, it'd be best if you ride. You're not afraid of horses, are you?"

"No. I'm not afraid. Just haven't ever been around them very much."

"We've got a string of really gentle trail horses. You

don't need to know much to ride 'em. They carry begin-
ners all summer long."

"Sure. I'll ride with you."

"Good." He nodded approval. "I'll get one of 'em
saddled up for you."

"Should I put Red Bird up?" Tonya asked.

"Yeah." Reid nodded. "I think we're done with her
for the day."

Tonya followed after him with the Appaloosa.

———∿∿∿———

"What's up with you and her?" Tonya asked as she
unsaddled the mare.

"What do you mean?"

"You and Wolf Woman."

"Her name's Haley," Reid corrected. "And it's none
of your business, Ton."

She heaved the saddle onto a nearby rack and then
turned to him, hands on hips. "I think it is my business,
Reid. I've been pretty patient, but I'm not going to
wait forever."

"I didn't ask you to. Not this time anyway. Matter of
fact, I don't seem to recall giving you any encouragement at all."

"No, you haven't," she agreed. "But I thought you
just needed more time."

"More time?" he repeated with a scoffing sound.
"Eternity wouldn't be long enough."

"What do you mean?"

"All right, Ton. I'll give it to you straight. There's
never going to be another 'us.'"

"Because of *her*?"

"No."

"Then why?" she asked, searching his eyes.

Reid compressed his mouth and leveled her with a stare. "I think you already know the answer to that."

"Jared," she whispered. "What did he tell you? I deserve to know."

"He told me you slept with him."

Her face blanched. "That son of a bitch. He had no right! It was a mistake, Reid. One that I've never repeated, but I didn't *cheat*. It happened *after* we broke up."

"How long after?"

She turned away and answered softly. "That night."

"Why Jared?" he asked. "Of all people, why did it have to be my brother?"

"I don't know, Reid. It just—"

"Happened," he finished for her. "I get it already." He heaved a regretful sigh. "Look, Ton, our families have been linked for a long time. I'm willing to put all this behind us if you are. If we're going to continue working together, I don't want things to be difficult. Can you handle it?"

"Yes," she said at length. "I can handle it, but it doesn't mean I have to like it."

"But you have to accept it." He rested his hand on her shoulder. "We were always friends first. I'd hate to lose that."

"Me too, Reid. If you really think Haley's the one you want, I won't make it awkward for you. You deserve to be happy. I just hope you're not making a mistake with her."

He offered a wry smile. "You and me both."

———

"That worked out real convenient now, didn't it?" Krista remarked once Reid was out of earshot.

"What do you mean?" Haley asked.

"You and Reid alone."

"I came out here on *business*."

"You could have sent someone else if you didn't want to see him," Krista argued. "My guess is that you *did* want to see him."

Haley went on the defensive. "Whether I did or didn't is none of your concern. Either way, it seems to me that Reid is quite able to look after himself."

Krista speared her with a resentful look. "You're wrong there, Dr. Cooper. My brother is very much my concern, and I'm troubled that he's still hung up on *you*."

Is he? Haley's heart skipped a beat. She really didn't know what to expect after the way they'd left things.

Krista continued, "He's a damned good man who's been through God knows what, and he doesn't deserve to have you or anyone else screw with his head."

Her genuine love and concern for Reid filled her eyes. It also softened Haley's response.

"I'm not the enemy, Krista. I'm just here doing my job."

"Are you saying Reid had nothing to do with it?"

"I didn't take the call as an excuse to come out here, if that's what you're thinking, but I certainly could have passed it on to someone else had I wanted to avoid him."

"So what exactly *are* you saying?"

"I'm not going to lie to you. It was a coincidence, but circumstances seem to keep throwing your brother and me together. I don't know what I feel for him, or what he feels for me, but rest assured, I'm *not* playing games with him."

"He wants to settle down. He wants to start a family. You don't strike me as that type."

That statement cut Haley to the core. "And what *type* is that?" she challenged. "Someone's wife? Someone's mother? Just because I come in a different package doesn't mean I don't want those things."

"People like you are usually more worried about population control than raising a family."

Krista was right about that. Jeffrey definitely fell into that category. It boggled her mind to know that Reid was so set on the very things that most men avoided— responsibility, commitment, marriage, and family. Jeffrey was pushing forty and had dodged all of it. Hell, he wouldn't even move in together. "Maybe you shouldn't judge people based solely on appearances."

"It's more than appearances, Haley. You could have had him five years ago. I think you know that. You could probably still have him now, but you've left him dangling on the hook. It's not right to take him for granted like that."

"What are you saying?"

"That it's time to fish or cut bait. Either tell him you want him or leave him the hell alone."

On those final words, Krista spun away.

Reid found Haley wearing a frown when he led two saddled horses to where she waited with her gear bag. He was relieved to see it smooth away at the sight of him. He hated this feeling of walking on uneven ground.

He felt like that a lot with her. And *only* with her. He was so uncertain of her, but at least she hadn't balked at riding alone with him.

She came toward him and reached for the sorrel's reins.

"Nope. That one's mine. Bud here's for you."

"Bud?" Her eyes widened when he handed her the reins to the behemoth bay. He'd forgotten just how tiny Haley was when he'd picked the draft-cross to carry her.

He grinned. "Yeah, short for Budweiser."

"You've got to be kidding." Her green gaze tracked upward to the saddle horn that was well above the top of her head and a stirrup that dangled at chin level. "I thought I was riding a horse, not climbing a mountain."

"Don't be intimidated. He's one of the gentlest and steadiest horses on the ranch. If you're ready, I'll give you a leg up." He dropped his reins and turned to help her mount.

"Won't your horse walk off?"

"Nope." He shook his head. "He ground ties. Most working ranch horses do. They're trained to stay put." Reid squatted and cupped his hands. "Reach up for that horn and be ready to throw your leg over." He boosted her with ease onto the horse's back.

"Hello, Bud." Haley reached down to stroke the horse's heavily crested neck. "You know, Reid, I feel like I'm straddling a barrel."

"I can promise he won't hurt you today," he said, as he proceeded to adjust her stirrups. "But tomorrow might be another story."

She gazed down at him with a panicked look. "What does that mean?"

He chuckled. "You'll be cursing a blue streak the minute you get out of bed and will probably be walking bowlegged for a few days after."

"Thanks a bunch, Reid. You know, a pony might have suited me much better."

"Maybe so, but we don't have any. Ponies are too smart for their own good, and most are mean little bastards to boot. They're always trying to run roughshod over the bigger horses. It's that Napoleon complex."

Haley laughed. "As one of the smaller people on this planet, I can certainly relate." Her laugh died when she noticed the rifle in his saddle holster. "You're bringing a gun?"

"Yeah. The ranch abuts thousands of acres of wilderness. You have to be prepared."

"I can understand bear spray, but I don't like guns, Reid."

"The gun's not going to hurt you. See?" He patted the butt. "It just sits there. I always carry it when I ride."

She scowled. "I'd rather you didn't this time."

"Sorry, Haley. I'm not leaving common sense behind just because it makes you uncomfortable. You can carry your bear spray if you like, but I'm taking my gun. Ready?" She returned a sulky nod but didn't offer any further protest. "Just keep your feet in the stirrups and the reins in your hands," he instructed while tying her gear bag to the back of the saddle.

They started out side by side, with Reid pointing out various landmarks around the ranch. Located ten miles outside of the town of Dubois, they were sheltered to the north by the Absaroka Mountains and to the south by the Wind River Range. Although mostly arid terrain, the vistas were breathtaking. They were also blessed with Chinook winds that kept it cool in the summer and melted the snow in the winter. He was proud of the place, but when Haley only made cursory replies to his remarks, he eventually gave up.

After about an hour, she finally broke her silence. "Your sister doesn't like me."

Ah, so she wasn't pissed off about the gun, after all; it was Krista that had her rattled.

Tension rolled off him with understanding. "Don't take it personally," he said. "She still wants to see Tonya and me back together and views you as a threat."

"Am I? A threat to that?"

Her direct question took him by surprise. He spun around to answer it head-on. "Dunno. Do you *want* to be?"

She hesitated. "I don't know. Maybe. But this is all really hard for me, Reid. I believe what I believe. I don't know *how* to be any different…even if I wanted to be."

"I don't want to change you, Haley. I'm just looking for you to meet me halfway. That's what it's about. There has to be some give and take on both sides. If you aren't prepared for that, we're done talking."

"I've only been involved in one other relationship, and it was nothing like this. There were never any major conflicts. Sure, we disagreed from time to time, but we never argued about anything substantial."

"You're talking about that professor guy."

"Yes. His name's Jeffrey," she corrected with a mild look of annoyance.

"Alright, *Jeffrey*," he conceded. "Are you still involved with him?"

"No. I broke it off. It's part of the reason I came here."

"How long were you together?"

"Almost five years."

"*Five years?*" His jaw tightened. "Did you love him?"

"No," she said softly. "I was infatuated at first, mostly with his intellect. At one time I thought there was more to it. I *wanted* it to be more, but it wasn't. I know that now. There was always something missing."

He cocked a brow. "So your Professor Perfect… wasn't?"

"No," she said. "He wasn't. I still care about Jeffrey and respect him as a colleague, but we drifted apart. We didn't want the same things. He wasn't interested in a long-term commitment."

He scowled. "Are you saying you are?"

She swallowed hard. "I might be…given the right circumstances."

"Just not with *me*."

She sighed. "I don't know, Reid. Part of me really wants to try, but I don't see how we could ever bridge our differences. Do you *honestly* think there is any way we could ever make a relationship work?"

"I think that all depends on how much we *want* to make it work. Do you want to, Haley?"

She slanted him an uncertain look. "I still don't know."

"But you're considering it?" he asked.

"Yes. I've been considering… I can't *stop* thinking about it… About you and me."

"And why's that?"

Her gaze wavered and then darted away.

"I'm listening," he encouraged.

"You see…the thing is…" She wet her lips. "When I was with Jeffrey, it was never like it is with you."

That reply eased the tightening in his chest.

"There. I've said it. Now you know. But just because we have a great physical connection doesn't mean we can build anything more on it."

"It's more than just physical," he argued.

"Okay, so maybe it is a little more," she confessed. "But is it enough?"

"Are you planning to stay in Wyoming?" he asked.

"I can't answer that either, Reid. I'm sorry, but I need more time to think."

"Fair enough." He digested her answer with a nod. "I can give you some space, but just know this up front: I'm not taking this halfway again. It's gonna be all or nothing with me, so you'd better think good and hard before you answer."

Chapter 18

THE TRAIL HAD NARROWED, SO REID RODE AHEAD OF her now, his form tall and straight in the saddle. As her gaze tracked over his wide back and broad shoulders, she felt a load slipping off her own. She'd tried to convince herself all along that their attraction was purely physical, but that was a lie. The physical chemistry was real enough, but it went deeper. If she confessed the truth, it always had. Her desire was for the man himself, not just his hotter-than-hell outer shell.

Reid had substance and principle. Unlike Jeffrey, he didn't pander to anyone. Nor did he tolerate politics or bullshit. She might not agree with him on most things, but he'd certainly earned her respect. Maybe it was stupid to think they could work it out, but their conversation and his patience with her had given her hope.

Reid abruptly pulled up his horse, pointing to the sky where a flock of turkey buzzards circled, a sure sign of carrion. "That way," he directed. "Don't know if it's Buckshot, but they're definitely feeding on something."

They turned up another narrow and rocky path that ran parallel to a deep ravine. The terrain made Haley's legs clamp around the horse and her hands clench the reins. As they approached the site of circling vultures, the horses snorted and balked, increasing her nervousness tenfold.

Just when she feared her horse would turn and bolt,

Reid came up alongside and took hold of Bud's bridle. "'Easy ol' boy," he said, soothing the fretful horse. "Looks like it's down there in the ravine. It's probably Buckshot," he declared grimly. "Horses have a sixth sense about these things. They always seem to know when it's one of their own."

He dismounted and then helped Haley do the same. "We'd best proceed the rest of the way by foot. It's too treacherous to ride."

"What about them?" she asked as he tethered the nervous horses. "Will they stay put?"

He cocked his head. "Let's just hope so."

She chewed her lip as he retrieved his rifle, but refrained from any comment about it. They moved cautiously down the rocky embankment, Reid leading the way. Several times he caught her as her footing slipped on loose rocks. Even in cowboy boots, Reid proved as sure-footed as a bighorn sheep.

The putrid smell of decay assailed them before they even reached the bottom. Haley fought her gag reflex. Reid offered his handkerchief. She accepted it gratefully, covering her nose and mouth with one hand as they approached the carcass. It was indeed a horse, or what remained of one. By the look of things, the kill was at least two days old.

"It's him." Reid nodded. "And something's been making a meal of him."

"It isn't a wolf kill," Haley declared with certainty. Although wolves and grizzlies were both known to scavenge, the hindquarters were still intact. Wolves almost always attacked from behind and devoured their prey the same way.

"Agreed," Reid said. "It's also half-buried, which means it was either a mountain lion or a grizzly. My first guess would be griz, but I don't relish getting up close and personal with either one of 'em." Reid grabbed her by the elbow. "C'mon. We have the answers we came for. Let's go."

"Just a minute," she protested. "We came all the way out here. Let me at least document the predation. If it was a grizzly, the WGF needs to know. You also have every right to file a claim with your insurance company."

"Look, Haley. You know as well as I do that there's *nothing* more dangerous or aggressive than a griz that's protecting his meal. I'm not about to risk my life or yours for a few hundred dollars. C'mon."

"But I only need a few seconds to take some pictures." Shaking off both his hand and his warning, she pulled out her phone, moving quickly around the carcass snapping shots of the carnage.

"I'm not screwing around," he warned. "We need to get the hell out of here. *Now*."

The brush stirred to life behind her. Reid's warning had come too late.

Haley's heart surged into her throat as a huge fur-covered body emerged. Her hands flew to her can of pepper spray but were too unsteady even to release it from the holster.

The bear let loose a bone-chilling growl and then charged.

"Hit the fucking dirt, Haley!" Reid bellowed.

His voice barely penetrated her consciousness. She recognized the command to play dead, but was utterly paralyzed by fear. The following seconds unfurled in a fog. A deafening roar filled her ears. Her body hit the ground with a bone-crushing force that drove the air from her lungs. Then the distinct smell of bear assaulted her nostrils.

She contracted into a ball, squeezing her eyes shut on a fervent prayer. *Dear God in heaven, please don't let me die!*

An explosion. A low groan. And then dead silence.

—⁓—

With his instincts screaming at him to protect, Reid reacted instantly to the attack, but he still wasn't fast enough. The bear charged, taking Haley down, but now his shot was clear. It was a monster, but at this close range, one well-placed cartridge took him out. Releasing a final agonizing roar, the bear crashed lifelessly to the ground.

His pulse still racing with adrenaline, Reid rushed to Haley. Dropping his rifle and kneeling beside her, his hands shook as he proceeded to assess the damage. She was pale, her skin clammy, her body trembling convulsively, but other than torn clothes and a few abrasions, she appeared unharmed.

"Y-you sh-shot it?" Her voice was a choked whisper.

"Yeah, I shot it."

"B-but I h-had b-bear spray."

He pulled her into his arms. "Shh," he soothed, gently, wiping the dirt and debris from her face. "You're babbling, sweetheart. It's a common shock response. No amount of pepper was going to stop that son of a bitch. Are you hurt?"

"I d-don't know. My head is throbbing real bad."

He gently palpated her scalp. "There's no blood, but you hit the ground pretty hard. Could be a concussion. Least I got him before he could do a dance on you. What else are you feeling?"

"Kind of numb."

"Numbness is shock too. Anything like this ever happened to you before?"

"N-no. Never."

"Count your blessings. I've seen it more times than I can count. Can you move your legs?"

"Y-yes. I think so."

"Think you can walk? I'd like to get you out of here and back to the ranch."

She sat up, looked wildly about and then began crawling around on all fours. Was she out of her mind?

"What the hell are you doing?" he asked.

"My phone. I've lost it. I need my phone."

"You get mauled by a griz and you're worried about your damned phone? Un-fucking-believable."

"You don't understand. Killing it is a felony, Reid. I'll need a picture to file a report. It's documentation for *your* sake."

He joined her on the ground, digging around through leaves, pine needles, and debris until they found it. Reid placed it in her hands with a shake of his head. She blew off the dirt and then scrambled back to the dead bear to take a few more pictures.

"Finished yet?" he asked impatiently.

"Yes. I'm finished."

He gave her a hand to stand up, but her legs almost instantly gave way. Before she could protest again, he scooped her into his arms. "Put me down, Reid. There's no way you can get back up that embankment carry-ing me."

"Oh yeah? Just watch me. For the record, you don't weigh much more than the pack I carried for eight years."

Needing a free arm to aid the climb, he hoisted her across his shoulders in a fireman's carry, and then proceeded to navigate the incline. To his immense relief, the horses were still where he'd left them. "Can you ride?"

"I think so," she murmured.

He hoisted Haley into the saddle, but she was shak-ing so hard she could barely hold the reins. "Just hold on, okay?"

"What are you doing?" she asked.

"Bud's a big boy. He can carry us both." He turned his own horse loose and slapped it on the rump. "This one knows the way home. He doesn't want to stay up here any more than we do."

Mounting the horse behind Haley, Reid guided them back to the ranch.

―᚜᚜᚜―

She didn't know when she'd fallen asleep, but in the far periphery of her consciousness, Haley was aware of the jolting of her battered body, of the soft snort of horses, and then the weightless sensation of being carried again.

When her eyes finally fluttered open, she was lying in a bed in an unfamiliar room with a ceiling and walls of rough-hewn log. It was a single room cabin, Spartan but adequate, with a tiny kitchenette and a breakfast bar, a table and two chairs, a love seat, and a queen bed. There was a wall-mounted TV above a small fireplace. A dog sprawled nearby with its tongue lolling.

"Where am I?" she whispered.

"My place." Reid appeared instantly, covering the floor in long strides and then squatting down beside her. The dog soon followed, nudging her hand with its cold, wet nose.

"I took over one of the guest cabins when I got home," Reid said. "I thought you'd prefer the privacy of it over the house where the family would all be gawking and hovering—only with the best intentions, of course. Mama's already been by to check on you twice, but I sent her away. I've stalled, but I'm afraid you won't be able to avoid them forever."

"Thanks." She smiled up at him and scratched behind the dog's floppy ears. "Who's this?"

"Jethro. He's a Bluetick Coonhound. They're supposed to be good at tracking mountain lions, but this one's not shown a whole lot of promise at anything, let alone hunting. Yet, he's somehow managed to insinuate himself into my place."

"Or maybe into your heart?" she suggested with a smile. "I didn't know you were such a softy, Reid."

He shrugged. "Least he's helped me watch over you."

"Has he? How long have I been asleep?"

"'Bout twelve hours. How's your head feeling?"

She lifted it tentatively from the pillow and then let it drop back again with a groan.

"Still throbbing, eh?" His brows met in a frown. "Should I take you to the hospital?"

"No. Honest. I'm fine. Just feeling a bit beat up."

"You hungry?" he asked.

"Maybe." She paused to assess her stomach, unable to determine if the churning was hunger or impending nausea. "I'm not sure."

"Mama brought vegetable soup. Wanna try some?"

"In a bit. I really need to get up first. Nature is calling." She pulled the blankets away and threw her legs over the side, suddenly realizing they were bare. She looked down to discover she wore nothing but a USMC T-shirt. "Who undressed me?" she asked.

"Who do you think?" His brows rose at her accusatory scowl. "I've seen it all before, remember?"

"But that was different. I was conscious then."

"You think I had my wicked way with you?"

"Of course not! It's just—" The fact that she was unconscious made her feel all too vulnerable.

"*Trust*, Haley. You need to learn it. Your clothes were torn and dirty. I pilfered some of Krista's for later, but thought this would be more comfortable for you to sleep in. C'mon. I'll help you to the john."

A wave of dizziness swept over her the moment her bare feet hit the floor. His arm came instantly around her waist. "You okay?"

"I will be. I just need a minute or two." She clutched his arm until the moment passed. "I haven't thanked you."

His jaw clenched. "It was a dumbass move to take you down there. I shouldn't have done it. It wasn't safe."

"You're not my keeper, Reid. I was doing my job, remember? It's not like you have any say in that."

"As your guide, safety *is* my job."

"I didn't hire you as my guide. I was doing an investigation. But there's no point arguing it any further," she said. "I freely admit I was wrong. I should have listened to you."

Her confession seemed to take him aback. But rather than the smug reply she half-expected, he acknowledged it with a grunt.

"I'm steady enough now," she said. "Can you just help me get across the room? I should be okay after that." He helped her to the bathroom, but then remained in the doorway. "I don't need an audience, Reid. I have a shy bladder."

"I'm not leaving you. What if you pass out?"

"I won't. I'm fine. Now please go."

He turned with reluctance, leaving the door cracked. Haley closed it sharply behind him. His sudden mother hen act was annoying as hell, but also mildly endearing.

After relieving herself, she clutched the sink and stared into the mirror, getting her first look at herself. *Ugh! What a mess*. Her hair was tangled in knots and scratches from the fall covered her face. She found a hairbrush and a toothbrush and set out to repair some of the damage. Although she'd washed her face, her body was still covered with dirt from rolling on the ground. She felt grimy and smelled like bear.

Thank God he'd taken it down before it'd gotten its claws into her. Grizzly claws were extremely lethal weapons. The memory of those fateful seconds struck her anew.

What if Reid hadn't been there? Or what if he'd gone along with her wishes and left the gun behind? She didn't want to think about it anymore. One confession of fault was her quota for the day. She couldn't bring herself to make another. They'd begun a reconciliation of sorts, but a lot of things were still up in the air.

Haley was suddenly aware that Reid was waiting on the other side of that door, and she found herself stalling. They were alone together in his cabin. He'd even undressed her. Now what?

She glanced longingly at the bathtub. Although she didn't feel stable enough to stand long enough for a shower, a bath would be soothing to her bruised body. She turned on the tap. Then knowing he'd probably bust down the door if she didn't come out soon, she opened it.

"Reid?"

"What, sweetheart?"

"I'm going to take a bath."

His broad shoulders suddenly filled the doorway. "I don't know if that's a good idea yet. I'm not about to leave you alone for that long."

"Then come in here with me."

His body stiffened and pupils flared. "In the tub?"

"No," she flushed. "I mean in the bathroom. You can sit beside me while I bathe."

"You're really pushing my self-control. You know that?"

"I'll pull the curtain."

"Won't make any difference. I'll still know you're naked in that tub."

"Yeah, Reid," she snorted. "I'm a truly irresistible sex goddess right now."

He came to her then, cupping her chin and tilting her face. "I think you underestimate your appeal." His big, warm hands dropped to her shoulders. "The thought of you wet and naked just switched off the thinking side of my brain." Even if he hadn't said it, the desire in his eyes was unmistakable.

He still wants me.

She swallowed hard, not knowing whether to respond to his remark or to the flicker he'd stirred to life inside her. The longer his gaze lingered on her, the stronger it became.

"I'm done thinking now too, Reid. Only hours ago I had my life flash before my eyes. I want to feel now." She wet her lips and laced her arms around his neck. "I want to feel *you*."

He exhaled an exasperated sigh. "As tempting as that offer is, I think we need to cool it for a while."

"Why?"

"Because an intense desire for sex is a common response to trauma. The shrinks even coined a term for it — 'terror sex.'"

"Do I look afraid?"

His gazed tracked involuntarily south, lingering on her nipples. They tightened into peaks before his eyes, evoking a similar hardening in his prick.

"You might feel differently about this later," he said. "I told you I'd give you some space. I intend to keep that promise. I'm not about to jump back into anything until I know exactly where I stand. I'm not taking that chance again."

"Where do you *want* to stand?" She flashed a slow and sexy grin as she slipped out of her panties, sending a surge of blood from his head to lower parts. His mind was rapidly losing focus, finding it harder to answer her questions. "Then again," she continued, snaking her arms around his neck, "we don't have to stand at all. It's much more comfortable sitting or lying down."

"Quit it, Haley." He reached up to encircle her wrists, bringing them behind her back, a position that pitched her breasts forward against his chest. Not helpful. At all. He abruptly released her. "*One* of us has to exercise a little common sense."

"Fine then." She jerked away, yanking the T-shirt over her head and throwing it at him. "Have it your way. You can just sit there and scrub my back, Mr. I-need-to-be-in-total-control-at-all-times."

He dropped onto the toilet lid. He'd resolved not to take her up on her offer, but damned if he'd deny himself the pleasure of watching. She bent to shut off the tap, intentionally taunting him with a prime view of her delectable ass. He sucked in a sharp breath.

Her coy smile said she knew damned well what she was doing to him. "It was your choice, Reid."

She reached a hand to his shoulder to steady herself as she dipped her toes into the water. Enough was enough.

He yanked her onto his lap. "Don't play with me, sweetheart. I promise you'll get far more than you bargained for."

"But that's exactly what I was counting on."

"I'm not screwing around here." In all truth, his resolve was weakening, his threats growing emptier by the second. It took all he had to turn her down, but he vowed he wasn't going to break this time. "I want to know *exactly* what I'm dealing with before we take this any further. I need your unconditional trust."

"What do you mean?"

"I mean that you have to stop jumping to conclusions and assuming the worst of me. You need to give me the benefit of the doubt when we disagree. *That's* what I'm asking for. What I expect. Those are my terms, Haley. I can't compromise on that. I'm an all-or-nothing deal."

He rose, deposited her in the bathtub, jerked the curtain closed, and walked out, leaving the door half open behind him. He leaned against the wall, his chest heaving, while he tried to will away a raging hard-on. He shut his eyes on a mumbled curse. Why did he always seem to get punished for doing the right thing?

Watching that grizzly attack had flipped a switch. The thought of losing her had nearly eviscerated him. He still had so much more to say to her, but she still wasn't near ready to hear it. Maybe she never would be, but until then, he swore he'd keep his dick zipped if it killed him.

~~~

Haley found a set of pink sweats sitting beside the sink when she got out of the tub. Apparently he didn't want to see her in his T-shirt anymore. His earlier rejection had stung, but she was too tired to think about it anymore. Although the bath had soothed her sore body, it had also made her incredibly sleepy.

She dressed and toweled her hair dry. When she emerged from the bathroom, the smell of homemade bread and a steaming bowl of vegetable soup greeted her. Her stomach reacted vociferously.

"So you're hungry after all." He spoke casually, as if nothing had happened. She wasn't sure what to make of that.

"Yeah. I am," she replied.

"Did the bath help?" His tone was a little too polite, his manner too reserved.

"It did. Immensely."

He might be able to ignore what happened—or better said, what didn't—but she couldn't deal with awkwardness. "I'm sorry," she blurted. "I shouldn't have pushed myself on you like that. I didn't mean to make you uncomfortable."

His mouth curved into a dry smile. "I was uncomfortable all right. Just not the way you imply." He laid his hands on her shoulders, his gaze holding hers. "Let me make one thing perfectly clear, Haley. It *wasn't* because I don't want you."

She chewed on that. "Then I guess I should thank you for not taking advantage of me."

"Let's forget it. Come and sit down before it gets cold."

Reid took a seat across from her, slouching back in his chair.

"Aren't you going to eat, too?" she asked, feeling self-conscious.

"I ate earlier while you were sleeping."

She sipped broth from her spoon, testing the temperature before diving into the bowl. The soup was wonderful, definitely not the Campbell's variety. "Your mom brought this over?"

"Yeah. I'm a lousy cook. I mostly eat at the house."

"But you don't live over there."

"No. The cabin's not much, but I need my own space. Eventually, I'd like to buy my own spread, but there's no reason to." His gaze met hers. "Not yet anyway."

"What kind of place do you want?" she asked.

"Probably a ranch like this one, but smaller."

"You want to stay in the same kind of business?"

He shrugged. "It's what I know. What I'm good at. 'Sides that, we've always made a decent living at it, which is more than many ranchers can say these days. What about you? Do you ever think about what you want a few years down the road?"

"I've started to," she said. "I think it began when Yolanda married last year. She already has a baby boy." She couldn't help the note of wistfulness.

His brows rose. "You want kids, Haley?"

"I do. I've always wanted a big family, maybe because it was always just me and my grandparents."

"That was partly your own choice, wasn't it?"

Her gaze narrowed. "They told you about my mother?"

"Yeah. Why didn't you want to live with her?"

"Because she never wanted me."

"She obviously had regrets later. She came for you, after all. Maybe you should make peace with her."

"I can never forgive her, and I don't want to talk about it. Why are you always trying to *reason* with me anyway?"

"Dunno." He shrugged. "It's just how I tick. I've always tried to look at both sides of every situation, even if it doesn't change my own opinion."

"I have a right to my feelings even if they don't make sense to you," she snapped.

"Absolutely," he agreed. "There's pie. Want some?"

"Pie is an unfair weapon, Reid." And he'd skillfully wielded it to diffuse her flare of temper. "Apple?" she asked hopefully.

"Yup. The best kind."

"It's my favorite, too. Yolanda makes a killer apple-jalapeño pie."

"Jalapeño peppers in pie?" He grimaced.

"Yup. Don't knock it 'til you try it. But it's best eaten with lots of ice cream."

She finished her soup while he cut two slices of pie. She suddenly realized just how comfortable she'd become sitting here with him. They'd been going on the last few minutes as if they were longtime friends. It struck her even harder that they hadn't even disagreed about anything besides her mother, but she'd even argued with her grandparents and Yolanda over that.

"You're joining me this time?" she remarked.

"Yup." He flashed a guilty grin. "Though I already had two pieces of it earlier."

"You're not afraid of getting fat?"

"Nope. I seem to burn it off." He looked almost boyish as he dug his fork into the pie.

Another flare of desire came out of nowhere. She could think of lots of ways to help him work off those calories. They ate stealing occasional glances at one another. The silence seemed companionable on the surface, but held an undercurrent of growing sexual tension.

When they finished, she watched him clear the table. He moved around the kitchen the same way he did everything—with confident ease. Fatigue once more overtaking her, Haley yawned and stretched.

"You wanna go back to bed?" he asked.

"Maybe. What time is it?"

"Probably getting close to sunup by now."

"You're kidding!"

"Nope. You slept a long time."

"So you've been up all night watching me?"

"It's the norm for me. Told you I don't sleep. Not much anyway. My body's conditioned to do without it."

"That's not normal, Reid. Not healthy."

"It's the way it is." He shrugged. "I crash for short periods when I need it."

"Come to bed with me."

He shook his head. "Told you, it's not gonna happen."

"No, Reid. I don't mean it like *that*. I just feel guilty about keeping you up all night. Just come and lie down with me. We'll stay dressed. I'll sleep better if you do." Haley climbed into the bed but stayed on top of the covers. She patted the space beside her. "Please, Reid."

He hesitated, then kicked off his boots. A moment later, the mattress sank beside her. Gravity alone rolled her up against him, not that she minded or tried to fight it.

"C'mere, Runt." He pulled her up close to his side.

"Runt?" she snorted. "I suppose that's better than some of the other names I've been called."

"You got picked on for your size?"

"Yup. And for the geeky glasses I wore until I was old enough for contacts."

"But now you're back to the geeky glasses."

"Now they serve a higher purpose," she argued.

"Do people really treat you differently because you wear them? Or it is because of the attitude you adopt when you wear them?"

"Attitude? What do you mean by that?"

"You know, that snotty Ivy-League elitism."

She pulled back with a frown. "You really think I act like *that*?"

"Intellectually superior? Sometimes you do, but it seems to be lessening. Then again," he teased, "maybe I'm just getting used to it."

"Yolanda says the same thing," she grudgingly confessed. "You're not perfect either, you know."

"Never said I was. But is there a particular imperfection that eats you?"

"Yes. There is. Why are you so damned unflappable? Doesn't anything ever get you worked up?"

"Besides you?" He flashed a crooked grin that made her heart flutter.

"I'm serious, Reid."

"So am I. I find you damned irritating, but I've learned to pick my battles. I've also learned that there just aren't that many things worth getting truly riled up about."

"What kind of things?" she asked. "What really and truly pisses you off?"

"You really want to know?"

"Yeah, I really do."

"Dishonesty, mainly. Liars, cheaters, and manipulators. People who take advantage of others' vulnerabilities and misfortunes. I've got no use for 'em."

"There are a lot of people like that in the world," Haley remarked.

"You got that right. And they better not ever mess with me or mine."

She chuckled. "You sound just like John Wayne when you talk like that. I can picture you in the saloon, in the corner, eyeing the bad guy with your six-shooter."

He shrugged. "I mean what I say, Haley." He pulled her closer. "I protect what's mine."

She lay snuggled under his arm with her head resting on his chest, listening to the low and rhythmic beat of his heart. She murmured softly. "Times may change, but I guess cowboys don't."

The sun was blazing through the windows when Reid woke up. "What the hell?" He snatched up his phone from the bedside nightstand. "Eight o'clock?" Had he really slept for four hours straight? That was the first time in years. He flung his legs over the bed and scrubbed the sleep from his eyes.

Haley didn't stir. For several minutes he just watched her. The sight of her filled his chest. She was snoring softly. He chuckled. He'd have to torment her about that. She'd hate knowing she snored. Then again, he'd probably have to record it before she'd ever believe him. He stood and stretched. Eager to get out of the clothes he'd slept in, he headed for the shower.

Haley awoke to a soft knock on the door. Her body was still one big ache from head to toe, but the dizziness and the throbbing in her head were gone. The bathroom door was closed and the shower was running, so she padded barefoot across the cabin to answer.

She opened it to find Krista standing there.

"You?" Reid's sister glared. "What are you doing here? Are those my sweats?"

"Yeah," Haley replied, suddenly embarrassed. "Reid borrowed them for me. I thought you knew. My clothes got shredded in the grizzly attack yesterday."

"You got attacked by a grizzly? Oh my God! I'm so sorry." She was suddenly contrite. "I didn't know anything about it. I stayed at Tonya's last night and just got home."

Haley stepped back from the door. "I guess you're looking for Reid?"

"Yeah. I was getting worried when I didn't see him this morning. Now I know why," she added dryly.

"Nothing happened between us, if that's what you're worried about."

"It's none of my business anyway, right? Please tell my brother I need to see him right away."

"Is something wrong?" Haley asked.

"As a matter of fact, yes. Another one of your *precious* wolves attacked one of my colts."

"It wasn't a wolf that killed Buckshot, Krista. We found his remains. All the evidence indicates a grizzly. It's how I nearly got mauled."

Krista planted her hands on her hip. "Well it *was* a wolf that got my horse. And I have proof. Half his tail is eaten off."

"Then it wasn't an intended kill," Haley said. "The pack must be training their young to hunt."

"Well, they aren't going to practice on any more of my horses! I'm telling you right now, Dr. Cooper, if I see a wolf anywhere near my stock, I'm shooting it."

"Please, Krista," Haley pleaded. "Let me help with this situation. It's my job."

"How?" Krista demanded. "What are you going to do about it?"

"I'll start by checking my logs to see if it's a pack we're monitoring. If so, we should be able to find the troublemaker and remove it. If not, we'll have to trap and collar them one by one until we determine which wolf is the culprit."

"And in the meantime, they're all free to wreak havoc on our stock? We have a business to run here, Dr. Cooper. We don't need our horses traumatized by predators that *you* people refuse to control."

"What's the trouble?" Reid asked.

Haley spun to find him standing behind her shirtless and toweling his hair. The vision made her mouth go dry.

"I'll tell you what's wrong," Krista said. "We've got a damned wolf problem, and I've got a colt with a missing tail to prove it."

"Then we're fortunate that Haley's here to help us deal with it," Reid replied evenly.

Krista's eyes widened. "I can't believe you just said that! All she wants to do is put freaking collars on them."

"It's the first step, Krista," Reid said. "They're still a protected species. We can't just kill them indiscriminately."

"*Indiscriminately?*" Krista repeated eyes blazing. "They're hunting wolves legally across two state lines, and we can't even shoot the ones that are harassing us in Wyoming?"

"Not yet," Reid said.

"And that's exactly why I'm here," Haley interjected. "Before they'll turn over management to the state, U.S. Wildlife Service needs to know the people of Wyoming will responsibly manage and not exterminate the wolves. I'm here to provide that evidence. If you shoot any of them without proper authorization, you're only hurting your own cause."

"She's right, Krista," Reid said. "It's a pain in the ass, but we need to go through the proper channels."

"Is that what you did with the griz, Reid?" she shot back. "Did you whip out your phone and call the feds to ask permission before pulling the trigger on that bear? Or do the same rules not apply to Dr. Cooper?"

"Don't be ridiculous, Krista," Reid said. "Her life was endangered."

"I don't want to hear it, Reid. I can't believe my brother, the U.S. Marine, has become such a traitor." She threw her hands in the air and spun away on her booted heels.

Reid stood behind Haley, his hands resting on her shoulders. Although he hadn't made any answering retort, she'd felt him stiffen at his sister's parting shot.

"You see?" Haley said softly. "She hates me. Your whole family is going to after this, aren't they?"

"Don't let her get to you. She'll come around…eventually. They all will."

"No. They won't," she insisted. "Why should they? It's time to face reality, Reid. I care about you. I truly do, but I care enough not to come between you and the people you love."

"It doesn't have to be one or the other," Reid insisted.

"Not to you and me perhaps, but based on Krista's reaction, your family is going to force a choice upon you whether you like it or not. I don't think I can live with that." She turned away unable to look him in the face. "I have to go now. Don't you see?"

"Please don't," Reid said.

"I'm sorry, Reid," she said in a choked voice, "but I think we both knew this couldn't work. I'll be back in a few days with a team to set traps."

Chapter 19

HALEY LEFT THE RANCH FEELING HEARTSICK BUT resolved that she'd done the right thing. She'd briefly fantasized that they might be able to work through their differences, but Krista's parting words had shattered that illusion.

She drove first to her rented condo, where she showered and changed clothes, then headed to the office to write up her reports on the horse depredation and the grizzly kill. She opened the door to find Jeffrey sitting behind her desk. "Jeffrey? What are you doing here?"

"Trying to track you down. You haven't answered any of my calls."

"I didn't get any. Then again, I've been in an area with no signal." She added dryly, "Cell phones always seem to work around here until you really need them."

"I was told you went out to investigate an alleged wolf depredation. What happened?"

"That was an adventure and a half. We went looking for a missing horse and had an unpleasant encounter with a grizzly."

"Really?" He rose, his eyes wide with concern. "Are you okay?"

"Yes. I'm all right, thanks to Reid."

His gaze narrowed. "Who's Reid?"

"The rancher. He's also a hunting guide. He had to shoot the grizzly."

"He *killed* it?"

"Yes, but he had no choice."

His expression darkened. "The hell he didn't. Don't you carry bear spray?"

"Of course I do! But have you ever tried to use it when a grizzly is charging? I panicked, Jeffrey. I couldn't think. Let alone move. That bear would have killed me."

"You know very well what to do in the case of a bear attack."

"Sure, I know *in theory*, but it's quite different when faced with the reality of eight hundred pounds of grizzly bearing down on you. Have *you* ever been attacked?"

"No. I always make it a point to give them a wide berth. Had you done the same, it probably wouldn't have happened. The bear would have left you alone once he knew you weren't a threat."

"He was protecting a kill. You know that changes all the rules."

"Did you document it?" he asked.

"Yeah. I took photos. Here. See for yourself." She dug into her purse for her phone, but came up empty. "Damn! I've lost it again!"

"Again?"

"Yes. I dropped my phone when the bear charged me. I finally found it and took pictures, but then must have left it behind at the ranch. I'll call Reid later and ask if he's seen it. What brings you to Wyoming anyway?"

"An emergency meeting of the board of directors. We flew into Jackson last night."

"The entire board?"

"Yes, along with a few key donors. We've leased a

retreat here in Jackson Hole. We're taking them into Grand Teton tomorrow for some wolf watching. You should join us."

"A corporate retreat? Isn't that a bit extravagant?" She was vividly reminded of all the times he'd denied her project funding.

"Not when our biggest donors want to see the wolves they sponsor. Sometimes it takes money to get money. And we are in serious need of money."

"Again? Why's that?"

"We're about to file another suit against the state of Idaho. We just got word that they've allowed the elk hunters to establish a bounty program for wolf kills."

"That's unconscionable!" Haley exclaimed.

"It gets worse," he said. "The state is not only in bed with the hunters, but they're even talking about bringing in a team of professionals to exterminate two entire packs in the Frank Church Wilderness."

"That's tantamount to hiring hit men."

"And precisely why I need you to help us stop it."

"*Me?* What can I do?"

"Come with us as a private guide. You can help us raise funds for the legal fees. I've said it before. No one can inspire donations like you can. Besides that, I've missed you." His hand came down on hers. "I'm going to be here for a few weeks. We can use it to catch up on lost time."

"Time, once lost, can *never* be recouped," she echoed Reid's words and pulled her hand away. "Why this sudden about-face, Jeffrey? I tried to talk you into taking a weekend together for the past year."

"Maybe it just took me a while to realize what I've been missing." He cupped her face, his brown eyes searching hers and then drifting down to her mouth. *Shit.* He was going to kiss her. She recognized the signs with a surge of panic.

"Am I interrupting something?"

Haley's gaze darted to the door. All the air sucked out of her lungs at the look on Reid's face. Although his tone was deceptively bland and his stride slow as he crossed the room, his eyes were glacial and his mouth compressed. "I thought you might be needing this." He dropped her iPhone on the desk.

"Reid..." She swallowed hard. "I...uh...this is..."

"Dr. Jeffrey Greene." Jeffrey stood and offered Reid his right hand, but kept his left one on Haley's shoulder.

Whether conscious or not, it was a possessive gesture she didn't like. She shrugged it off in annoyance. "Jeffrey's a colleague of mine. He's here for an important meeting," she heard herself babble.

Reid's gaze met hers and held. "You don't have to explain. I'm well aware of your *relationship*. Just came to return your phone, *Dr. Cooper.*"

Her stomach tied in a knot as he tipped his hat and walked out. Her first impulse was to run after him and explain, but what was there to say? In reality, she'd done nothing wrong. Still, she felt riddled with guilt.

Jeffrey's brows rose in subtle mockery. "Your grizzly-shooting knight errant I presume?"

"He's also a decorated marine scout sniper."

"Ah!" Jeffrey smirked. "An equal-opportunity killer. How heartening to know that all species are on the same footing with him."

"That's not funny, Jeffrey," she protested. "He's not like that. At all."

"Not a killer? You said he shot the bear dead."

"And I told you that he didn't have a choice. It was a justified kill."

"You think so? How can you be certain? How do you *know* he didn't use that horse carcass to bait the bear?"

She hesitated only for a millisecond. Maybe she and Reid didn't agree on many issues, but his integrity was incontestable. "He didn't. I know him, Jeffrey. He would *never* do anything so underhanded or unethical."

"From your own account, he didn't even *try* any non-lethal means of controlling the bear."

"You weren't there, so don't judge," she snapped. "Would you really place that bear's life over mine?"

"Of course not. Don't twist my words."

"I'm tired of all this posturing, Jeffrey. Most of the people here are only trying to protect their livestock and livelihoods. How can we fault them for that?"

"The wolves and grizzlies have as much right to be here as the people do. In fact, they have even more right, as they were here *first*."

"But we've already made amends by reintroducing wolves. They're thriving now and have vastly exceeded our recovery goal. So are grizzlies, but they're now encroaching into areas we hadn't expected them to."

"We can't change their nature." He gave a fatalistic shrug. "Bears and wolves will roam."

"All the more reason for us to help find a solution that people can live with. We need to do a better job of *tracking* where they go. All this money we're wasting on lawsuits would be much better spent on GPS and radio collars."

"So you'd collar every single wolf?"

"If necessary, yes."

"We don't have unlimited resources. Just who do you expect to monitor them?" He gave a derisive snort. "The hunters?"

"Don't mock me, Jeffrey. There are tens of thousands of people who watch wolves as a hobby. They even spend considerable dollars doing it. Why not train some of them to monitor the packs? We could even set up a central control system that would allow people all over the world to help. In essence it would be an early warning system. I believe we could prevent a majority of human–predator conflicts this way."

"Too complicated and expensive," he said, dismissing the idea out of hand.

"It isn't!" she insisted. "I'm certain we could raise enough money for the collars, and the wolf-watchers would do it for the sheer joy of it. If people and wolves are to coexist, it's our responsibility to meet the ranchers and hunters halfway. Many conflicts could be prevented if we just put the right measures in place."

"And when we *can't* prevent conflicts?"

"If it's a problem animal, we'd have no choice but to remove it."

"*Remove?* So in the end you advocate killing the very animals we're fighting to protect?"

"I suppose there's little choice but selective euthanasia, once all other means are exhausted, but we are far from that point. Why does it really have to be a *fight*, Jeffrey? Why is it always us against them? It's not unreasonable that they want us to control the wolves that we brought in. Why can't we all work together to manage the situation?"

"Because *they* only see one solution."

"Maybe that's because we haven't done *our* job. Why has there been no talk about breeding control? Zoos around the country have used contraception for decades. The BLM has even adopted a contraceptive vaccine for use in feral horses. I've been trying to get funding to test this with wolves for the past three years, but I keep getting shot down."

"Because it would be a waste of time and money," he argued. "They *want* to hunt wolves. It's sport to them. You can't *reason* with people who kill for pleasure—people like your *friend* Reid."

"I told you he's not like that."

"So you insist… What is he to you, Haley?"

"An old friend. I knew him back in California."

"So you're screwing him," he stated matter-of-factly. "I suppose that explains everything."

"What the hell does that mean?" she snapped. This was a side of Jeffrey she'd never seen before, a nasty side she hadn't even known existed.

"It means, Dr. Cooper, that you seem to have lost your objectivity."

"Really? Objectivity might be the single thing I've gained since accepting this job."

"So now you'd bite the hand that feeds you?"

"I don't understand. What has any of this got to do with you?"

He smiled smugly. "Everything. How do you think you got this job?"

"I received a call from a recruiter."

"And *why* do you think *you* were on their A-list?"

"Because of my work. My reputation."

"So sorry to burst your bubble, but *I* chose you. You're here because *I* put you here. The organization needed someone in place that we could count on. Our Washington connection made sure it was you. Unfortunately, you're turning out to be quite the disappointment."

She was stunned speechless. How could she have been unknowingly manipulated? Was she really that naïve? That gullible?

Bits and pieces of the last six years flashed through her mind—that first winter she'd spent alone in Alaska, the spying she'd done on the wolf hunters, all the work she'd done on his research without pay or even due credit. She recalled countless hours she'd volunteered for fund-raising. At the time, she'd chalked it all up as paying her dues, but now the ugly truth reared its head. Even the relationship she'd regarded as one of mutual respect was nothing more than a well-orchestrated seduction. Her eyes had finally opened. Jeffrey had controlled, manipulated, and used her. He'd played her from the very start.

Jeffrey picked up her phone and began scrolling through her photos. "You took pictures of the horse and the grizzly?"

"Yes, I documented everything."

"I'm glad you're so thorough." He tucked the phone into his pocket. "It'll help our cause."

Haley's throat tightened. "You wouldn't. You can't, Jeffrey!" She stood toe-to-toe and jutted her chin. "Give my phone back! I'm not going to let you politicize this!"

"Really?" His lips curved into another condescending smile. "And just how do you propose to stop me?"

Haley watched him walk out. Her chest was so tight

she could hardly breathe. She felt betrayed and so many other things she couldn't even categorize.

Reid.

She had to call him and explain. But Jeffrey had taken her phone, and Reid's number was programmed into her contacts. Should she call the ranch?

With trembling fingers, Haley Googled the number and then picked up her desk phone. He wouldn't be there yet, but she could at least leave a message. She had to warn him what Jeffrey was up to.

Reid's words about dishonesty rang a peal in her brain. Jeffrey might have political clout beyond what she'd realized, but Reid Everett wouldn't let this deception go unanswered. And he sure as hell would't go down without a fight. The only question was whether he'd ever trust *her* again after this.

She chewed her thumb as the phone rang and rang. It was the sixth ring before someone finally answered. "Two Rivers Ranch and Everett Expeditions, Krista speaking."

Shit! Why did it have to be Reid's sister who answered? Haley almost hung up in despair. "Krista? This is Haley Cooper. I need to get in touch with Reid."

"You've got his number."

"No. I don't. It's in my phone, and I've lost it."

"Yeah. I heard about that. He's bringing it to your office. Why don't you just dial it?"

"He already brought it back to me."

"Then why—"

"Look, I can't explain all that right now. It's imperative that I get in touch with him. Could you please ask him to call me?"

Silence.

"Please Krista," she begged. "It is really, truly urgent that I speak to him."

"I'll pass on the message when I see him." *Click*.

She might as well have said "when hell freezes over."

Haley stared at the receiver feeling helpless. She needed to act, but what could she do? If she went out to the ranch to warn Reid, she'd only give Jeffrey more time to wreak whatever havoc he had planned. If he meant to cause trouble for Reid with the Feds, which is what she suspected, her best course would be to go straight to Jim at Wyoming Game and Fish. She didn't know what he could do but at least he was a friend to the Everetts.

She phoned the Cody WGF office.

"I'm sorry, Dr. Cooper," his assistant said. "Jim's gone to Cheyenne for a big meeting between WGF and the Board of Outfitters."

"When will he be back?" Haley asked.

"In the Cody Office? Not until Monday morning. You could try his cell phone, but he probably has it turned off. That's why your call came to me."

"Thanks. If he calls in, would you please ask him to ring me? It's urgent," Haley added.

"Is there another officer who might be able to help you?"

"No. I don't think so. I really need to speak to Jim."

Haley hung up with a sigh of despair. There was no way she could let this situation fester until Monday, but Jim was six hours away. Then again, if she drove to Cheyenne tonight, maybe she could head things off before Jeffrey did irreparable harm.

Reid left Haley's office before he lost it completely. He was already seeing the world through a fiery red haze. *Jeffrey*. What the fuck kind of pussy name was that anyway?

The moment he walked in and realized who was putting the moves on Haley, he'd wanted to smash the son of a bitch's face in. He knew he was overreacting, but he couldn't help himself.

He and Haley had made huge strides in the last forty-eight hours. *The words* had even been on the tip of his tongue more than once, until Krista had come along and fucked it all up.

Even then Haley had gone as far as to say she *cared* about him, whatever the hell that meant. But once more, he'd let her go without a fight. He'd let her walk away because he was too chicken shit about another rejection to open his mouth. He was damned if he'd bare his heart without at least a token sign of reciprocation.

Fuck that shit.

It was past time to fess up. He was in love with her. *Goddammit*. The longer he thought about it, the more certain he was.

She'd left her phone behind, but he hadn't really needed the excuse to follow her into Jackson. He'd come to her office prepared to finally tell her straight out, to lay it all on the line — whether she was ready to hear it or not. Then he'd walked in on her about to lip-lock with Jeffrey.

He knew she wasn't into it, could see it on her face, but he was still filled to the brim with jealous rage.

His choices were to walk it off or drink it off before saying—or worse, *doing*—something he couldn't take back. So he'd left. But instead of heading back to the ranch, he had a couple of beers at the Cowboy and then drove back to her office hoping to catch her alone.

He'd cooled down enough to talk, but to his rising frustration, she'd already left. Worse, they were *both* gone. He just hoped not together.

He punched her number into his phone. He'd take her to dinner. Maybe back to that Italian place, since they'd never actually gotten to the meal last time. After that, he'd just have to play it by ear. Three rings later, a male voice answered. Reid jerked the phone back from his ear to scowl at the number. It was hers, all right.

Forcing himself to breathe, he disconnected. He went to pocket the phone, glared at it again, and then with a long, colorful stream of Marine Corps expletives, pitched it out the window.

The next morning, Haley was waiting outside the Board of Outfitters Offices before they even opened. Jim pulled up with raised brows, Starbucks in hand. "Dr. Cooper? What are you doing here?"

"I needed to talk to you."

"Now?"

"Yes, Jim. It's vital or I wouldn't have come all the way down here."

His gray brows furrowed. "What is it?"

"Can we go somewhere more private?"

"Sure thing. How about my truck? It's parked right over there." He indicated a white Dodge Ram.

"Do you know Dr. Jeffrey Greene of the Wolf Recovery Alliance?" she asked once she was certain no one would overhear.

His frown deepened. "Only by reputation."

"He is...*or was*...my boss. He showed up yesterday with a group of board members who plan to sue Idaho over their wolf management plan."

"I'd heard. They're also one of the plaintiffs in a similar suit against Wyoming."

"He's going to make major trouble for Reid."

"How's that possible?"

"Reid and I had an encounter with a grizzly when I went out to the Everett place to investigate. He had to shoot it. I took pictures to support my report, but Jeffrey is planning to use them to promote the WRC's agenda. He's going to state that Reid baited the bear to kill it."

"There will be a major shit storm if he does."

"That's what I'm afraid of. I need your help, Jim. I have my full report for U.S. Fish and Wildlife right here. I was hoping to turn it in before Jeffrey can cause any damage. I'm willing to make a sworn statement to the USFW and the Board of Outfitters. There was no wrongdoing on Reid's part."

Jim shook his head. "Hate to say the truth doesn't matter, but if the WRC manages to circulate the lie, there's no putting that tiger back in its cage."

"What do you mean? Reid is innocent."

"But he'll still be tried in the court of public opinion. There are lots of people who've received death threats for less. Either way, it can't go well for him."

The kitchen went dead silent the moment Reid walked in. His hand froze on the coffeepot. "Something up?" He grew increasingly disconcerted as his gaze tracked from Krista to his mother and father.

"You might say that," his father replied. "I take it you haven't seen the morning paper."

"Nope. What has you all so worked up?"

"Your mug shot," Krista replied. "You made the national news, Reid."

His father slid a copy of the *Casper Star-Tribune* across the breakfast bar.

Reid snatched it up. "What the hell?" His pulse thundered as he read the headline. ABOVE THE LAW: WYOMING HUNTING GUIDE BAITS AND KILLS PROTECTED GRIZZLY. "Holy shit! How could this have happened?"

"It's also in *USA Today*." Krista handed him the article on her iPad. "They're all accusing you of grizzly-baiting."

Reid quickly Googled "Wyoming bear baiting." At least a half-dozen related articles popped up, all featuring Haley's photographs of him, the horse carcass, and the dead bear.

"It's a damned lie!" he cried. "That's not how it happened."

"But it's still all over the Internet," Krista said. "Can you sue her?"

"Haley?"

"Yeah. It was her, wasn't it?"

He groped desperately for any other explanation, only to come up empty-handed. It was *her* phone. She'd *insisted* on taking pictures. He remembered the near-kiss between her and Jeffrey. He'd thought she wasn't into it. He was such a deluded jackass! He'd thought she loved him, or was at least starting to. The realization that she'd played him was a knife in his gut.

"I don't know," he replied woodenly, still unable to believe it. "But one thing is for certain: the Feds are gonna be all over this like flies on shit."

His father stood and laid a hand on his shoulder. "Don't worry about a thing, Son. I'm calling Jared right now to take this up with the lawyers. He's already in Cheyenne for the Board of Outfitters meeting. They'll stand behind you, but I promise this is gonna get real ugly real fast. The board won't have any choice if the Feds insist on suspending your license."

"Again?" Reid shut his eyes in disbelief.

Fool me once, shame on you. Fool me twice… The adage hit him like a sledgehammer.

"I'm afraid that's the least of your worries," his father continued. "You could be facing a felony charge over this, but I promise we'll fight it tooth and nail."

"What are you gonna do, Reid?" Krista asked.

"Hell if I know." He gave a defeated sigh. How could he have been such an idiot over her?

"I'll tell you what he's gonna do." His father snatched up the latest copy of *Eastman's Hunting Journal*, stabbing a page with his index finger. "It says right here that Idaho Fish and Game are looking for a professional hunter to eliminate two wolf packs."

"What has that got to do with me?" Reid asked.

"Everything, Son. This group that's causing you so much strife came up here to sue Idaho over this issue. Seems to me if they wanna play dirty, you can hit them back right where it hurts the most. Take the job. I've got connections. If I make the call, the contract is yours." His eyes searched Reid's. "What do you want to do?"

Reid didn't hesitate long. He'd had enough. The job would offer solitude and time to think. And with all of his plans gone up in a puff of smoke, it was time to get the hell out of dodge. He nodded to his father. "Make the call."

Chapter 20

A WEEK LATER, HALEY PULLED INTO THE EVERETT ranch. Her stomach knotted with trepidation as she knocked lightly on the door. To her relief, it wasn't Krista, but an older woman who answered. She was tall and thin with vaguely familiar features.

"Mrs. Everett?" she began. "I'm Haley Cooper, a friend of Reid's."

The warm smile evaporated from her face. "I know *exactly* who and what you are, Dr. Cooper. And you are no friend to my son or to his family."

"Please! Listen to me, Mrs. Everett!" Haley cried, sensing the door was about to slam in her face. "I had nothing to do with it. It's all a big misunderstanding. I've been trying to reach Reid for almost a week, but he doesn't answer my calls. It's urgent that I talk to him."

"I'm sorry. My son isn't here," she responded tight-lipped.

"When will he be back?"

"I don't know. He's on an extended trip. I've got nothing more to say to you, Dr. Cooper."

"Wait! I can explain everything!"

The door swung only marginally wider as Krista appeared behind her mother. "I'll *bet* you can," she snorted. "Haven't you already caused my brother enough grief?"

"Did you ever give him my message?" Haley asked.

"I called before any of this happened. I was trying to warn him about it. You *must* remember that. Someone stole the pictures from my phone. I had nothing to do with any of this."

"Someone?" Krista's brows met in doubt. "Like who?"

"His name's Jeffrey Greene. He's the head of the Wolf Recovery Alliance. I used to work for him."

"You mean before you came to Wyoming to spy on us?"

"That's not how it was. Not why I came here. I'm as much a victim in all this as Reid is."

"I doubt it. You aren't about to face a felony charge, are you?"

"That's what I'm trying to say. Reid isn't going to be charged with anything. I've given my sworn testimony to U.S. Fish and Wildlife about what really happened. I want Reid to know I'm trying to make things right."

"Why should we believe anything you say?"

"Do you honestly think I would have come here if I were guilty of setting Reid up?"

"Maybe…" Krista chewed her lip and then shook her head. "Probably not."

"I've also quit my job. Call Jim Banks if you don't believe me."

Krista blinked in surprise. "You really quit?"

"Yes. I gave my notice as soon as I knew Reid was in the clear. I refuse to be used and manipulated any longer. Please tell me where he is."

Krista looked to her mother.

Mrs. Everett regarded Haley with a narrowed gaze. "Do you have anything *else* to say to my son?"

"Yes," Haley confessed. "As a matter of fact, I do. I have a lot more to say to him, but the rest is private. I need to tell him face-to-face."

After another pause, Mrs. Everett's mouth curved into a slow smile. "In that case, c'mon in, Dr. Cooper." She swung the door wide open. "It seems we might have something to talk about after all."

———

River of No Return Wilderness
Salmon River Canyon, Idaho

After collecting her equipment, Haley set out for Idaho, determined to track down Reid. The rangers at the Salmon Idaho station had informed her that he'd packed in with a horse and three mules carrying enough supplies to last a month. They told her Reid would probably work his way from the ranger cabin he'd be using as a base camp to the river where they'd be dropping his supplies, but precisely where he was now, no one seemed to know.

Given that he was somewhere unspecified in the second-largest wilderness in the continental U.S., her quest seemed all too much like hunting for a needle in a haystack. If that wasn't already daunting enough, with no roads for over eighty miles, she had only two approaches, either by chartering a plane and landing on one of the backcountry airstrips or by jet boat for the fifty-mile trek up the raging River of No Return.

To Haley, either option was more terrifying than any ride on Mickey's Fun Wheel.

Choosing what she considered the lesser of two

evils, she boarded the jet boat at Corn Creek with her two packs and Reid's hunting dog. His family had sent Jethro, thinking he'd help her find Reid. But with the grizzly encounter still fresh in her memory, she was glad to have the dog's protection, as well as his company.

Mountains splayed out in all directions, flanking her as they traveled up the Salmon River Canyon. The unspoiled wilderness, alternating between treacherous rocky embankments speckled with bighorn sheep to heavily forested sections of Douglas fir and lodgepole pine, took her breath away.

But while others on the jet boat laughed and squealed whenever the boat rocked and listed, the numerous sections of the white water made Haley's heart hammer and knuckles whiten. She squeezed her eyes shut on a prayer that it would be over soon, but it was several hours before they approached the section where Reid would eventually make camp.

They finally pulled up along a sandy stretch of river, where Haley and Jethro disembarked with two packs containing a week's worth of food and equipment. They'd dropped off the other passengers at a rafting launch about twenty miles back. Now it was only Haley and the river outfitter.

"You sure you're going to be okay out here all by yourself?" the guide asked, looking reluctant to leave her.

"Yes. I've spent weeks at a time camping out in national parks in Alaska, Montana, and Wyoming. I'll be fine," she replied with more confidence than she actually felt. She really had camped out for long stretches—just never completely alone.

"When do you want me to come back?"

"Five days," she replied. "I'll be waiting right here. But if I'm not, please feel free to send a posse," she ended with a hollow laugh. She reached down to scratch Jethro's head, inhaling a shaky breath as she watched the boat launch back into the river.

Minutes later, she found herself completely on her own in a vast, nearly untouched wilderness, a place numerous predators called home, and clueless as to where to begin her search.

With daylight growing short, she decided to make camp. Careful to avoid any stretches of brush where an animal might conceal itself, she chose a spot in the open to set up her tent. She then went about collecting wood for her fire pan. Although her campfire would be small, she hoped Reid would see it and come to her. If he didn't, she resolved to put Jethro on the scent first thing in the morning.

—∿∿—

After two weeks of complete isolation, Reid was having second thoughts. He didn't mind being alone. That was the sole benefit of this whole gig. He finally had time to get his fucked-up head back together. At the time, he'd known bailing was a chicken shit thing to do, but he had a deep-seated need to get away from everything after Haley's betrayal.

Taking the job as a wolf killer had been a purely knee-jerk reaction. Now he faced serious qualms about his decision. It wasn't that he had issues with hunting in general. He believed to his core in responsible game management, but it hardly seemed ethical to introduce a species to a wilderness area, protect it for two decades, and then summarily exterminate it.

On the other hand, the wolf population in Idaho was booming, while the elk numbers were way down. And elk hunting was vital to the state economy. Ergo, the state's answer was to get rid of all the wolves. Not just a handful, but to eradicate entire packs. Issuing wolf hunting and trapping permits to sportsmen, however, had proven ineffectual. The vast majority of sport hunters had come up empty-handed. Wolves were too cunning. Hence the need for a professional, and Reid was uniquely qualified.

In the first week he'd caught four wolves in traps and shot two others. Problem was, he didn't feel right about it. Killing wolves purely to increase the elk population for hunters was doing the wrong thing for all the wrong reasons. And now that he'd faced up to his self-centered and petty motives for taking the job, the question remained of what he was going to do about it. Should he stay on and finish the contract or head back home to possible felony charges?

All things considered, it was a no-brainer.

Tomorrow he'd collect the remaining traps, pack up his shit, and go back to face the music.

Haley awoke just before dawn to a chorus of howling wolves. She lay in her sleeping bag for the longest time just listening. Although the lupine choir aggravated Jethro, their proximity didn't instill any fear in Haley. She found an odd sort of comfort in it. Wolves were her whole life, or had been for the last five years.

She wondered what would happen to her now that she'd quit her job. Teaching didn't appeal. No doubt Jeffrey would do his best to blackball her anyway. Perhaps this was the ideal time to pursue research full time? All she needed to do was secure enough funding. And fund-raising was her particular talent.

Jethro nudged her out of her ruminations. With wolves so close, she leashed him before exiting the tent. His natural instinct would be to track them, so she'd have to keep him close. A pack would rip a dog to shreds in an instant. Wolves' hunting style was the one thing about them she could never completely reconcile. Other predators killed their prey before eating them.

Wolves ate them alive.

After a quick breakfast of granola bars and powdered milk, she bathed in the frigid river, dressed, cleaned up the campsite, and prepared to depart. "C'mon, Jethro. You have a job to do."

Pulling one of Reid's T-shirts from her pack, she let the dog get his fill of his scent. She paused, shirt in hand, purely to indulge her own senses. Shutting her eyes, she drank in his musky essence with a deep sniff that sent a ripple of desire coursing through her. But the T-shirt was no substitute for the real thing. Not even close. She had a lot of things to say when she found him, but *talking* wouldn't necessarily be her first priority.

Having made his decision to leave, Reid set out early to collect his traps. He'd laid out over a dozen in areas where he'd seen signs of wolves and had filled almost half of them the first week. Once he'd gathered them all, he planned to work his way toward the supply drop site on the river. He'd be over a week early, but planned to make the best of his situation on a river heavily populated with fish. Although it was too late in the season for steelhead, he had an excellent chance of landing a Chinook salmon. At least he'd eat well while waiting for the boat to arrive.

Unlike all the others he'd collected, the last trap wasn't empty when Reid arrived. A young wolf greeted him, growling and snarling with hackles raised.

Shit. He hadn't planned on taking any more, but the deed was half done already. Dismounting from his horse, he unsheathed his rifle and approached by foot. "This just isn't your lucky day now, is it?" Reid raised the gun with a resigned sigh and took aim.

The wolf went silent, staring him down with its intense golden eyes.

His finger relaxed on the trigger. He lowered the rifle with a shake of his head.

He just couldn't do it. He was finished.

"Looks like I was wrong. You're one lucky bastard after all."

—⁓—

Haley always carried a compass and a GPS, but neither did much good when you didn't even know your destination. She'd set out in a general northeasterly direction, but the dog had yet to show any sign of picking up Reid's scent.

Growing thirsty and frustrated, Haley dropped her pack and sat on a stump to rehydrate. She had the bottle poised to drink when Jethro began circling, whining, and pulling on the leash. She froze at a sound in the near distance. A bark? Was it a dog? She listened more intently, recognizing the lower-pitched, shorter bark of a single wolf.

Was it injured? Or maybe trapped? She couldn't risk her life over it, but also couldn't ignore it without investigating. Haley took quick inventory. She had bear spray, but that was iffy with wolves. She also had her tranquilizer gun and a few darts, but drugging took time. Provided she could keep him from harm, Jethro was her best defense.

She relaxed her tight grip on the leash. Given encouragement, the dog let out a howl and then half led, half dragged Haley through a quarter mile of brush and brambles.

She spotted the horse and mules first. *Reid?* It *had* to be him.

At the sight of its master, Jethro let out a howl and jerked wildly on the leash, yanking it completely out of her hand. Haley stumbled after him.

Reid spun around, freezing with a look of abject shock. For several seconds he didn't move, speak, or even bat an eye.

"Reid!" she gasped, breathless from the chase. "I can't believe we found you."

"What the *hell* are *you* doing here?"

"Looking for you. Why do you think I would have come?"

"I don't know. Maybe to take pictures of me brutally slaughtering wolves?" One brow rose above a stare that gave her chills. His tone was equally glacial. "Or did you bring a whole film crew with you this time?"

Her heart, filled to the brim with joy only a minute ago, sank deep into her stomach. But how could she blame him after what happened? Of course that's what he'd think.

"Please, Reid. It's not like that at all. You have to let me explain."

"What are you doing with my dog?" He posed the question through gritted teeth.

"Your brother said he'd help me find you."

"My brother?" He looked confused. "Jared sent him with you?"

"Yes. And your mom gave me one of your shirts."

"My mother? Why would they—"

"Because they know I didn't do it, Reid. Jeffrey did. He stole my phone and used the pictures to spread his propaganda and lies. I tried to call and warn you, but Krista didn't trust me."

"So what are you saying?"

"That there's no case against you. I went down to Cheyenne and filed my reports with both the Feds and the Board of Outfitters. We can't undo the damage, of course, but there won't be any charges."

His expression remained wary, but his chest fell on a deep exhale.

"The wolves are innocent too, Reid," she said softly. "You have every right to be angry about what happened, but they don't deserve extermination for it."

His gaze and tone softened. "I know that… Now."

She took a step closer. He did the same.

"So you came here to tell me I can go back?"

Haley bit into her lip. "That was part of it."

He cocked his head. "Only *part*?"

Her mouth was suddenly so dry she wasn't sure any more words would come out. She swallowed twice. But it didn't help. "Yes, Reid. There's something a whole lot more important I have to tell you."

He waited, his expression impassive.

Her pulse raced. It was the moment of truth, but she didn't know if she could finally voice what was in her heart. Her gaze suddenly darted to the object in his hands. "What are you doing with a snare pole?"

"A responsible trapper always packs one. It comes in handy in the event of catching something you didn't intend to."

"And you did?" Even as she asked the question, she spotted the wolf about thirty feet away. So did Jethro. Thankfully, Reid was quick to grab his collar.

"I don't think it's hurt. I was getting ready to release it. Wanna help?"

Haley gaped. "Did you say *release*?"

"Yes. But it'd be a lot easier, not to mention safer, with another set of hands."

She instantly dropped her pack. "Of course I'll help."

"Chances are this guy's gonna bolt straight into the brush when I let go, but I can't take a chance on him attacking one of us."

"What do you want me to do?"

"Grab my rifle just in case," Reid commanded.

She reluctantly retrieved the rifle while Reid secured the dog at a safe distance from the wolf. He then took up the snare pole. It took several minutes for Reid to get the snare over the snapping wolf's head. They moved quickly after that. Reid used both his hands and his body to subdue the animal. Haley laid down the rifle to release the wolf from the trap. She was relieved to see he'd used the padded version. The animal's leg appeared swollen from limited circulation, but there was no outward sign of injury.

"Pick up the gun." Reid jerked his head toward the discarded rifle. "It's already loaded and chambered. You only need to take the safety off. It's that little lever on the side."

"I can't do it, Reid. I can't shoot it."

"I'm not asking you to shoot. It's just a precaution." Reluctantly, Haley complied.

"Ready?" Reid stood and slowly backed off to the pole's maximum reach, which was only about four feet.

Haley nodded. "I'm ready."

"Just don't shoot *me*, okay?" Reid returned an uncertain smile.

Reid released the snare and leaped back. The animal shook its head but didn't move. Instead, it held its ground, baring its huge teeth in a snarl. Haley's throat constricted as its golden eyes tracked from her to Reid and back again.

"He's not showing much appreciation, is he?" Reid took a step to shield her, his eyes never leaving the wolf. "Now give me the gun." He reached for the rifle. "I'm giving him about thirty seconds to either disappear or be dispatched. Get behind me, Haley. Move slowly." Reid continued his own deliberate retreat.

"But he's just frightened, Reid," she protested. "Look at his tail—"

"I don't want to hear any more. I gave him a fair chance." He raised the rifle. "Last time, buddy. Get the hell out of here if you know what's good for you."

"Go! Scram!" Haley hissed.

For a terrifying second the wolf looked as if it would lunge, but then spun around and bolted into the brush. Haley collapsed against him as Reid lowered the rifle.

"You really would have done it?" she asked.

"If he hadn't backed down? Damn straight."

"I don't understand you at all, Reid. If you came here to hunt wolves, why did you release him?" she asked.

"Because it was wrong to come out here."

"You were doing it only to hurt me?"

"Mostly," he confessed. "But it was a petty way for me to lash out at you."

"I'm sorry, Reid. I swear to you I had nothing to do with that grizzly business." She gazed into his face, praying he'd accept her words as truth.

"I believe you," he replied.

She exhaled a lungful of relief.

"Why else would you come all the way out here?" he said.

"I had another reason, Reid…a much more personal reason."

"And what's that?" he prompted.

Her heart galloped violently in her chest. Now that the moment had come for her finally to confess her feelings, she felt herself faltering. Again. "Maybe this isn't the best time."

"Maybe not," he pressed. "But I'm thinking I might want to hear it anyway."

She drew a fortifying breath and then exhaled a long gush of words. "I've been unfair to you, Reid. I see that now. Horribly unfair. You said to make things work we'd have to meet in the middle. Well, here I am."

She gestured to the endless expanse of forest with a nervous laugh. "Meeting you right smack in the middle of nowhere."

She searched his face for any encouraging sign, but his expression remained unreadable. Her eyes burned and her tongue felt too thick, but she forced herself to continue, "I came to tell you... What I need to say is..."

"What, sweetheart?" he finally prompted in a husky voice.

Sweetheart? The endearment was all the encouragement she needed. "I'm ready now, Reid," she blurted. "That is, if you still—"

Without warning his big arms came crushing around her, squeezing her tight. His mouth claimed hers, branding her with his hot, hungry kiss that stole all her remaining breath.

She shut her eyes on a moan. Their tongues tangled. Her knees went weak.

In seconds he had her reeling like a drunk.

Dear God, how had she lived so long without this? Without him?

She shoved his hat off to curl her fingers in his hair. His hands slid down her back to cup her ass, lifting her clean off the ground. She clamped her legs around his waist, embracing him with her whole body, but it still wasn't enough. They'd kissed many times before, but this was different. It was fevered and feral and almost frantic, as if they'd broken through some kind of barrier.

They were both panting when he finally broke the kiss. Reid raked a hand though his hair, looking as wild and desperate as she felt. "You're right about one thing, sweetheart. You couldn't have picked a more inconvenient time and place if you'd tried."

———∿∿∿———

Reid devoured her mouth once more before reluctantly setting her on the ground. He had some things to tell her too. Lots of things. But they'd have to wait just a little bit longer. Although the surrounding wilderness cried out to his primitive side to claim her in the most primal way, he held himself in check. Once he started, he intended to finish.

His mind raced until locking onto the perfect setting for what he had in mind. "C'mon. There's something I want to show you."

Moving with fast efficiency, he stripped the gear from the back of his saddle, moving it to the pack mules to make room for her. He then untied the dog, hoping the dumb mutt would have the sense to stay close. He mounted the horse first and then helped Haley up behind him.

She gazed at him in bewilderment. "Where are we going?"

"You'll see soon enough."

It took a while to locate the overgrown trail that led back toward the river. They traveled several miles parallel to the waterway with her breasts at his back and her hands clasped on his hips. It was agony to want her so badly and to be so close. Soon, he told himself.

They waded on horseback up an icy stream running through a narrow canyon with two-hundred-foot cliffs on either side. Her grip tightened on him the deeper the water got. It had risen to the horse's belly. Jethro swam happily beside them, seemingly oblivious to the frigid water.

"You'd better bring your legs up," he warned, "or you're going to get a soaking."

She wrapped them around him about the same time a blast of arctic water filled his boots. Thankfully, it didn't get any deeper. After a distance, the gorge widened to a large mouth. He'd found it—one of the best-kept secrets in this entire two-and-a-half-million-acre wilderness.

Reid guided the horses and mules up the embankment where moss-covered cliffs soared above a small clearing. Gushing from these cliff faces were numerous natural water jets blanketing the entire area in a fine mist. Interacting with the sunlight, the mist created rainbows all around.

Catching her first glimpse of it, Haley inhaled on a gasp. "This place is amazing. It's like some kind of geothermal fairyland."

"It gets better still," Reid said.

He'd stumbled onto the hot springs a week earlier and had spent the better part of a day exploring it. "There's a great place to make camp right there." He pointed to an open space, just large enough for a couple of tents.

After helping her down from the horse, he set straight to work unpacking the gear while she tended to the animals. An hour later, they'd established a temporary claim on this secluded piece of paradise.

"C'mon." Reid took her by the hand. "It's time to show you the best part." He led her down an overgrown trail to a sandy-bottomed pool of the clearest crystal blue.

"It's the most beautiful thing I've ever seen," she whispered.

"Yes," he replied, his eyes never leaving hers. "Now I've got something to say to you." He clasped her chin, tipping her head up. "Since you've come all the way out here, I have to assume you're finally ready to hear it. If I'm wrong about that, and you're not, I'm asking you to speak up now, before I make a giant ass of myself."

"You're not wrong," she whispered.

"Good." He gave a short, dry laugh. "I'd hate to think I wasted all this scenery."

He slid his hands down to her shoulders. "I've been waiting a long time for the right woman, Haley, one I can both love and respect. I've been waiting because I don't compromise, because I've never settled for second best. I've been waiting for *you*."

He paused, giving her time to absorb his words.

"We were meant to be together. I've been patient, hoping you'd eventually see that too, but every time I thought we might be getting close…"

"I panicked," she said. "I panicked because this didn't feel like I expected it to. Like I thought it was supposed to. I thought when it happened it would be warm and wonderful, but it wasn't like that with us…well, not completely. I felt vulnerable, scared, insecure—"

"Welcome to my world." He gave another dry laugh. "I spent eight years in a war zone and never felt any of those things until Haley Cooper came along—all five-foot-nothing of you. Even now, you have the power to devastate me. Do you know that?"

"Then maybe it's time I laid those fears to rest." She brought her hands up to his face. "I love you, Reid. I know that now." Her green gaze never wavered. "I think I've been in love with you for quite a while, but I wouldn't acknowledge it because it didn't fit. I thought love had a certain formula. I thought it had to be built on friendship and shared ideals. I thought all *we* had together was shared lust... I was wrong."

He shut his eyes on a groan of relief. She'd finally given him what he desired most.

Haley had surprised the hell out of him by showing up like she had. But then again, she'd never done anything in half-measures. Her passion was one of the things he loved most about her, but he needed not just her body, but her heart. He might be able to take the first, but she had to give him the rest. He never would have opened his mouth if he hadn't thought she reciprocated at least *some* of his feelings, but he'd still harbored some doubts. Until now.

"If that's really how you feel," he said, "I think it's time to lay it *all* on the line."

Her forehead wrinkled. "I thought we just did that."

The uncertainty clouding her eyes made his pulse drum in his ears, but he'd already crossed the point of no return. There was no holding back now. He took a fortifying breath. "That was only half of it. There's more. I want you, Haley... I want to spend the rest of my life with you."

———— ⁓⁓⁓ ————

She couldn't believe the words that just spilled from his mouth. But it still seemed impossible. "This is all happening so fast."

"Hardly." His mouth curved sardonically. "It's been almost seven years since you slapped that twenty on the pool table. *Seven years*, sweetheart. It's a snail's pace.

I'm offering you everything I have. Everything I am."
He caressed her face. "Marry me, Haley. Let's prove
to the whole world that two strong people with widely
differing views can make it work."

"Do you honestly think we can?" she asked.

"Depends on how much we want it," he repeated his
earlier reassurance.

"I do, Reid. More than anything, but—"

He silenced her with a finger to her lips. "We're
smart people. We can figure it all out." The same finger
gently traced her mouth. "Marry me, Haley. I swear I'll
love, honor, and cherish you, if you'll let me."

She could hardly breathe for the pounding in her
chest. He'd just offered her everything she'd ever
wanted, voiced everything she'd never thought to hear
in her wildest dreams.

She swallowed hard, taking the biggest leap of faith
ever. "Yes, Reid. I'll marry you."

The answer was barely out of her mouth before his
lips claimed hers in a long, lush kiss, the kind that sent
ripples of desire all the way to her toes. His hot mouth
moved slowly up her neck to hover at her ear. His hands
cupped her breasts, his thumbs teasing her nipples. His
breath was hot and humid on her skin. "When is the boat
coming back for you?"

"In four days," she replied. "I told him to send out a
posse if I'm not back by then."

"Then that only gives us ninety-six hours." He
grinned, big and sexy. "We'd better not waste any of it."

Between fevered kisses, they kicked off boots and
peeled off clothing. Moments later, a squeal ripped from
her throat as Reid pulled her into the crystal clear pool.

The steamy water engulfed them, but nothing compared to the heat of his hands and mouth.

He settled on a natural ledge, pulling her onto his lap. She wound her arms around him and shut her eyes, suffusing her senses in the feel of his hard, muscular thighs supporting her body and his hungry mouth feasting on her breasts.

Writhing with need, she reached for his erection, jutting large, hard, and proud between them. "I want you inside me, Reid," she gasped. "Please."

He suddenly tensed, his breath leaking out in a long, unnerving hiss.

"What's wrong?"

"Shit! I don't have protection. Do you?"

"No," she replied in dismay.

He shook his head on a sigh. "Don't worry about it, sweetheart. I'm happy to take care of you."

"No, Reid. That's not enough for me. I *need* you inside me." After their heartfelt exchange, the prospect of anything less made her feel cheated.

He stared back at her in protracted silence, the tension of the moment stretching out.

"Are you sure?" he asked. "I promise you I'm safe, but—"

Safe? She almost laughed. With Reid Everett, safe was the last word that ever came to her mind. "I'm certain," she replied. "I want to feel all of you and I want you to feel all of me. All or nothing, right? I want you to come inside me, Reid."

His pupils flared, darkening his irises to cobalt. "Sweetheart, if you want a bareback ride, I'll make a cowgirl out of you yet."

She threw her head back on a cry of pleasure as he pierced and filled her. They merged and melded with mingled moans and synchronous sighs. Kissing, nipping, groaning, and gasping, they embraced the sweet, wet friction. Harder. Deeper. Careening into a climax as pure and primordial as their surroundings.

—⁓—

Hours later, after making love again, they lay in joined sleeping bags, gazing up at a nighttime sky exploding with brilliant stars. Haley had never felt more content, or more in harmony with the world. Everything was so right when it was only the two of them. It was only when the outside world came crashing in that things always fell apart.

But they wouldn't be alone forever. Once they went back, would they discover that it was all just a delusion? Would their differences lead to constant discord and strife?

"Reid?"

"What, Runt?" He nuzzled into her hair.

"What's going to happen when we get back? You know I don't fit into your world."

"I'm not asking you to."

"Do you think your family will accept me?"

"They will if they want to be part of our lives," he replied solemnly.

"Are you going to go back to outfitting?"

"I don't know."

"Is there something else you want to do instead?"

"I don't know that either, although I have a few ideas." He ran his tongue around the shell of her ear.

"Like what? You need to stop that now, Reid. This

is a serious discussion. Tell me what you've been think-ing about."

He shook his head. "Not yet. It's a bit premature to discuss. I want to do a bit of research first."

"Don't be so mysterious," she persisted.

"That's me," he remarked dryly. "Mr. Enigma."

"C'mon, Reid," she cajoled. "Tell me. Maybe I can even help. Research is very much what I do, remember?"

"You truly want to know?"

"Yes!"

"It's going to be really anticlimactic now."

"I want to hear it," she insisted.

"All right. Maybe you do, especially since it concerns wolves."

She regarded him quizzically. "Wolves?"

"Yes. I've been thinking a lot, Haley. This whole situation has gotten so far out of hand. There's gotta be a better, more proactive method of managing it. A lot of folks seem to think the silver bullet is killing more wolves, but reducing their numbers is only a partial solution. As long as there are *any* wolves, they're gonna compete with hunters and threaten livestock. That's a real problem when people are fighting just to make ends meet.

"But there are programs in place—"

"But they don't always work. You gotta understand how it is with ranchers, Haley. Once they move their cattle out to summer range, they only do spot checks a few times a week, sometimes less. They can't afford to spend all day babysitting cows. On the other hand, if they aren't around to witness a predator attack, they may never find the carcass to report. No carcass means no reimbursement."

"I understand that, but what more can we do that we aren't already doing?"

"Ever heard of range riders?" he asked.

Her forehead wrinkled. "Aren't they just cowboys?"

"They're the old-school kind, the kind that stay with a herd for the entire grazing season, moving cattle around, doctoring whatever needs to be doctored, and watching out for the stock. They don't kill predators, but they do haze with rubber bullets, flash rounds, or shellcrackers. Some of the big commercial cattle operations use them to minimize losses while grazing stock on public lands."

"So where are you going with all this?" she asked.

"I'd like to start a range rider program and recruit returning vets. There're a lot of good men and women out there who are having trouble adjusting to civilian life. And a lot of them can't find jobs. They already have survival skills and arms training. They just need to learn about the livestock. It's only a seasonal gig and wouldn't pay a whole lot, but it could give people who need it time to decompress and get their heads together, just like I have out here in the wilderness." He added with a dry laugh, "When all I've had is my own company, it hasn't taken me long to figure a lot of shit out."

"It's a brilliant idea, Reid, but how could small ranches afford to hire these riders?"

"That's the dilemma. For this to work, I think it would have to be a co-operation between the Feds, ranchers, and conservation groups. That leads to the research part I was talking about."

"But I can help you with that," she said. "God knows I have enough experience with grant writing. I did almost all of Jeffrey's for him. I'm certain a number of veterans' organizations would get on board, and I'd be happy to contact some the conservation groups that set funds aside for projects like this."

"So you support the idea? It's something you could get behind?"

"Absolutely," she assured him. "And it looks like I'll have plenty of time to devote to it since I'm now unemployed."

"What do you mean? What happened to your job?"

"I quit. Maybe it wasn't the smartest thing to do with nothing else lined up, but I couldn't stay after everything that happened. Problem is, Jeffrey has a lot of clout and will likely retaliate. I may not be able to find another position."

"What about that independent study you wanted to do?"

She snorted. "The one I've been denied funding on for three years?"

"Yeah, that one. Why not apply for an independent grant?"

"I admit the thought occurred to me after Jeffrey shot me down again."

"Screw Jeffrey. He has his own agenda."

"He used me, Reid, and I'm sorry you had to suffer for it."

"Don't worry about it, sweetheart. There's nothing you could have done."

"How can you be so damned nonchalant about all this?" she asked.

He turned her face to his and brushed her lips in a soft and tender kiss. "Because I have everything I want right here. Everything I need. *You*. In the great scheme of things, nothing else matters."

Haley nuzzled into his chest, breathing him in with a blissful sigh. How could she ever have doubted him? Just as Yolanda had said, he was everything she needed to bring her life into balance. He was a warrior and a lover—tender, sensitive, passionate, attentive, masterful when he had to be, but still willing to give up control. As a husband, she knew he would love and respect, provide, and protect. And as a father...

"What are the chances?" Reid's softly spoken question eerily echoed her thoughts.

"I don't know," she whispered. "It probably wasn't very smart or safe."

She gazed up at him with a sudden onset of guilt. She hadn't even considered that he might resent being rushed into fatherhood. She'd been far too caught up in the moment, in her need for him, even to care.

"And if you are?" He softly stroked her hair. "Any regrets?"

"Honestly?"

"Yes. Always. There isn't room for anything but honesty between us, Haley."

She shook her head. "No regrets, Reid. Not a single one. I'd do it again in a heartbeat."

To her relief, the wrinkle eased from his brow. "Glad to hear it, Runt." A slow, sexy smile spread over his face. "It might take me a little longer than a heartbeat, but I'll be happy to oblige you." Rolling on top of her, his eagerness for an encore emerged between them as his tongue sought hers in a long, lush kiss. "Then again..." He pulled back, chuckling. "Maybe not."

Epilogue

Frank Church Wilderness, Central Idaho
Six months later

"TARGETS SIGHTED," THE PILOT ANNOUNCED.

The helicopter zoomed in on the wolf pack, easily identifiable with the barren trees and heavy snow cover. There were six in all—groggy, lethargic, and slow to react after gorging on the nearby elk carcass. And Reid hoped to get them all.

He locked his sights on the largest of the bunch, presumably the alpha male and took careful aim. "Steady now," he commanded the pilot. A second later, he squeezed the trigger. "Hit," he declared. "One down. Five to go."

By now the wolves had roused from their post-feast torpor and were in motion. Hovering and swooping close to the ground, the helicopter gave chase to the howling pack. One by one, Reid took his shots. After hitting the last, he gave the signal for the pilot to land.

Minutes later, they leaped out of the chopper, gear in hand. They had a narrow time window to get the job done. The tranquilizer darts were fast-acting and had already begun to take effect, but they wouldn't last long. The snow was deep. By the time they reached the first wolf, Haley was breathless and flushed.

"Are you all right, sweetheart?" Reid asked.

"I'm fine," she replied, still panting as she dropped her pack. "It's just hard to move fast carrying all this extra weight."

In truth, it hadn't slowed her down near enough for his peace of mind, but when Haley set her mind to something, she was unstoppable. His wife's energy and tenacity never ceased to impress and amaze him.

They handled the wolf with the usual caution. Haley's drug of choice was a paralytic agent that left the animal immobilized, but still conscious, a fact that always made Reid a bit nervous. Reid muzzled the wolf as an added safety precaution and then stood guard over her, assisting as needed while Haley took blood and recorded the animal's gender and vital signs. She then placed a radio collar around its neck. Working with fast and confident efficiency, they were finished within ten minutes. After administering the reversal drug, they moved on to the next wolf.

The second wolf was female, which meant she got a dose of the new contraceptive vaccine they were testing, along with a special GPS collar for closer monitoring. In less than an hour, they'd collared the entire pack. He was glad this was the last excursion until spring. They were too close to the wolves' breeding season to do any more. Any further contraceptive vaccines would only be wasted.

"I think that was our record, Reid." Haley grinned as she gathered up her supplies. "Who would have known we'd make such a perfect team?"

"I did," he replied smugly.

Haley laughed in reply as he boosted her back into the chopper.

Reid's eyes never left her beautiful, wind-burned face during the twenty-minute flight. Watching Haley work with the wolves, he recognized that she was in her true element, and his heart swelled with pride. She'd been relentless in her quest for subsidies and grants for her contraception study, and her efforts had paid off in spades. She'd received enough funding to support a ten-year study.

Their next greatest challenge had been to obtain study subjects. This is where Reid's family had surprised him. They'd thrown themselves behind Haley's pet project, using all of their substantial clout to gain the cooperation of state wildlife services in Wyoming, Idaho, and Montana. It was a priceless gesture from his family, and one that gave Haley the sense of acceptance she so deeply craved.

They didn't speak again until after landing at the Salmon Heliport. It was too loud to be heard on the chopper anyway. A few minutes later, he handed her up into the truck. He barely had the engine running before she'd shed out of her coat. "Aren't you cold?" he asked.

"I was while on the helicopter, but mainly because of the wind. Now I'm getting hot. It hits me at really weird times, Reid."

"Good thing I like the cold," he said. "Else you'd freeze my ass off."

She laughed. "Now that would be a crime. You already know how fond I am of your ass. I still think it's much nicer than Hugh Jackman's, and he flaunted his big time in the last Wolverine movie."

Reid shuddered. "That was a visual I did *not* need, sweetheart."

She laughed. "Are we staying here tonight or driving home?"

"I s'pose that's your call," he replied.

"I'm pretty tired, but I'm even more homesick," she said. "I'd really love to sleep in our own bed tonight."

He would too. After a week of motels and rough camping, he was glad that they were finally free to head back home. "Are you sure you're up to the trip?" he asked, concerned about the dark circles shadowing her eyes.

"I'm fine, really, Reid, as long as you don't mind driving. If I get too sleepy, I'll just take a nap."

"Here." He handed her a pillow from the backseat. "I'll wake you up when we get into Wyoming."

"I'm not *that* tired yet."

"Are you hungry?" he asked. "If you want to get something, we should stop here in town. There won't be many options once we get on the highway."

"I'm always hungry, Reid, but I have juice and granola bars in my pack. I'll survive until we hit Wyoming." She shook her head with a giggle and then threw the pillow in the back. "What a mother hen you're becoming."

"I take care of what matters to me, and you top that list."

"You're first on mine too, Reid," she returned with a soft smile, and then curled up against his chest. He put the truck in gear and drove the next twenty miles lost in his thoughts. He thought she'd nodded off until she broke the silence. "It's getting close to Christmas."

"Yup."

"We haven't talked about how we're going to spend it."

"Nope," he replied, watching her in his peripheral vision.

"So…do you have any thoughts on the subject?"

"As a matter of fact I do," he replied. "Thoughts and plans."

"Care to elaborate, Reid? I'm not sure I like playing twenty questions."

"Seems to me we have several options."

"I'm listening."

"Since it's our first Christmas together, we might want to spend it alone. Or, if you prefer, we're always welcome up at the ranch."

"You said several options. What's the third?" she asked.

"We *could* drive out to California and spend it with your grandparents."

"Really, Reid?" Her face lit up. "You'd do that?"

"Absolutely. Only seems right. You haven't seen them in almost a year."

"But will your family be disappointed if we don't spend it with them?"

"A little." He shrugged. "But they'll get over it."

"We've come a long way, haven't we? Your family and me. I never could have imagined it, especially Krista."

"She never really disliked you. She just wanted to see me with Tonya and thought you were the only reason it didn't work out. She didn't know anything about Ton and Jared. Everything changed once I told her. Krista's always been fiercely loyal to me."

"Don't I know it," she replied dryly.

"Speaking of family, there's something else I've been wanting to talk to you about."

"What's that?"

"Your mom, Haley. I'm wondering if you might be feeling a tad bit softer toward her now."

She exhaled a long sigh. "I don't know. Maybe part of me does, but the other half feels more resentful than ever."

"Then maybe you can just concentrate on that first part?" he suggested.

"Why are you bringing it up out of the blue like this?"

"Because she'd like to see you at Christmas. She'd like to be part of your life."

Haley's brows met in a scowl. "You've spoken with her?"

"Not directly."

"Then how?" she demanded.

"Your grandpa told me. Just think about it, okay? We could drive through Washington on our way to California. That way you could visit however long you like—twenty minutes or twenty hours. Totally your choice. I'd just like to see you mend your fences with her. Especially now. I think you'd be happier if you did."

"But I *am* happy," she insisted.

"You might be even happier knowing the truth about your parents, especially with the baby coming. Have you ever thought about tracking down your father?"

"I lied when you asked me that once before. I told you I hadn't, but the truth is I'm afraid."

"Of what, sweetheart?"

"Rejection, Reid. What if he really is the dog I've always believed he was?"

"But what if he isn't? Worst-case scenario, he's the man you already think he is, but maybe he isn't. What if he has regrets about the past and is equally fearful of rejection from you? What if he never knew about you at all? I'm not gonna force the issue, but just consider it, okay?"

"I will," she replied. After a moment she added, "It's really sweet of you to care about all that, Reid."

His hand came off the wheel to grip hers. "I care about *you*. Everything that matters to you, matters to me. Which brings up another subject I've been waiting to discuss."

"What's that?"

"Wolves. Or rather wolf control."

"What do you mean?"

"You remember that range rider idea I had?"

"Of course I remember."

"I have some thoughts on how to get it started."

"Do you? Tell me, Reid."

"A couple of weeks ago I got a call from an old buddy of mine who's having some wolf troubles. He's got a big spread, about five thousand acres, I think. He's expecting a new crop of calves soon and is getting worried about driving them into the mountains for summer grazing. He says he lost a number of high-dollar cows to predators last year."

"Is he using fladry?" she asked.

"No. It's not practical in the mountains."

"Then I suppose we could collar them and try to weed out the culprits," she suggested.

He shook his head. "But then the damage is already done. On top of all that, it isn't just depredations that he has to fret about, but aborted fetuses and low-body condition of their stock due to stress from predators. Do you see how it is?"

"I'm starting to," she said.

"Dirk told me he's looking for some ranch hands to watch over the herd. I asked him about hiring some vets. I think his place would make an ideal pilot program."

"What did he say?"

"He's interested. He knows better than most how it is. He had a helluva time adjusting."

"Why's that?"

"He lost half his leg in Afghanistan."

"And he's still running a ranch?"

"Yup. Moreover, he's about to expand his operation. He just signed a grazing lease for twelve hundred acres owned by his brother's fiancée."

"So what's the next step?" she asked.

"We need to go up there and meet face-to-face. Iron out some details about how we're going to do this."

"When do you want to go? I'd love to meet him."

"*Them*," Reid corrected. "I forgot to mention he's getting married. I know her too. We all used to rodeo back in the day. Her name's Janice. You'll like her. He's invited us to their wedding in February. It's going to be small and private."

"The best kind," she said.

"Oh yeah? So you didn't miss that whole bridesmaid-and-bouquet-tossing thing?"

"Maybe a little," she confessed, then broke into a mischievous grin. "But you more than made up for it with the honeymoon."

They'd rushed things a bit once they'd learned about the baby, but he had no regrets about any of it. He'd waited long enough already. After the civil ceremony, he'd surprised her with a honeymoon cabin at Dunton

Hot Springs outside Telluride, Colorado. He'd seen it listed in *Forbes* as one of the ten most romantic places in the U.S. *Forbes* was right. They didn't leave their cabin for three days. Although most of the amenities were wasted, at least they'd had the benefit of a private hot pool and five-star room services.

The memory stirred him to life. "Do you recall that first night we spent at the hot spring?"

"Do I?" She gave a throaty chuckle. "It's kind of hard to forget." She slid their joined hands from her thigh up to her protruding belly. "Unlike you, I have a daily reminder of it."

He reached under her sweater to caress her bare skin. The thought of the life growing inside her never ceased to fill him with awe. "Since you mention it, what does the doc say about..."

"Sex, Reid?" She grinned. "You can't say it? I can. You've corrupted me. I can even say *orgasm* now," she exaggerated the word. "Yolanda would be very proud."

"Well, don't say it anymore unless you want me to pull the truck over."

"Really?" She arched a brow. "Is that a dare, Reid?"

"It's a *promise*."

"In that case I'd better choose my words very carefully. How about *multiple screaming orgasms*?"

"That's a damned tall order to fill in a truck, sweetheart."

"Oh." Her mouth drooped in disappointment.

Two miles later he turned off the highway, answering her confused look with a lecherous grin. "But there's a motel just up the road."

SLOW HAND

THE FASTEN SEAT BELT SIGN GLARED LIKE A
malevolent beacon.

Clutching both armrests with clammy palms and
white knuckles, Nikki diverted her terrified gaze from
the sign to the window, where lightning slashed the
black clouds. She then looked in panic to the seat pocket
in front of her, vainly seeking the little white paper bag.

*Dear God, don't let me get sick! Breathe, Nikki.
Just breathe.*

As if on cue, the plane took another turbulent lurch,
sending bile to the back of her throat.

Was this foul weather some kind of dark omen? What
would happen if lightning struck the plane? Or would
they just run out of fuel while circling the blackened
skies above Denver?

She hated flying. Always had. Maybe it was irrational, but she despised any situation that placed her fate
under anyone else's control. On a normal day she didn't
even like being a passenger in a car. Flying, however,
literally put her life in a perfect stranger's hands, so she
avoided it at all costs.

Until now.

But Atlanta to Sheridan, Montana, was over two thousand miles, an impossible drive with only a three-day bereavement leave.

She closed her eyes, willing away the nausea churning her stomach, wishing she had never received the fateful phone call, and hoping that this entire episode was just a very bad dream. She didn't know why she'd felt such a strong obligation to get on the damn plane in the first place. He'd bailed out when she was only seven, after all. Followed by over twenty years of stone-cold silence.

Then the letter arrived.

It had come to her with a Bozeman, Montana, postmark, but no return address. Still, she had known it was from *him*. She hadn't opened it, but she hadn't destroyed it either. Instead, it sat in a state of purgatory in her desk drawer—untouched for eighteen months. Well, that wasn't quite right either, for she had *touched* it often enough. Picked it up, turned it over, smelled the familiar Marlboro scent, and thrown it back in the drawer again. Everything short of actually opening it. The letter represented a virtual Pandora's box of heartaches that she just wasn't willing to experience again. So, she'd buried it. Chapter closed. Until the blasted phone call with news that unleashed a gale of emotions about a man she'd hardly known.

Hours later she'd torn the letter open, devouring every line as if starved. She wished she'd never read it because then she wouldn't have cared. But she had, and she did. But now it was too late.

He was gone.

They would never get to say what needed saying. She would *never* see his face again. The letter left her with a relentless ache in the middle of her chest, a pain that she suspected would continue to eat at her until she followed this through. In the end, she'd had no choice but to suffer the motion sickness and face her near-paralyzing fear of flying.

The garbled voice of the captain jarred into her wildly rambling thoughts. Three precious words were all she understood, but also all she cared about—*cleared for landing*.

—◠◠◠—

Nikki anxiously waited another fifteen minutes before the plane actually hit the tarmac. It had barely reached the Jetway before she flipped the seat buckle and snatched the shoulder strap of her oversized purse, the one she'd barely managed to cram under the seat to begin with. A struggle to release it ensued, eating up valuable seconds before she could escape from the flying deathtrap. One last tug and it lurched free, only to have the contents spill helter-skelter all over the floor.

"Help me, sweet Jesus," she murmured, more curse than prayer.

She scrambled to collect her cell phone, tubes of lipstick, feminine products, and miscellaneous other objects that littered the floor. By the time she'd gathered everything up and crawled out from under the seat, passengers were jamming the aisle.

Shit! With nothing else to do but stand there with her neck craned to avoid the overhead compartments, she turned on her cell phone to check for messages, but the digital clock sent her heart lurching into her throat. *Double shit!* Her connection to Bozeman was scheduled to depart in eighteen minutes! Even if she could squeeze out of this sardine can, she'd never make it across the behemoth Denver airport to her next gate. *Could this trip possibly get any worse?*

Hell yes, was the answer when she arrived, winded and flustered, at gate fifty in Terminal C to find stranded passengers camping around the counter.

"Please, you've got to help me," Nikki pleaded with the gate agent. "I didn't even want to make this trip to begin with, but my father has passed away. I *have* to get on this flight."

"I'm sorry for your loss, miss." The agent's gaze barely flickered up from the computer monitor. Although the words were sympathetic, the voice was anything but. "I have done all I can. The next flight is already overbooked due to the inclement weather and all the earlier cancellations. I have you on standby, but I wouldn't get my hopes up. I can confirm you on our noon departure tomorrow."

"Tomorrow? You mean I'll be stuck here overnight?"

The woman glanced up with an exasperated sigh. "We can provide a room and meal voucher." She gazed over Nikki's shoulder and beckoned to the next passenger.

"Wait! You don't understand! I *have* to be there."

Nikki felt a burning sensation behind her eyes. *Keep it together, Nikki. You've already made an ass of yourself in front of a hundred strangers. Don't you dare cry.*

"I'm sorry, miss." The agent's face was completely

impassive, now looking past Nikki as if she wasn't there. "Next in line, please."

With eyes blurring with tears she still refused to acknowledge, Nikki spun around but found no vacant seats close to the gate. Lacking any other options, she threw herself to the floor beside her bag, fished out a Kleenex from her purse, and blew her nose loud enough to draw some stares. Well, *more* stares.

What had possessed her to break down into near-hysterics over a man she'd hardly known? She shook her head, drew in a ragged breath, and scrubbed her face with her palms. For a moment she deliberated turning back, catching the next flight to Atlanta, but that would be cowardly.

And Nikki was no coward.

She'd proven it enough times in her life. Except for flying, that is, but she'd even braved *that* horror when she'd had to. She drew another long and shaky breath in an effort at composure, glaring back at those who still gaped at her, reserving her best glower for the cowboy she'd caught staring at her ass. He was slouched in his seat with his Stetson hat and ostrich Lucchese boots, his long legs stretched out and crossed at the ankles, taking up all the surrounding floor space as if he owned it.

God, how I hate arrogant, swaggering cowboys.

She'd had a bellyful of them with their tall boots, big hats, monster trucks, Red Man, and NASCAR. It was one of the reasons for getting the hell out of Toccoa ten years ago—to avoid repeating all of her past mistakes involving no-account cowboys. At least greater Atlanta had a more diversified mix of losers and players—the only two breeds of male she'd identified so far—unfortunately, *by dating them*.

When Marlboro Man rose to talk to the gate agent, she assumed he must also be on standby. She slanted a covetous glance at his seat the moment he'd vacated, as did several other people. Well hell, if she didn't take it, someone else certainly would. She stood and slid into it, noting with surprise that it was still warm. Somehow it seemed weird to be absorbing a total stranger's body heat in such an intimate place.

After his exchange with the agent, Mr. Look-How-Damned-Hot-I-Am headed away from the gate area. *Thank God for small favors*. The jerk actually had the balls to tip his hat at her with a smirk that said *I'm God's gift to womankind*. Perhaps he'd decided to take the noon flight tomorrow, which made her wonder what the chances were—

"Paging passenger Powell. Passenger Powell, please come to gate number fifty."

———～～～———

It was her ass he'd noticed first—actually, he couldn't avoid it since it was parked right in front of him at eye level. Clad in tight denim, supported by legs that went *all the way up*, it was a mighty fine, shapely, womanly ass, the kind a man liked to fill his hands with.

His interest piqued, Wade's gaze roamed higher to light brown hair that fell in waves over her shoulders. With her back to him, he couldn't see her face or judge her age, nor could he hear a word she spoke with George Strait crooning in his earbuds. Still, he was an observer by nature, and his innate ability to read body language had been further

honed by his profession. Lacking any other distraction,
he watched her, playing a game with himself to see how
much of her story he could discern by her actions alone.

The youngish woman attached to the prime ass had
a boarding pass in hand that she flapped at the apathetic
gate agent whose attention appeared fully engaged in
tapping on the keyboard, and staring into her monitor
like it was a crystal ball. After a time, the wooden-faced
woman glanced up and shook her head. Further fruitless
argument ensued, at which point Wade pulled out his
earbuds to eavesdrop.

Hot Ass wasn't getting on the flight.

She spun around giving Wade the first glimpse of her
face. With red blotches staining her neck and cheeks,
and mascara and snot streaming down her face, what a
hot mess Hot Ass turned out to be. She threw herself to
the floor beside her bag, a vision of pure woebegone.

"I have to say good-bye," she repeated to herself in a
choked whisper.

Ah hell! Her desolate expression and pathetic words
sent Wade surging to his feet with a groan. He'd been
bred to do the right thing, especially where women, chil-
dren, and animals were concerned, and the right thing
now was to give up his damned seat—even though this
was the last flight to Bozeman tonight and he had a court
date in Virginia City at nine a.m.

He glanced at his watch. It was nearly six. If he
rented a car, he could be on the road within the hour,
and if he drove through the night, he'd hit Virginia City
by six a.m. He figured he could crash for an hour in his
office and still make his appearance, albeit not in his
most pristine condition.

Having set his course, he stashed his iPod and earbuds, threw his carry-on over his shoulder, and approached the desk. After a few minutes of low conversation, Wade turned to leave, tipping his hat and flashing his killer smile at Hot Ass as he passed. Having appropriated his seat, she averted her face with a guilty look.

Seconds later when the garbled PA system called out her almost indistinguishable name, he couldn't help glancing over his shoulder to catch her surprise.

—◊◊◊—

An hour after leaving the airport, Wade was nursing a number of regrets about his impulsive decision. Driving from Denver to Virginia City wasn't the most inspired idea he'd ever had, but then again, he'd always been a soft touch where women were concerned, especially pretty ones in distress. Now he'd pay for it...again.

In reality, the entire trip had been a bust. He should have known the ol' man would back out of the deal. Dirk must have jumped on the opportunity to undermine Wade the moment his back was turned, or more rightly, the moment he'd boarded the plane for Denver. Not that it would have taken much work for his brother to persuade their father. Wade had been a fool to think the lure of cash would overcome four generations of fealty to the land, regardless of the pressing circumstances. Ranching ran bone-deep in all the Knowltons—*all but him*.

Still, it had come close. Closer this time than he would have expected.

Allie, of course, was pissed as a wet cat, having spent weeks brokering the deal. She'd already refused his invitation for lunch after the thwarted closing. If he'd been stuck in Denver, he wouldn't have been welcome in her bunk tonight.

He realized he was getting damned tired of her using sex to manipulate him. For nearly four years they'd played it fast and loose, which had suited him just fine. Work took up most of his time anyway, but now Allie had begun to press for commitments he wasn't ready to make. From the moment he'd met her in Denver, she'd acted like he was a bonus to the six-figure commission she'd expected—the one she'd just lost.

Hell, we've all lost out on this one—who knows when or if another offer might come along in this shitty economy.

Like most private ranches in these times, the Flying K had teetered on the brink of foreclosure for years. The Knowltons had forged on in the false hope that the next year would be better, but it never was. It was just no damn good any more. They needed to sell out while they still could, but Dirk had refused. Instead, he'd been willing to hazard everything, the ranch and his family's entire economic future, on the slim chance that his breeding experiments would pay off.

"Damn you to hell, Dirk!"

Wade was bone weary, stretched to the breaking point, but his family showed little appreciation for his efforts, and he'd worked too friggin' hard to keep them above water to watch it all go down the drain. Perhaps he and Allie could still salvage the deal? As soon as he got back to Twin Bridges he, Dirk, and the ol' man would have a serious "come to Jesus" meeting.

He had a lot of time to strategize with an eleven-hour drive ahead of him. But two hours out of Denver had him yearning for the good old days when he could have done it in about eight—the days before they'd reinstated a speed limit on Montana highways. At least the weather had cleared, and he'd left late enough to have missed the outbound commuter traffic.

As for Allie, he supposed the rift was no great loss. Although he wouldn't be getting any for a while after this fiasco, he'd survived lengthy dry spells before—even during his marriage. Given Allie's recent change in attitude, it wouldn't hurt to put some distance between them anyway. He'd never been a player, but maybe it was time to seek out greener grazing.

His mind wandered back to the girl at the airport. He still marveled at the impulse that had spurred him to give up his seat. He wondered what might have happened had he been stranded in Denver with her. Maybe he would have offered her dinner. Maybe she would have accepted. And maybe they would have shared a room at the airport Hilton. He then shrugged it off as another lost opportunity, a sorry addition to all the rest.

Wade plugged his iPod into the audio jack of the rental car and scrolled impatiently through various playlists in search of something to help the two cans of Red Bull keep his eyes open for the all-night driving marathon. He settled on the blaring sounds of Big and Rich.

I'm a dynamite, daddy, I'll put the rhythm in your blues, I'm not a wishy-washy boy like you're used to...

Yeah. That was the ticket. Part country, part urban madness. Much like him.

Grinning, he punched the accelerator of the Dodge Avenger. And like any good cowboy, Wade drove off into the sunset.

Chapter 2

IT WAS AFTER ELEVEN WHEN NIKKI LANDED IN Bozeman. Expecting to arrive hours earlier, she'd reserved a rental car, but after collecting her bags and proceeding to the Thrifty counter, she found it dark and abandoned. She glanced down the row of rental car desks in mounting frustration. All of them were closed. *Damn it all! What now?*

The bank of hotel courtesy phones caught her eye next. That was it. She'd just call a hotel with an airport shuttle and get the car in the morning. She was dead tired and in no shape to drive almost a hundred miles in total darkness on unfamiliar roads anyway. It would be smarter to pick up her car early in the morning and then depart for Sheridan. She could live with a few hours delay. At least she wasn't stuck in Denver.

Satisfied with this plan, she picked up the phone, reserved a room at the Holiday Inn Express in Bozeman, and settled on the bench at the shuttle pickup. Up until now she hadn't thought through many of the details and the flight delays had screwed everything up even worse. Now she had to put her mind to reordering her priorities.

The mortuary had already held his body for an entire week before anyone had tracked her down. She wondered if he would have wanted cremation or a burial. She didn't even know him well enough to say. Did he have any friends who mourned him? No one aside from the mortuary had even tried to contact her. Had he left a will? She didn't know that either. She supposed she'd have to contact the attorney's office to find out. She rolled her eyes at the prospect of dealing with blood-sucking lawyers.

First things first, Nikki. Get some sleep. Get to Sheridan. Sign whatever you have to. See him properly buried. Then, get the hell out of Montana. It seemed like a solid plan.

Nikki was the sole passenger when the shuttle pulled up in front of a brightly lit entrance to the hotel lobby. With an exhausted groan, she dragged her bags inside and up to the front desk. Surely a hot shower and a clean bed would make everything right again.

"Hi, I'm Nicole Powell." She greeted the night clerk with a weary smile. "I called a few minutes ago from the airport."

"Welcome to the Holiday Inn Express, Miss Powell," he replied. "I'll be happy to check you in. All I need is a credit card."

"No problem." Nikki plopped her purse on the counter and fished inside, but her blindly groping fingers failed to encounter anything approximating calfskin. "I'm sorry. I can't seem to find my wallet. Just another minute, OK? It's a new bag." She fully opened the mouth of the leather abyss and reached inside again, only to come up short for a second time.

With rising panic, Nikki dumped her entire bag on the counter.

Two sets of keys, miscellaneous makeup items, a cell phone, address book, Tampax, and her checkbook—many of the same things she'd collected when they'd spilled out under the seat of the airplane. *But no wallet.*

She shook the bag upside down in disbelief. *Oh shit!* She'd lost her damned wallet on the plane! With a flushed face and shaking hands, she began cramming everything back into her purse. "I'm sorry. I seem to have lost my wallet. Will you take a check?"

"Certainly. I just need a driver's license and credit card."

"But I don't have them. My license and credit cards were in my wallet."

The clerk shook his head with an impassive expression. "I'm sorry, Miss Powell. We can't accept a personal check without proper identification."

"But I need a room. Surely there's *something* we can work out."

"Is there someone you can call? A friend or family member?"

Nikki stared at him, scrambling to make sense of this situation. She was stranded at a motel in Bozeman, Montana, without a room, money, or identification. Worse, there wasn't a soul she could think of to help her in the middle of the night. Her mother was out of the question. She couldn't even remember the last time they'd spoken. Since her grandparents died, her sister Shelby was the only family member she'd maintained any contact with, but Shelby was a total screwup. There was no one.

"No." Nikki shook her head.

"Do you have any business associates, perhaps?"

"Look, I only have two numbers, the Sheridan

mortuary and a law office. Do you really think either one is going to answer the phone at this time of night?"

His smile thinned. "I'm sorry, but we can't accommodate you without payment. This is a hotel. We are in business to sell rooms."

Overcome with a growing sense of helplessness, Nikki turned away to dig desperately inside her purse for her cell phone. Not putting much stock in the mortuary, she decided to try the lawyer. Finding the number, she punched it on a whispered prayer.

———

Wade's lids were drooping, and his vision blurring when the sound of his tires bumping the road reflectors jarred him fully alert. He swore aloud and shook his head to clear away the cobwebs. Where the hell was he anyway? Wyoming? Yeah, now he remembered. He'd just passed through Casper—the halfway point. The caffeine had already worn off and he still had a good five hours to go.

By now he was cursing both Hot Ass for provoking his stupid act of chivalry and his Momma for raising him to be a gentleman. Would he have given up his seat if the girl had been old or ugly? Yeah, on the first account anyway. His grandma would roll over in her grave if he'd let some elderly woman get stranded. But ugly was a matter for debate. Attractive women made fools of men.

The vibration of his phone suddenly jolted him. He jerked it out of his holster, noting the unfamiliar area code with a scowl. Who the devil outside his family, or maybe Allie, would be calling him at this ungodly hour?

"Wade here," he growled, half expecting a wrong number.

"Excuse me?" a female voice responded. "I was trying to reach Evans and Knowlton Law Firm."

"This is Wade Knowlton of Evans and Knowlton."

"Thank God!" she answered with a near-sob.

"Look, ma'am, this is my private line and it's after midnight. I suggest you call me back tomorrow during normal business hours." He paused. "How did you even get this number anyway?"

"Your office had a recording to call this number in the event of an emergency. This *is* an urgent matter."

"It had better be life or death," he warned. His response was ill-tempered and lacked his normal courtesy, but he was dog tired.

"It is." She paused. "Well, death anyway."

"All right, you've got my attention. Now what are you going to do with it?"

"I have an emergency."

"I thought we'd already established that, Miss—"

"I'm so sorry—I thought I said. This is Nicole Powell."

"Powell? Sorry. Doesn't ring any bells."

"My father is...was...Raymond Powell. He just passed away. You were recommended by the Sheridan mortuary."

The first rays of understanding in this bizarre conversation had begun to dawn. "Ah. Then you wish me to handle the probate."

"Yes, I suppose so."

"Then I once more suggest that you call back in the morning. There's nothing I can do for you right now."

"But there is—"

Given his fatigue and foul mood, Wade made no

attempt to restrain his sarcasm. "You have my sincere condolences for your loss, Miss Powell, but I fail to see how this is an emergency…given that he's already dead."

"But it's not him. It's me that needs your help, Mr. Knowlton. I've just arrived in Montana and I've lost my wallet. I have no money. No ID. No room for the night. I'm so sorry to burden you, but aside from the mortuary, your office was the only number I had. I just found it on a scrap of paper in my purse. Please, is there anything you can do to help me?"

"I'll do what I can," he replied, his ill humor somewhat dissipated. "How do you suggest I assist you?"

"I need a short-term loan, maybe a few hundred dollars, until I get my ID and credit cards back."

"Look, ma'am. While I don't wish to appear hardhearted, I don't know you from Eve."

"But surely my father must have left some cash or something of value I could borrow against."

"I have no clue about your father's state of affairs and am nowhere near my office even to find out. And while I don't wish to make either of our lives more difficult, it isn't as easy as all that anyway. You have to understand there are legal waters to navigate in cases like this."

"Please." He detected a quaver in her voice. "I am truly in a bind."

Her tone of desperation struck a nerve. Remembering the woman in Denver, Wade pinched the bridge of his nose with a sigh. *Twice in one night? Incredible.*

Giving up his airline seat had already cost him time and money, two hundred dollars with the extra fee charged for the one-way car rental. He knew nothing about this woman, yet he was already damn close to offering his own credit card, but there were limits to his generosity to strangers—even female ones. Still, he couldn't refuse her request for help.

"Where are you, Miz Powell?"

"In the lobby of the Holiday Inn Express at Bozeman. I couldn't get a room without my credit card. I'm going to have the same problem getting a rental car. I'm stranded here." He thought he heard a muffled sniff. *Aw hell.* The tears were about to fall. The last thing he needed was to deal with a hysterical woman on no sleep.

"Where are you headed?" he asked.

"To Sheridan."

"Then it's your lucky night, darlin'. I'm going to Virginia City and Sheridan isn't too far out of the way. I'm on my way to Bozeman right now to pick up my vehicle as I've been out of town on business. I'm still several hours away, but if you can hang on for a while, I'll pick you up."

"Really? Thank you so much. I truly appreciate your help, Mr. Knowlton."

"Don't worry 'bout a thing, Miz Powell," he offered in the most soothing tone he could muster. "It's been a rough night for both of us, but everything looks brighter in the light of day."

"I never could have imagined getting into a situation like this. It's a horrible feeling."

"I think in a few hours you'll see that your situation isn't near as dire as you thought."

"Why's that?"

"I'll be there to treat you to a Starbucks by six."

WATCH FOR THE NEXT BOOK IN VICTORIA VANE'S
HOT COWBOY NIGHTS SERIES

A COWBOY'S WHISPER

COMING SOON FROM SOURCEBOOKS CASABLANCA

Acknowledgments

I am ever grateful to my loving husband of thirty-plus years for supporting my writing career during many ups and downs. I also wish to express my appreciation to my critique partner, Violetta Rand, for helping me through some rough spots, and to my wonderful friends Jill, Ivy, and Annette, for taking the time to give this an early read and for sharing their invaluable feedback. I would like to acknowledge all of the wonderful people at Sourcebooks who helped to bring this story to life, especially my editor, Deb Werksman, for her continued faith in me. Last but certainly not least, I wish to thank Dawn Adams and photographer Claudio Marinesco for my incredible book covers.

About the Author

Victoria Vane is an award-winning author of smart and sexy romance. Her works range from historical to contemporary settings and include everything from wild comedic romps to emotionally compelling erotic romance. Her books have received numerous reviewer awards and nominations, including the 2014 RONE Award for *Treacherous Temptations* and *Library Journal* Best E-Book Romance of 2012 for the Devil DeVere series. Look for more smoking-hot contemporary Western romances in 2015.